The Stowmarket Mystery

Or, A Legacy of Hate

By Louis Tracy

Originally published in 1904

The Stowmarket Mystery
Or, A Legacy of Hate

© 2010 Resurrected Press
www.ResurrectedPress.com

Published by Intrepid Ink, LLC

Intrepid Ink, LLC provides full publishing services to authors of fiction and non-fiction books, eBooks and websites. From editing to formatting, to publishing, to marketing, Intrepid Ink gets your creative works into the hands of the people who want to read them.
Find out more at www.IntrepidInk.com.

ISBN 13: 978-1-935774-26-6

Printed in the United States of America

FOREWORD

The Stowmarket Mystery introduces Reginald Brett, described as a barrister-detective. Brett is the model of the gentleman detective, a wealthy, educated lawyer well placed to move in the circles of the British elite. He would later figure is several other mysteries by Louis Tracy including *The Albert Gate Mystery*.

The book also introduces another character, who would figure in a later book, *The Strange Case of Mortimer Fenley*. This character is Mr. Winter of Scotland Yard. While in *The Stowmarket Mystery* Winter is portrayed as a slightly dull policeman completely lacking in imagination, in *The Strange Case of Mortimer Fenley* he holds the rank of Superintendent and takes the lead in the investigation. Clearly, a decade of experience did wonders for his detection skills, though he relies heavily on his underling Furneaux.

Several bits of history play a role in *The Stowmarket Mystery*. The first is the Scottish rebellion of 1745, which is the root of the curse that plagues the Frazer-Hume family. In that event a Scottish army led by Bonnie Prince Charlie invaded England and marched south threatening to unseat the British monarch until they were defeated at the battle of Culloden. The Humes, like many Scottish families had members on both sides of the conflict. As is usual, the ones on the winning side assumed the family's estates while the losers were driven into exile.

The second event is the opening up of Japan. Until the 1850's, Japan had been a closed country. No foreigners were allowed entry except for a very limited Dutch presence. In 1853 a fleet led by the American Admiral Perry sailed into Uraga harbor and demanded that the country be opened to Americans. The European great powers also made their claims, and it is during these events that the Japanese Katana that figures in *The Stowmarket Mystery* came into the possession of the Frazer-Hume family.

The final point of interest is the reference to The Black Museum, Scotland Yard's collection of artifacts associated with its most famous cases.

Louis Tracy, in *The Stowmarket Mystery*, has provided the reader with a fine puzzle, where secret is piled on secret, and no one is who they seem.

Note: This book contains terms that are not socially acceptable in modern society. Resurrected Press has opted to publish the book with its original integrity intact, driving home the evolution of words and their usage.

About the Author

Louis Tracy (1863-1928) was a British journalist and author. He wrote numerous books both under his own name and using the pseudonyms Gordon Holmes and Robert Fraser. He shared these pseudonyms and collaborated with P.M. Shiel on a number of works. Among his books are *The Wings of Morning* (1903), *The Stowmarket Mystery* (1904), and *Number Seventeen* (1916).

Greg Fowlkes
Editor-In-Chief
Resurrected Press
www.ResurrectedPress.com

TABLE OF CONTENTS

1
"THE STOWMARKET MYSTERY"

"Mr. David Hume."

Reginald Brett, barrister-detective, twisted round in his easy-chair to permit the light to fall clearly on the card handed to him by his man-servant.

"What does Mr. David Hume look like, Smith?" he asked.

"A gentleman, sir."

Well-trained servants never make a mistake when they give such a description of a visitor. Brett was satisfied.

"Produce him."

Then he examined the card.

"It is odd," he thought. "Mr. David Hume gives no address, and writes his own cards. I like his signature, too. Now, I wonder"

The door was thrown open. A tall, well-proportioned young man entered. He was soberly attired in blue serge. His face and hands bore the impress of travel and exposure. His expression was pleasing and attractive. In repose his features were regular, and marked with lines of thought. A short, well-trimmed beard, of the type affected by some naval men, gave him a somewhat unusual appearance. Otherwise he carried himself like a British cavalry officer in mufti.

He advanced into the room and bowed easily. Brett, who had risen, instantly felt that his visitor was one of those people who erect invisible barriers between themselves and strangers.

"My errand will occupy some time, perhaps half an hour, to permit of full explanation," said Mr. Hume. "May I ask–"

"I am completely at your service. Take that chair. You will find it comfortable. Do you smoke? Yes. Well, try those cigarettes. They are better than they look."

Mr. Hume seemed to be gratified by this cordial reception. He seated himself as requested, in the best light obtainable in a north-side Victoria Street flat, and picked up the box of cigarettes.

"Turkish," he announced.

"Yes."

"Grown on a slope near Salonica."

"Indeed? You interest me."

"Oh, I know them well. I was there two months ago. I suppose you got these as a present from Yildiz Kiosk?"

"Mr. Hume, you asked for half an hour, Make it an hour. You have touched upon a subject dear to my heart."

"They are the best cigarettes in the world. No one can buy them. They are made for the exclusive use of the Sultan's household. To attempt to export them means the bastinado and banishment, at the least. I do not credit you with employing agents on such terms, so I assume an Imperial gift."

The barrister had been looking intently at the other man during this short colloquy. Suddenly his eyes sparkled. He struck a match and held it to his visitor, with the words:

"You are quite right, Mr. David Hume-Frazer."

The person thus addressed neither started, nor sprang to his feet, nor gasped in amazement He took the match, lit a cigarette, and said:

"So you know me?"

"Yes."

"It is strange. I have never previously met you to my knowledge. Am I still a celebrity?"

"To me–yes."

"A sort of distinguished criminal, eh?"

"No man could be such a judge of tobacco and remain commonplace."

"'Pon my honour, Mr. Brett, I think you deserve your reputation. For the first time during eighteen months I feel hopeful. Do you know, I passed dozens of acquaintances in the streets yesterday and none of them knew me. Yet you pick me out at the first glance, so to speak."

"They might do the same if you spoke to them, Mr."

"Hume, if you please."

"Certainly. Why have you dropped part of your surname?"

"It is a long story. My lawyers, Flint & Sharp, of Gray's Inn, heard of your achievements in the cases of Lady Lyle and the Imperial Diamonds. They persuaded me to come to you."

"Though, personally, you have little faith in me?"

"Heaven knows, Mr. Brett, I have had good cause to lose faith. My case defies analysis. It savours of the supernatural."

The barrister shoved his chair sideways until he was able to reach a bookcase, from which he took a bulky interleaved volume.

"Supernatural," he repeated. "That is new to me. As I remember the affair, it was highly sensational, perplexing—a blend of romance and Japanese knives—but I do not remember any abnormal element save one, utter absence of motive."

"Do you mean to say that you possess a record of the facts?" inquired Hume, exhibiting some tokens of excitement in face and voice as he watched Brett turning over the leaves of the scrap-book, in which newspaper cuttings were neatly pasted, some being freely annotated.

"Yes. The daily press supplies my demands in the way of fiction—a word, by the way, often misapplied. Where do you find stranger tales than in the records of every-day life? Ah, here we are!"

He searched through a large number of printed extracts. There were comments, long reports, and not a few notes, all under the heading: "The Stowmarket Mystery."

Hume was now deeply agitated; he evidently restrained his feelings by sheer force of will.

"Mr. Brett," he said, and his voice trembled a little, "surely you could not have expected my presence here this morning?"

"I no more expected you than the man in the moon," was the reply; "but I recognised you at once. I watched your face for many hours whilst you stood in the dock. Professional business took me to the Assizes during your second trial. At one time I thought of offering my services."

"To me?"

"No, not to you."

"To whom, then?"

"To the police. Winter, the Scotland Yard man who had charge of the business, is an old friend of mine."

"What restrained you?"

"Pity, and perhaps doubt. I could see no reason why you should kill your cousin."

"But you believed me guilty?"

The barrister looked his questioner straight in the eyes. He saw there the glistening terror of a tortured soul. Somehow he expected to find a different expression. He was puzzled.

"Why have you come here, Mr. Hume?" he abruptly demanded.

"To implore your assistance. They tell me you are the one man in the world able to clear my name from the stain of crime. Will you do it?"

Again their eyes met. Hume was fighting now, fighting for all that a man holds dear. He did not plead. He only demanded his rights. Born a few centuries earlier, he would have enforced them with cold steel.

"Come, Mr. Brett," he almost shouted. "If you are as good a judge of men as you say I am of tobacco, you will not think that the cowardly murderer who struck down my cousin would come to you, of all others, and reopen the story of a crime closed unwillingly by the law."

Brett could, on occasion, exhibit an obstinate determination not to be drawn into expressing an opinion. His visitor's masterful manner annoyed him. Hume, metaphorically speaking, took him by the throat and compelled his services. He rebelled against this species of compulsion, but mere politeness required some display of courteous tolerance.

"It seems to me," he said, "that we are beginning at the end. I may not be able to help you. What are the facts?"

The stranger was so agitated that he could not reply. Self-restrained men are not ready with language. Their thoughts may be fiery as bottled vitriol, but they keep the cork in. The barrister allowed for this drawback. His sympathies were aroused, and they overcame his slight resentment.

"Try another cigarette," he said, "I have here a summary of the evidence. I will read it to you. Do not interrupt. Follow the details closely, and correct anything that is wrong when I have ended."

Hume was still volcanic, but he took the proffered box.

"Ah," cried Brett, "though you are angry, your judgment is sound. Now listen!"

Then he read the following statement, prepared by himself in an idle moment:

"The Stowmarket Mystery is a strange mixture of the real and the unreal. Sir Alan Hume-Frazer, fourth baronet, met his death on the hunting-field. His horse blundered at a brook and the rider was impaled on a hidden stake, placed in the stream by his own orders to prevent poachers from netting trout. His wife, née Somers, a Bristol family, had pre-deceased him.

"There were two children, a daughter, Margaret, aged twenty-five, and a son, Alan, aged twenty-three. By his will, Sir Alan left all his real and personal estate to his son, with a life charge of £1,000 per annum for the daughter. As he was a very wealthy man, almost a millionaire, the provision for his daughter was niggardly, which might be accounted for by the fact that the girl, several years before her father's death, quarrelled with him and left home, residing in London and in Florence. Both children, by the way, were born in Italy, where Sir Alan met and married Miss Somers.

"The old gentleman, it appeared, allowed Miss Hume-Frazer £5,000 per annum during his life. His son voluntarily continued this allowance, but the brother and sister continued to live apart, he devoted to travel and sport, she to music and art, with a leaning towards the occult—a woman divorced from conventionality and filled with a hatred of restraint.

"Beechcroft, the family residence, is situated four miles from Stowmarket, close to the small village of Sleagill. After his father's death, the young Sir Alan went for a protracted tour round the world. Meanwhile his first cousin, Mr. David Hume-Frazer, lived at Beechcroft during the shooting season, and incidentally fell in love with Miss Helen Layton, daughter of the rector of Sleagill, the Rev. Wilberforce Layton."

Hume stirred uneasily in his chair, and the barrister paused, expecting him to say something. But the other only gasped brokenly: "Go on; go on!"

"Love lasts longer than death or crime," mused Brett.

He continued:

"In eighteen months Sir Alan the fifth—all heirs had same name—returned to Beechcroft, about Christmas. His cousin had been called away on family business, but returned for a New Year's Eve ball, given by Mrs. Eastham, a lady of some local importance. Sir Alan and Helen Layton had followed the hounds together three times during Christmas week. They were, of course, old friends.

"David sent from Scotland–his father's estate was situated close to Inverness–some presents to his future wife, his cousin, and others. The gift to Sir Alan was noteworthy and fatalistic–a handsomely inlaid Japanese sword, with a small dagger inserted in a sheath near the top of the scabbard. David reached Beechcroft on the day of the ball. Relations between the cousins seemed to the servants to be cool, though the coolness lay rather with the baronet, and David, a year older, it may be here stated, was evidently taken by surprise by Sir Alan's attitude.

"The three young people went to the ball, and shortly after midnight there was something in the nature of a scene. Sir Alan had been dancing with Miss Layton. They were in the conservatory when the young lady burst into tears, hurried to find David, and asked him to take her at once to her carriage. Mrs. Eastham was acting as chaperon to the girl, and some heated words passed between her and the two young men.

"Evidence showed that Sir Alan had bitterly upbraided Miss Layton on account of her engagement, and hinted that David had taken an unfair advantage of his (Alan's) absence to win her affections. This was absolutely untrue. It was denied by the two most concerned, and by Mrs. Eastham, who, as a privileged friend, knew all the facts. The young men were in a state of white heat, but David sensibly withdrew, and walked to the Hall.

"Mrs. Eastham's house was close to the lodge gates, and from the lodge a straight yew-shaded drive led to the library windows, the main entrance being at the side of the house.

"In the library a footman, on duty in the room, maintained a good fire, and the French windows were left unfastened, as the young gentlemen would probably enter the house that way. David did, in fact, do so. The footman quitted the room, and a few minutes later the butler appeared. He was an old favourite of David's. He asked if he should send some whisky and soda.

"The young man agreed, adding:

"'Sir Alan and I have commenced the year badly, Ferguson. We quarrelled over a silly mistake. I have made up my mind not to sleep on it, so I will await his arrival. Let me know if he comes in the other way.'

"The butler hoped that the matter was not a serious one.

"'Under other circumstances it might be,' was the answer, 'but as things are, it is simply a wretched mistake, which a little reasonable discussion will put right.'

"The footman brought the whisky and soda.

"Twenty minutes later he re-entered the room to attend to the fire. Mr. David Hume-Frazer was curled up in an arm-chair asleep, or rather dozing, for he stirred a little when the man put some coal in the grate. This was at 1 a.m. exactly.

"At 1.10 a.m. the butler thought he heard his master's voice coming from the front of the house, and angrily protesting something. Unfortunately he could not catch a single word. He imagined that the 'quarrel' spoken of by David had been renewed.

"He waited two minutes, not more, but hearing no further sounds, he walked round to the library windows, thinking that perhaps he would see Sir Alan in the room.

"To his dismay he found his young master stretched on the turf at the side of the drive, thirty feet from the house. He rushed into the library, where David was still asleep and moving uneasily–muttering, the man thought:

"'Come quickly, sir,' he cried, 'I fear something has happened to Sir Alan. He is lying on the ground outside the house, and I cannot arouse him.'

"Then David Hume-Frazer sprang to his feet and shouted:

"'My God! It was not a dream. He is murdered!'
"Unquestionably"

But the barrister's cold-blooded synopsis of a thrilling crime proved to be too much for his hearer's nerves. Hume stood up. The man was a born fighter. He could take, his punishment, but only on his feet.

Again he cried in anguish:

"No! It was no dream, but a foul murder. And they blame me!"

2
DAVID HUME'S STORY

Brett closed the book with a snap.

"What good purpose can it serve at this time to reopen the miserable story?" he asked.

Curiously enough, Hume paid no heed to the question. His lips quivered, his nostrils twitched, and his eyes shot strange gleams. He caught the back of his chair with both hands in a grasp that tried to squeeze the tough oak.

"What else have you written there?" he said, and Brett could not help but admire his forced composure.

"Nothing of any material importance. You were arrested, after an interval of some days, as the result of a coroner's warrant. You explained that you had a vivid dream, in which you saw your cousin stabbed by a stranger whom you did not know, whose face even you never saw. Sir Alan was undoubtedly murdered. The dagger-like attachment to your Japanese sword had been driven into his breast up to the hilt, actually splitting his heart. To deliver such a blow, with such a weapon, required uncommon strength and skill. I think I describe it here as 'un-English.'"

Brett referred to his scrap-book. In spite of himself, he felt all his old interest reawakening in this remarkable crime.

"Yes?" queried Hume.

The barrister, his lips pursed up and critical, surveyed his concluding notes.

"You were tried at the ensuing Assizes, and the jury disagreed. Your second trial resulted in an acquittal, though the public attitude towards you was dubious. The judge, in summing up, said that the evidence against you 'might be deemed insufficient.' In these words he

conveyed the popular opinion. I see I have noted here that
Miss Margaret Hume-Frazer was at a Covent Garden
Fancy Dress Ball on the night of the murder. But the
tragic deaths of her father and brother had a marked
influence on the young lady. She, of course, succeeded to
the estates, and decided at once to live at Beechcroft.
Does she still live there?"

"Yes. I am told she is distinguished for her charity
and good works. She is married."

"Ah! To whom?"

"To an Italian, named Giovanni Capella."

"His stage name?"

"No; he is really an Italian."

Brett's pleasantry was successful in its object. David
Hume regained his equanimity and sat down again. After
a pause he went on:

"May I ask, Mr. Brett, before I tell you my part of the
story, if you formed any theories as to the occurrence at
the time?"

The barrister consulted his memoranda. Something
that met his eyes caused him to smile.

"I see," he said, "that Mr. Winter, of Scotland Yard,
was convinced of your guilt. That is greatly in your
favour."

"Why?"

Hume disdained the police, but Brett's remark evoked
curiosity.

"Because Mr. Winter is a most excellent officer, whose
intellect is shackled by handcuffs. 'De l'audace!' says the
Frenchman, as a specific for human conduct. 'Lock 'em
up,' says Mr. Winter, when he is inquiring into a crime.
Of course, he is right nine times out of ten; but if, in the
tenth case, intellect conflicts with handcuffs, the
handcuffs win, being stronger in his instance."

Hume was in no mood to appreciate the humours of
Scotland Yard, so the other continued:

"The most telling point against you was the fact that
not only the butler, footman, and two housemaids, but

you yourself, at the coroner's inquest, swore that the small Japanese knife was in its sheath during the afternoon; indeed, the footman said it was there, to the best of his belief, at midnight. Then, again, a small drawer in Sir Alan's writing-table had been wrenched open whilst you were alone in the room. On this point the footman was positive. Near the drawer rested the sword from which its viperish companion had been abstracted. Had not the butler found Sir Alan's body, still palpitating, and testified beyond any manner of doubt that you were apparently sleeping in the library, you would have been hanged, Mr. Hume."

"Probably."

"The air of probability attending your execution would have been most convincing."

"Is my case, then, so desperate?"

"You cannot be tried again, you know."

"I do not mean that. I want to establish my innocence; to compel society to reinstate me as a man profoundly wronged; above all, to marry the woman I love."

Brett amused himself by rapidly projecting several rings of smoke through a large one.

"So you really are innocent?" he said, after a pause.

David Hume rose from his chair, and reached for his hat, gloves, and stick.

"You have crushed my remaining hope of emancipation," he exclaimed bitterly. "You have the repute of being able to pluck the heart out of a mystery, Mr. Brett, so when you assume that I am guilty"

"I have assumed nothing of the kind. You seem to possess the faculty of self-control. Kindly exercise it, and answer my questions, Did you kill your cousin?"

"No."

"Who did kill him?"

"I do not know."

"Do you suspect anybody ?"

"Not in the remotest degree."

"Did he kill himself?"

"That theory was discussed privately, but not brought forward at the trial. Three doctors said it was not worthy of a moment's consideration."

"Well, you need not shout your replies, and I would prefer to see you comfortably seated, unless, of course, you feel more at ease near the door."

A trifle shamefacedly, Hume returned to his former position near the fireplace–that shrine to which all the household gods do reverence, even in the height of summer. It is impossible to conceive the occupants of a room deliberately grouping themselves without reference to the grate.

Brett placed the open scrap-book on his knees, and ran an index finger along underlined passages in the manner of counsel consulting a brief.

"Why did you give your cousin this sword?"

"Because he told me he was making a collection of Japanese arms, and I remarked that my grandfather on my mother's side, Admiral Cunningham, had brought this weapon, with others, from the Far East. It lay for fifty years in our gun-room at Glen Tochan."

"So you met Sir Alan soon after his return home?"

"Yes, in London, the day he arrived. Came to town on purpose, in fact. Afterwards I travelled North, and he went to Beechcroft."

"How long afterwards? Be particular as to dates."

"It is quite a simple matter, owing to the season. Alan reached Charing Cross from Brindisi on December 20. We remained together–that is, lived at the same hotel, paid calls in company, visited the same restaurants, went to the same theatres–until the night of the 23rd, when we parted. It is a tradition of my family that the members of it should spend Christmas together."

"A somewhat unusual tradition in Scotland, is it not?"

"Yes, but it was my mother's wish, so my father and I keep the custom up."

"Your father is still living?"

"Yes, thank goodness!"

"He is now the sixth baronet?"

"He is not. Neither he nor I will assume the title while the succession bears the taint of crime."

"Did you quarrel with your cousin in London?"

"Not by word or thought. He seemed to be surprised when I told him of my engagement to Helen, but he warmly congratulated me. One afternoon he was a trifle short-tempered, but not with me."

"Tell me about this."

"His sister is, or was then, a rather rapid young lady. She discovered that certain money-lenders would honour her drafts on her brother, and she had been going the pace somewhat heavily. Alan went to see her, told her to stop this practice, and sent formal notice to the same effect through his solicitors to the bill discounters. It annoyed him, not on account of the money, but that his sister should act in such a way,"

"Ah, this is important! It was not mentioned at the trial."

"Why should it be?"

"Who can say? I wish to goodness I had helped your butler to raise Sir Alan's lifeless body. But about this family dispute. Was there a scene—tears, recriminations?"

"Not a bit. You don't know Rita. We used to call her Rita because, as boys, we teased her by saying her name was Margharita, and not Margaret"

"Why?"

"She has such a foreign manner and style." "How did she acquire them?"

"She was a big girl, six years old, and tall for her age, when her parents settled down in England. She first spoke Italian, and picked up Italian ways from her nurse, an old party who was devotedly attached to her. Even Alan was a good Italian linguist, and given to foreign manners when a little chap. But Harrow soon knocked them out of him. Rita retained them."

"I see. A curious household. I should have expected this young lady to upbraid her brother after the style of the prima donna in grand opera."

"No. He told me she laughed at him, and invited him to witness the trying on of a fancy dress costume, the 'Queen of Night,' which she wore at a *bal masqué* the night he was murdered."

"When did she get married?"

"Last January, at Naples, very suddenly, and without the knowledge of any of her relatives."

"She had been living at Beechcroft nearly a year, then?"

"Yes, she went South in the winter. The reason she gave was that the Hall would be depressing on the anniversary of her brother's death. She had become most popular in the district. Helen is very fond of her, and was quite shocked to hear of her marriage. The local people do not like Signor Capella."

"Why?"

"It is difficult to give a reason. Miss Layton does not indulge in details, but that is the impression I gather from her letters."

Hume paused, and Brett shot a quick glance at him.

"Finish what you were going to say," he said.

"Only this—Helen and I have mutually released each other from our engagement, and in the same breath have refused to be released. That is, if you understand"

The barrister nodded.

"The result is that we are both thoroughly miserable. Our respective fathers do not like the idea of our marriage under the circumstances. We are simply drifting in the feeble hope that someday a kindly Providence will dissipate the cloud that hangs over me. Ah, Mr. Brett, I am a rich man. Command the limits of my fortune, but clear me. Prove to Helen that her faith in my innocence is justified."

"For goodness' sake light another cigarette," snapped the barrister. "You have interfered with my line of thought. It is all wriggly."

Quite a minute elapsed before he began again.

"What caused the trouble at Mrs. Eastham's ball?"

"I think I can explain that. It seems that Alan's father told him to get married"

"Told him!"

"Well, left instructions."

"How?"

"I do not know. I only gathered as much from my cousin's remarks. Well, it was not until his final home-coming that he realised what a beautiful woman the jolly little girl he knew as a boy had developed into. She was just the kind of wife he wanted, and I fancy he imagined I had stolen a march on him. But he was a thoroughly straightforward, manly fellow, and something very much out of the common must have upset him before he vented his anger on me and Helen."

"Have you any notion"

"Not the least. Pardon me. I suppose you were going to ask if I guessed the cause?"

"Yes."

"It is quite unfathomable. We parted the best of friends in London, although he knew all about the engagement. We met again at 6 p.m. on New Year's Eve, and he was very short with me. I can only vaguely assume that some feeling of resentment had meanwhile been working up in him, and it found expression during his chat with Helen in the conservatory."

"Did you use threats to him during the subsequent wrangle?"

"Threats! Good gracious, no. I was angry with him for spoiling Miss Layton's enjoyment. I called him an ass, and said that he had better have remained away another year than come back and make mischief. That is all. Mrs. Eastham was far more outspoken."

"Indeed. What did she say?"

"She hinted that his temper was a reminiscence of his Southern birth, always a sore point with him, and contrasted me with him, to his disadvantage. All very unfair, of course, but, you see, she was the hostess, and Alan had upset her party very much."

"So you walked home, and resolved to hold out the olive branch?"

"Most decidedly. I was older, perhaps a trifle more sedate. I knew that Helen loved me. There were no difficulties in the way of our marriage, which was arranged for the following spring. Indeed, my second trial took place on the very date we had selected. It was my duty to use poor Alan gently. Even his foolish and unreasonable jealousy was a compliment."

Brett threw the scrap-book on to the table. He clasped his hands in front of his knees, tucking his heels on the edge of his chair.

"Mr. Hume," he said slowly, gazing fixedly at the other, "I believe you. You did not kill your cousin."

3
THE DREAM

"Thank you," was the quiet answer.

"You hinted at some supernatural influence in relation to this crime. What did you mean?"

"Ah, that is the unpublished part of the affair. We are a Scots family, as our name implies. The first Sir Alan Frazer became a baronet owing to his services to King George during the '45 Rebellion. There was some trouble about a sequestered estate—now our place in Scotland—which belonged to his wife's brother, a Hume and a rebel. Anyhow, in 1763, he fought a duel with Hume's son, his own nephew by marriage, and was killed."

"Really," broke in Brett, "this ancient history"

"Is quite to the point. Sir Alan the first fought and died in front of the library at Beechcroft."

The barrister commenced to study the moulding in the centre of the ceiling.

"He was succeeded by his grandson, a little lad of eight. In 1807, after a heavy drinking bout, the second Sir Alan Hume-Frazer cut his throat, and chose the scene of his ancestor's duel for the operation."

"A remarkable coincidence!"

"In 1842, during a bread riot, the third baronet was stabbed with a pitchfork whilst facing a mob in the same place. Then a long interval occurred. Again a small child became the heir. Three years ago the fourth baronet expired whilst the library windows were being opened to admit the litter on which he was carried from the hunting-field. The fate of the fifth you know."

Brett's chair emitted a series of squeaks as he urged it closer to the wall. At the proper distance he stretched out his leg and pressed an electric bell with his toe.

"Decanters and syphons, Smith," he cried, when the door opened.

"Which do you take, whisky or brandy, Mr. Hume?" he inquired.

"Whisky. But I assure you I am quite serious. These things"

"Serious! If my name were Hume-Frazer, nothing less than a runaway steam-engine would take me to Beechcroft. I have never previously heard such a marvellous recital."

"We are a stiff-necked race. My uncle and cousin knew how strangely Fate had pursued every heir to the title, yet each hoped that in his person the tragic sequence would be broken. Oddly enough, my father holds that the family curse, or whatever it is, has now exhausted itself."

"What grounds has he for the belief?"

"None, save a Highlander's readiness to accept signs and portents. Look at this seal."

He unfastened from his waistcoat his watch and chain, with a small bunch of pendants attached, and handed them to Brett. The latter examined the seal with deep interest. It was cut into a bloodstone, and showed a stag's head, surmounted by five pointed rays, like a crown of daggers.

"I cannot decipher the motto," he said; "what is it?"

"*Fortis et audax.*"

"Hum! 'Strong and bold.' A stiff-necked legend, too."

He reached to his bookcase for Burke's "General Armoury." After a brief search, he asked:

"Do you know anything about heraldry?"

"Nothing whatever."

"Then listen to this. The crest of your, house is: 'A stag's head, erased argent, charged with a star of five rays gules.' It is peculiar."

"Yes, so my father says; but why does it appeal to you in that way?"

"Because 'erased' means, in this instance, a stag's head torn forcibly from the body, the severed part being jagged like the teeth of a saw. And 'gules' means 'red.' Now, such heraldic rays are usually azure or blue."

"By Jove, you have hit upon the old man's idea. He contends that those five blood-coloured points signify the founder of the baronetcy and his four lineal descendants. Moreover, the race is now extinct in the direct succession. The title goes to a collateral branch."

Brett stroked his chin thoughtfully.

"It is certainly very strange," he murmured, "that the dry-as-dust knowledge of some member of the College of Heralds should evolve these armorial bearings with their weird significance. Does this account for your allusion to the supernatural?"

"Partly. Do not forget my dream."

"Tell it to me."

"During the trials, my counsel, a very able man, by the way—you know him, of course, Mr. Dobbie, K.C.—only referred to the fact that I dreamed my cousin was in some mortal danger, and that my exclamation 'He is murdered!' was really a startled comment on my part induced by the butler's words. That is not correct. I never told Mr. Dobbie the details of my dream, or vision."

"Oh, didn't you? Men have been hanged before to-day because they thought they could construct a better line of defence than their counsel."

"I had nothing to defend. I was innocent. Moreover, I knew I should not be convicted."

The barrister well remembered the view of the case taken by the Bar mess. Even the redoubtable Dobbie was afraid of the jury. His face must have conveyed dubiety with respect to Hume's last remark, for the other continued eagerly:

"It is quite true. Wait until I have concluded. After the footman brought the whisky and soda to the library that night I took a small quantity, and pulled an easy-chair in front of the fire. I was tired, having travelled all the preceding night and part of the day. Hence the warmth and comfort soon sent me to sleep. I have a hazy recollection of the man coming in to put some coal on the fire. In a sub-conscious fashion I knew that it was not my cousin, but a servant. I settled down a trifle more comfortably, and everything became a blank. Then I thought I awoke. I looked out through the windows, and, to my astonishment, it was broad daylight. The trees, too, were covered with leaves, the sun was shining, and there was every evidence of a fine day in early summer. In some indefinite way I realised that the library was no longer the room which I knew. The furniture and carpets were different. The books were old-fashioned. A very handsome spinning-wheel stood near the open window. There was no litter of newspapers or magazines.

"Before I could begin to piece together these curious discrepancies in the normal condition of things, I saw two men riding up the avenue, where the yew trees, by the way, were loftier and finer in every way than those really existing. The horsemen were dressed in such strange fashion that, unfortunately, I paid little heed to their faces. They wore frilled waistcoats, redingotes with huge lapels and turned-back cuffs, three-cornered hats, and gigantic boots. They dismounted when close to the house. One man held both horses; the other advanced. I was just going to look him straight in the face when another figure appeared, coming from that side of the hall where the entrance is situated. This was a gentleman in very elegant garments, hatless, with powdered queue, pink satin coat embroidered with lace, pink satin small-clothes, white silk stockings, and low shoes. As he walked, a smart cane swung from his left wrist by a silk tassel, and he took a pinch of snuff from an ivory box.

"The two men met and seemed to have a heated argument, bitter and passionate on one side, studiously scornful on the other. This was all in dumb show. Not a word did I hear. My amazed wits were fully taken up with noting their clothes, their postures, the trappings of the horses, the eighteenth century aspect of the library. Strange, is it not, I did not look at their faces?"

Hume paused to gulp down the contents of his tumbler. Brett said not a word, but sat intent, absorbed, wondering, with eyes fixed on the speaker.

"All at once the dispute became vehement. The more stylishly attired man disappeared, but returned instantly with a drawn sword in his hand. The stranger, as we may call him, whipped out a claymore, and the two fought fiercely. By Jove, it was no stage combat or French duel. They went for each other as if they meant it. There was no stopping to take breath, nor drawing apart after a foiled attack. Each man tried to kill the other as speedily as possible. Three times they circled round in furious sword-play. Then the stranger got his point home. The other, in mortal agony, dropped his weapon, and tried with both hands to tear his adversary's blade from his breast. He failed, and staggered back, the victor still shoving the claymore through his opponent's body. Then, and not until then, I saw the face of the man who was wounded, probably killed. It was my cousin, Alan Hume-Fraser."

David Hume stopped again. His bronzed face was pale now. With his left hand he swept huge drops of perspiration from his brow. But his class demands coolness in the most desperate moments. He actually struck a match and relighted his cigarette.

"I suppose you occasionally have a nightmare after an indigestible supper, Mr. Brett," he went on, "and have experienced a peculiar sensation of dumb palsy in the presence of some unknown but terrifying danger? Well, such was my exact state at that moment. Alan fell, apparently lifeless. The stranger kissed his blood-stained sword, which required a strong tug before he could disengage it, rattled it back into the scabbard, rejoined his companion, and the two rode off, without once looking back. I can see them now, square-shouldered, with hair tied in a knot beneath their quaint hats, their hips absurdly swollen by the huge pockets of their coats, their boots hanging over their knees. They wore big brass spurs with tremendous rowels, and the cantles of their saddles were high and brass-bound.

"Alan lay motionless. I could neither speak nor move. Whether I was sitting or standing I cannot tell you, nor do I know how I was supposed to be attired, A darkness came over my eyes. Then a voice–Helen's voice– whispered to me, 'Fear not, dearest; the wrong is avenged.' I awoke, to find the trembling butler shouting in my ear that his master was lying dead outside the house. Now, Mr. Brett, I ask you, would you have submitted that fairy tale to a jury? I was quite assured of a verdict in my favour, though the first disagreement almost shook my faith in Helen's promise, but I did not want to end my days in a criminal lunatic asylum."

He did not appear to expect an answer. He was quite calm again, and even his eyes had lost their intensity. The mere telling of his uncanny experience had a soothing effect. He nonchalantly readjusted his watch and chain, and noted the time.

"I have gone far beyond my stipulated half hour," he said, forcing a deprecatory smile.

"Yes; far beyond, indeed. You carried me back to 1763, but Heaven alone knows when you will end."

"Will you take up my case?"

"Can you doubt it? Do you think I would throw aside the most remarkable criminal puzzle I have ever tackled?"

"Mr. Brett, I cannot find words to thank you. If you succeed–and you inspire me with confidence–Helen and I will strive to merit your lifelong friendship."

"Miss Layton knows the whole of your story, of course?"

"Yes; she and my father only. I must inform you that I had never heard the full reason of the duel between the first Sir Alan and his nephew. But my father knew it fairly well, and the details fitted in exactly with my vision. I can hardly call it a dream."

"What was the nephew's name?"

"David Hume!"

Brett jumped up, and paced about the room.

"These coincidences defy analysis," he exclaimed. "Your Christian name is David. Your surname joins both families. Why, the thing is a romance of the wildest sort."

"Unhappily, it has a tragic side for me."

"Yes; the story cannot end here. You and your fiancée have suffered. Miss Layton must be a very estimable young lady–one worth winning. She will be a true and loyal wife."

"Do you think you will be able to solve the riddle? Someone murdered my cousin."

"That is our only solid fact at present. The family tradition is passing strange, but it will not serve in a court of law. I may fail, for the first time, but I will try hard. When can you accompany me to Stowmarket?"

The question disconcerted his eager auditor. The young man's countenance clouded.

"Is it necessary that I should go there?" he asked.

"Certainly. You must throw aside all delicacy of feeling, sacrifice even your own sentiments. That is the one locality where you don't wish to be seen, of course?"

"It is indeed."

"I cannot help that. I must have the assistance of your local and family knowledge to decide the knotty points sure to arise when I begin the inquiry. Can you start this afternoon?"

"Yes."

"Very well. Come and lunch with me at my club. Then we will separate, to meet again at Liverpool Street. Smith! Pack my traps for a week."

Brett was in the hall now, but he suddenly stopped his companion.

"By the way, Hume, you may like to wire to Miss Layton. My man will send the telegram for you."

David Hume's barrier of proud reserve vanished from that instant. The kindly familiarity of the barrister's words to one who, during many weary days, suspected all men of loathing him as a murderer at large, was directed by infinite tact.

Hume held out his hand, "You *are* a good chap," he said.

4
THROUGH THE LIBRARY WINDOW

Hume did not send a telegram to the Sleagill Rectory. He explained that, owing to the attitude adopted by the Rev. Wilberforce Layton, Helen avoided friction with her father by receiving his (Hume's) letters under cover to Mrs. Eastham.

The younger man was quick to note that Brett did not like this arrangement. He smilingly protested that there was no deception in the matter.

"Helen would never consent to anything that savoured of subterfuge," he explained. "Her father knows well that she hears from me constantly. He is a studious, reserved old gentleman. He was very much shocked by the tragedy, and his daughter's innocent association with it. He told me quite plainly that, under the circumstances, I ought to consider the engagement at an end. Possibly I resented an imputation not intended by him. I made some unfair retort about his hyper-sensitiveness, and promptly sent Helen a formal release. She tore it up, and at the same time accepted it so far as I was concerned. We met at Mrs. Eastham's house—that good lady has remained my firm friend throughout—and I don't mind telling you, Brett, that I broke down utterly. Well, we began by sending messages to each other through Mrs. Eastham. Then I forwarded to Helen, in the same way, a copy of a rough diary of my travels. She wrote to me direct; I replied. The position now is that she will not marry me without her father's consent, and she will marry no one else. He is aware of our correspondence. She always tells him of my movements. The poor old rector is worried to know how to act for the best. His daughter's happiness is at stake, and so my unhappy affairs have drifted aimlessly for more than a year."

"The drifting must cease," said Brett decisively. "Beechcroft Hall will probably provide scope for activity."

They reached Stowmarket by a late train. Next morning they drove to Sleagill–a pretty village, with a Norman church tower standing squarely in the midst of lofty trees, and white-washed cottages and red-tiled villa-residences nestling in gardens.

"A bower of orchards and green lanes," murmured the barrister as their dog-cart sped rapidly over the smooth highway.

Hume was driving. He pointed out the rectory. His eyes were eagerly searching the lawn and the well-trimmed garden, but he was denied a sight of his divinity. The few people they encountered gazed at them curiously. Hume was seemingly unrecognised.

"Here is Mrs. Eastham's house," he said, checking the horse's pace as they approached a roomy, comfortable-looking mansion, occupying an angle where the village street sharply bifurcated. "And there is Beechcroft!"

The lodge faced the road along which they were advancing. Beyond the gates the yew-lined drive, with its selvages of deep green turf, led straight to the Elizabethan house a quarter of a mile distant. The ground in the rear rose gently through a mile or more of the home park.

Immediately behind the Hall was a dense plantation of spruce and larch. The man who planned the estate evidently possessed both taste and spirit. It presented a beautiful and pleasing picture. A sense of homeliness was given by a number of Alderney cattle and young hunters grazing in the park on both sides of the avenue. Beechcroft had a reputation in metropolitan sale-rings. Its two-year-olds were always in demand.

"We will leave the conveyance here," announced Brett "I prefer to walk to the house."

The hotel groom went to the horse's head. He did not hear the barrister's question:

"I suppose both you and your cousin quitted Mrs. Eastham's house by that side-door and entered the park through the wicket?"

"Yes," assented Hume, "though I fail to see why you should hit upon the side-door rather than the main entrance."

"Because the ball-room is built out at the back. It was originally a granary. The conservatory opens into the garden on the other side. As there was a large number of guests, Mrs. Eastham required all her front rooms for supper and extra servants, so she asked people to halt their carriages at the side-door. I would not be surprised if the gentlemen's cloak-room was provided by the saddle-room there, whilst the yard was carpeted and covered with an awning."

Brett rattled on in this way, heedless of his companion's blank amazement, perhaps secretly enjoying it.

Hume was so taken aback that he stood poised on the step of the vehicle and forgot to slip the reins into the catch on the splashboard.

"I told you none of these things," he cried.

"Of course not. They are obvious. But tell this good lady that we are going to the Hall."

Both the main gate and wicket were fastened, and the lodge-keeper's wife was gazing at them through the bars.

"Hello, Mrs. Crowe, don't you know me?" cried Hume.

"My gracious, It's Mr. David!" gasped the woman.

"Why are the gates locked?"

"Mrs. Capella is not receiving visitors, sir."

"Is she ill?"

"No, sir. Indisposed, I think Mr. Capella said."

"Well, she will receive me, at any rate."

"No doubt, sir, it will be all right."

She hesitatingly unbarred the wicket, and the two men entered. They walked slowly up the drive. Hume was restless. Twice he looked behind him.

He stopped.

"It was here," he said, "that the two men dismounted."

Then a few yards farther on:

"Alan came round from the door there, and they fought here. Alan forced the stranger on to the turf. When he was stabbed he fell here."

He pointed to a spot where the road commenced to turn to the left to clear the house. Brett watched him narrowly. The young man was describing his dream, not the actual murder. The vision was far more real to him.

"It was just such a day as this," he continued. "It might have been almost this hour. The library windows"

He ceased and looked fixedly towards the house. Brett, too, gazed in silence. They saw a small, pale-faced, exceedingly handsome Italian—a young man, with coal-black eyes and a mass of shining black hair—scowling at them from within the library.

A black velvet coat and a brilliant tie were the only bizarre features of his costume. They served sufficiently to enhance his foreign appearance. Such a man would be correctly placed in the marble frame of a Neapolitan villa; here he was unusual, *outré*, "un-English," as Brett put it.

But he was evidently master. He flung open the window, and said, with some degree of hauteur:

"Whom do you wish to see? Can I be of any assistance?"

His accent was strongly marked, but his words were well chosen and civil enough, had his tone accorded with their sense. As it was, he might be deemed rude.

Brett advanced.

"Are you Signor Capella?" he inquired.

"Mr. Capella. Yes."

"Then you can, indeed, be of much assistance. This gentleman is Mrs. Capella's cousin, Mr. David Hume-Frazer."

"Corpo di Baccho!"

The Italian was completely taken by surprise. His eyebrows suddenly stood out in a ridge. His sallow skin could not become more pallid; to show emotion he flushed a swarthy red. Beyond the involuntary exclamation in his own language, he could not find words.

"Yes," explained the smiling Brett, "he is a near relative of yours by marriage. We were told by the lodge-keeper that Mrs. Capella was indisposed, but under the circumstances we felt assured that she would receive her cousin—unless, that is, she is seriously ill."

"It is an unexpected pleasure, this visit."

Capella replied to the barrister, but looked at Hume. He had an unpleasant habit of parting his lips closely to his teeth, like the silent snarl of a dog.

"Undoubtedly. We both apologise for not having prepared you."

Brett's smooth, even voice seemed to exasperate the other, who continued to block the library window in uncompromising manner.

"And you, sir. May I ask who you are?"

"My name is Brett, Reginald Brett, a friend of Mr. Hume's—who, I may mention, does not use his full surname at present."

The Italian was compelled to turn his glittering eyes upon the man who addressed him so glibly.

"I am sorry," he said slowly, "but Mrs. Capella is too unwell to meet either of you to-day."

"Ah! We share your regrets. Nevertheless, as a preliminary to our purpose, you will serve our needs equally well. May we not come in?"

Capella was faced with difficult alternatives. He must either be discourteous to two gentlemanly strangers, one of them his wife's relative, or admit them with some show of politeness. An Italian may be rude, he can never be *gauche*. Having decided, Capella ushered them into the library with quick transition to dignified ease.

He asked if he might ring for any refreshments. Hume, who glared at his host with uncompromising hostility, and had not taken any part in the conversation, shook his head.

Brett surprised both, for different reasons, by readily falling in with Capella's suggestion.

"A whisky and soda would be most grateful," he said.

The Italian moved towards the bell.

"Permit me!" cried Brett.

He rose in awkward haste, and upset his chair with a loud crash on the parquet floor.

"How stupid of me!" he exclaimed, whilst Hume wondered what had happened to flurry the barrister, and Capella smothered a curse.

A distant bell jangled. By tacit consent, there was no further talk until a servant appeared. The man was a stranger to Hume.

Oddly enough, Brett took but a very small allowance of the spirit. In reality, he hated alcohol in any form during the earlier hours. He was wont to declare that it not only disturbed his digestion but destroyed his taste for tobacco. Hume did not yet know what a concession to exciting circumstances his new-found friend had made the previous day in ordering spirits before luncheon.

When the servant vanished, Capella settled himself in his chair with the air of a man awaiting explanations. Yet he was restless and disturbed. He was afraid of these two. Why? Brett determined to try the effect of generalities.

"You probably guess the object of our visit?" he began.

"I? No. How should I guess?"

"As the husband of a lady so closely connected with Mr. Hume"

But the Italian seemed to be firmly resolved to end the suspense.

"Caramba!" he broke in. "What is it?"

"It is this. Mr. Hume has asked me to help him in the investigation of certain"

The library door swung open, and a lady entered. She was tall, graceful, distinguished-looking. Her cousinship to Hume was unmistakable. In both there was the air of aristocratic birth. Their eyes, the contour of their faces, were alike. But the fresh Anglo-Saxon complexion of the man was replaced in the woman by a peach-like skin, whilst her hair and eyebrows were darker.

She was strikingly beautiful. A plain black dress set off a figure that would have caused a sculptor to dream of chiselled marble.

"A passionate, voluptuous woman," thought Brett. "A woman easily swayed, but never to be compelled, the ready-made heroine of a tragedy."

Her first expression was one of polite inquiry, but her glance fell upon Hume. Her face, prone to betray each fleeting emotion, exhibited surprise, almost consternation.

"You, Davie!" she gasped.

Hume went to meet her.

"Yes, Rita," he said. "I hope you are glad to see me."

Mrs. Capella was profoundly agitated, but she held out her hand and summoned the quick smile of an actress.

"Of course I am," she cried. "I did not know you were in England. Why did you not let me know, and why are you here?"

"I only returned home three days ago. My journey to Beechcroft was a hasty resolve. This is my friend, Mr. Reginald Brett. He was just about to explain to Mr. Capella the object of our visit when you came in."

Neither husband nor wife looked at the other. Mrs. Capella was flustered, indulging in desperate surmises, but she laughed readily enough.

"I heard a noise in this room, and then the bell rang. I thought something had happened. You know–I mean, I thought there was no one here."

"I fear that I am the culprit, Mrs. Capella. Your husband was good enough to invite us to enter by the window, and I promptly disturbed the household."

Brett's pleasant tones came as a relief. Capella glared at him now with undisguised hostility, for the barrister's adroit ruse had outwitted him by bringing the lady from the drawing-room, which gave on to the garden and lawn at the back of the house.

"Please do not take the blame of my intrusion, Mr. Brett," said Margaret, with forced composure. "You will stay for luncheon, will you not? And you, Davie? Are you at Mrs. Eastham's?"

Her concluding question was eager, almost wistful. Her cousin answered it first.

"No," he said. "We have driven over from Stowmarket."

"And, unfortunately," put in the barrister, "we are pledged to visit Mrs. Eastham within an hour."

The announcement seemed to please Mrs. Capella, for some reason at present hidden from Brett. Hume, of course, was mystified by the course taken by his friend, but held his peace.

Capella brusquely interfered:

"Perhaps, Rita, these gentlemen would now like to make the explanation which you prevented."

He moved towards the door. So that his wife could rest under no doubt as to his wishes, he held it open for her.

"No, no!" exclaimed Brett. "This matter concerns Mrs. Capella personally. You probably forget that we asked to be allowed to see her in the first instance, but you told us that she was too unwell to receive us."

For an instant Margaret gazed at the Italian with imperious scorn. Then she deliberately turned her back on him, and seated herself close to her cousin.

Capella closed the door and walked to the library window.

Hume openly showed his pained astonishment at this little scene. Brett treated the incident as a domestic commonplace.

"The fact is," he explained, "that your cousin, Mrs. Capella, has sought my assistance in order to clear his name of the odium attached to it by the manner of Sir Alan Hume-Frazer's death. At my request he brought me here. In this house, in this very room, such an inquiry should have its origin, wherever it may lead ultimately."

The lady's cheeks became ashen. Her large eyes dilated.

"Is not that terrible business ended yet?" she cried. "I little dreamed that such could be the object of your visit, Davie. What has happened"

The Italian swung round viciously.

"If you come here as a detective, Mr. Brett," he snapped, "I refer you to the police. Mr. Hume-Frazer is known to them."

5
FROM BEHIND THE HEDGE

The man's swarthy rage added force to the taunt. David Hume leaped up, but Brett anticipated him, gripping his arm firmly, and without ostentation.

Margaret, too, had risen. She appeared to be battling with some powerful emotion, choking back a fierce impulse. For an instant the situation was electrical. Then the woman's clear tones rang through the room.

"I am mistress here," she cried, "Giovanni, remain silent or leave us. How dare you, of all men, speak thus to my cousin?"

Certainly the effect of the barrister's straightforward statement was unlooked-for. But Brett felt that a family quarrel would not further his object at that moment. It was necessary to stop the imminent outburst, for David Hume and Giovanni Capella were silently challenging each other to mortal combat. What a place of ill-omen to the descendants of the Georgian baronet was this sun-lit library with its spacious French windows!

"Of course," said the barrister, speaking as quietly as if he were discussing the weather, "such a topic is an unpleasant one. It is, however, unavoidable. My young friend here is determined, at all costs, to discover the secret of Sir Alan's murder. It is imperative that he should do so. The happiness of his whole life depends upon his success. Until that mystery is solved he cannot marry the woman he loves."

"Do you mean Helen Layton?" Margaret's syllables might have been so many mortal daggers.

"Yes."

"Is David still in love with her?"

"Yes."

"And she with him?"

David Hume broke in:

"Yes, Rita. She has been faithful to the end."

A very forcible Italian oath came from Capella as he passed through the window and strode rapidly out of sight, passing to the left of the house, where one of the lines of yew trees ended in a group of conservatories.

Margaret was now deadly white. She pressed her hand to her bosom.

"Forgive me," she sobbed. "I do not feel well. You will both be always welcome here. Let no one interfere with you. But I must leave you. This afternoon"

She staggered to the door. Her cousin caught her.

"Thank you, Davie," she whispered. "Leave me now. I will be all right soon. My heart troubles me. No. Do not ring. Let us keep our miseries from the servants."

She passed out, leaving Hume and the barrister uncertain how best to act The situation had developed with a vengeance. Brett was more bewildered than ever before in his life.

"That scoundrel killed Alan, and now he wants to kill his own wife!" growled Hume, when they were alone.

Brett looked through him rather than at him. He was thinking intently. For a long time—minutes it seemed to his fuming companion—he remained motionless, with glazed, immovable eyes. Then he awoke to action.

"Quick!" he cried. "Tell me if this room has changed much since you were last here. Is the furniture the same? Is that the writing-table? What chair did you sit in? Where was it placed? Quick, man! You have wasted eighteen months. Give me no opinions, but facts."

Thus admonished, scared somewhat by the barrister's volcanic energy, Hume obeyed him.

"There is no material change in the room," he said. "The secretaire is the same. You see, here is the drawer which was broken open. It bears the marks of the implement used to force the lock. I think I sat in this chair, or one like it. It was placed here. My face was turned towards the fire, yet in my dream I was looking through the centre window. The Japanese sword rested here. I showed you where Alan's body was found."

The young man darted about the room to illustrate each sentence. Brett followed his words and actions without comment. He grabbed his hat and stick.

"We will return later in the day," he said. "Let us go at once and call on Mrs. Eastham."

"Mrs. Eastham! Why?"

"Because I want to see Miss Helen Layton. The old lady can send for her."

Hume needed no urging. He could not walk fast enough. They had gone a hundred yards from the house when Brett suddenly stopped and checked his companion.

Behind the yew trees on the left, and rendered invisible by a stout hedge, a man was running–running at top speed, with the labouring breath of one unaccustomed to the exercise. The barrister sprang over the strip of turf, passed among the trees, and plunged into the hedge regardless of thorns. He came back instantly.

"There is a footpath across the park, leading towards the lodge gates. Where does it come out?" he asked, speaking rapidly in a low tone.

"It enters, the road near the avenue, close to the gates. It leads from a farmhouse."

"A lady is walking through the park towards the lodge. Capella is running to intercept her. Come! We may hear something."

Brett set off at a rapid pace along the turf. Hume followed, and soon they were near the lodge. Mrs. Crowe saw them, and came out.

"Stop her!" gasped Brett.

Hume signalled the woman not to open the gate. She watched them with open-mouthed curiosity. The barrister slowed down and quietly made his way to the leafy angle where the avenue hedge joined that which shut off the park from the road.

He held up a warning hand. Hume stepped warily behind him, and both men looked through a portion of the hedge where briars were supplanted by hazel bushes.

Capella was standing panting near a stile. A girl, dressed in muslin, and wearing a large straw hat, was approaching.

"Great Heavens! It is Helen!" exclaimed Hume.

Brett grasped his shoulder.

"Restrain yourself," he whispered earnestly. "Luckily, Capella has not heard you. I regret the necessity which makes us eavesdroppers, but it is a fortunate accident, all the same. Not a word! Remember what is at stake."

They could not see the Italian's face. His back was heaving from the violence of his exertion. Miss Layton was walking rapidly towards the stile. Obviously she had perceived the waiting man, and she was not pleased.

Her pretty face, flushed and sunburnt, wore the strained aspect of a woman annoyed, but trying to be civil.

It was she who took the initiative.

"Good day, Mr. Capella," she said pleasantly. "Why on earth did you run so fast?"

"Because I wished to be here before you, Miss Layton," replied the man, his voice tremulous with excitement.

"Then I wish I had known, because I could have beaten you easily if you meant to race me."

"That was not my object."

"Well, now you have attained it, whatever it may have been, please allow me to get over the stile. I will be late for luncheon. My father wished me to ascertain how Farmer Burton is progressing after his spill. He was thrown from his dog-cart whilst coming from the Bury St. Edmund's fair."

It was easy for the listeners behind the hedge to gather that the girl's affable manner was affected. She was really somewhat alarmed. Her eyes wandered to the high road to see if anyone was approaching, and she kept at some distance from the Italian.

"Do not play with me, Nellie," said Capella, in agonised accents. "I am consumed with love of you. Can you not, at least, give me your pity?"

"Mr. Capella," she cried, and none but one blind to all save his own passionate desires could fail to note her lofty disdain, "how can you be so base as to use such language to me?"

"Base! To love you!"

"Again I say it—base and unmanly. What have I done that you should venture to so insult your charming wife, not to speak of the insult to myself? When you so far forgot yourself a fortnight ago as to hint at your outrageous ideas regarding me, I forced myself to remember that you were not an Englishman, that perhaps in your country there may be a social code which permits a man to dishonour his home and to annoy a defenceless woman. I cannot forgive you a second time. Let me pass! Let me pass, I tell you, or I will strike you!"

Brett, in his admiration for the spirited girl who, notwithstanding her protestations, seemed to be anything but "defenceless," momentarily forgot his companion.

A convulsive tightening of Hume's muscles, preparatory to a leap through the hedge, warned him in time.

"Idiot!" he whispered, as he clutched him again.

Were not the others so taken up with the throbbing influences of the moment they must have heard the rustling of the leaves. But they paid little heed to external affairs. The Italian was speaking.

"Nellie," he said, "you will drive me mad. But listen, carissima. If I may not love you, I can at least defend you. David Hume-Frazer, the man who murdered my wife's brother, has returned, and openly boasts that you are waiting to marry him."

"Boasts! To whom, pray?"

"To me. I heard him say this not fifteen minutes since."

"Where? You do not know him. He could not be here without my knowledge."

"Then it is true. You do intend to marry this unconvicted felon?"

"Mr. Capella, I really think you are what English people call 'cracked.'"

"But you believe me—that this man has come to Beechcroft?"

"It may be so. He has good reasons, doubtless, for keeping his presence here a secret. Whatever they may be, I shall soon know them."

"Helen, he is not worthy of you. He cannot give you a love fierce as mine.

Nay, I will not be repelled. Hear me. My wife is dying. I will be free in a few months. Bid me to hope. I will not trouble you. I will go away, but I swear, if you marry Frazer, neither he nor you will long enjoy your happiness!" The girl made no reply, but sprang towards the stile in sheer desperation.

Capella strove to take her in his arms, not indeed with intent to offer her any violence; but she met his lover-like ardour with such a vigorous buffet that he lost his temper.

He caught her. She had almost surmounted the stile, but her dress hampered her movements. The Italian, vowing his passion in an ardent flow of words, endeavoured to kiss her.

Then, with a sigh, for he would have preferred to avoid an open rupture, Brett let go his hold on Hume. Indeed, if he had not done so, there must have been a fight on both sides of the hedge.

He turned away at once to light a cigarette. What followed immediately had no professional interest for him.

But he could not help hearing Helen's shriek of delighted surprise, and certain other sounds which denoted that Giovanni was being used as a football by his near relative by marriage.

Mrs. Crowe came out of her cottage.

"What's a-goin' on in the park, sir?" she inquired anxiously.

"A great event," he said. "Faust is kicking Mephistopheles."

"Drat them colts!" she cried, adding, after taking thought; "but we haven't any horses of them names, sir."

"No! You surprise me. They are of the best Italian pedigree."

Meanwhile, he was achieving his object, which was to drive Mrs. Crowe back towards the wicket.

Helen's voice came to them shrilly:

"That will do, Davie! Do you hear me?"

"Why, bless my 'eart, there's Miss Layton," said Mrs. Crowe.

"What a fine little boy this is!" exclaimed Brett, stooping over a curly-haired urchin. "Is he the oldest?"

"Good gracious, sir, no. He's the youngest."

"Dear me, I would not have thought so. You must have been married very early. Here, my little man, see what you can buy for half-a-crown."

"What a nice gentleman he is, to be sure," thought the lodge-keeper's wife, when Brett passed through the smaller gate, assured that the struggle in the park had ended.

"Just fancy 'im a-thinkin' Jimmy was the eldest, when I will be a grandmother come August if all goes well wi' Kate."

The barrister signed to the groom to wait, and joined the young couple, who now appeared in the roadway. A haggard, dishevelled, and furious man burst through the avenue hedge and ran across the drive.

"Mrs. Crowe," he almost screamed, "do you see those two men there?"

"Yes, sir."

The good woman was startled by her master's sudden appearance and his excited state.

"They are never to be admitted to the grounds again. Do you understand?"

"Yes, sir."

Capella turned to rush away up the avenue, but he was compelled to limp. Mrs. Crowe watched him wonderingly, and tried to piece together in her mind the queer sounds and occurrences of the last two minutes.

She had not long been in the cottage when the butler arrived.

"You let two gentlemen in a while ago?" he said.

"I did."

"One was Mr. David and the other a Mr. Brett?"

"Oh, was that the tall gentleman's name?"

"I expect so. Well, here's the missus's written order that whenever they want to come to the 'ouse or go anywheres in the park it's O.K."

Mrs. Crowe was wise enough to keep her own counsel, but when the butler retired, she said:

"Then I'll obey the missus, an' master can settle it with her. I don't hold by Eye-talians, anyhow."

6
AN OLD ACQUAINTANCE

Helen was very much upset by the painful scene which had just been enacted. Its vulgarity appalled her. In a little old-world hamlet like Sleagill, a riotous cow or frightened horse supplied sensation for a week. What would happen when it became known that the rector's daughter had been attacked by the Squire of Beechcroft in the park meadow, and saved from his embraces only after a vigorous struggle, in which her defender was David Hume-Frazer, concerning whom the villagers still spoke with bated breath?

Of course, the girl imagined that many people must have witnessed the occurrence. The appearance of Brett, of the waiting groom, and of a chance labourer who now strode up the village street, led her to think so.

She did not realise that the whole affair had barely lasted a minute, that Brett was Hume's friend, the man-servant a stranger who had seen nothing and heard little, whilst the villager only wondered, when he touched his cap, "why Miss Layton was so flustered like."

Brett attributed her agitation to its right cause. He knew that this healthy, high-minded, and athletic young woman went under no fear of Capella and his ravings.

"What happened when you jumped the hedge?" he said to Hume.

"I handled that scoundrel somewhat roughly," was the answer. "It was Nellie here who begged for mercy on his account."

"Ah, well, the incident ended very pleasantly. No one saw what happened save the principals, a fortunate thing in itself. We want to prevent a nine days' wonder just now."

"Are you quite sure?" asked Miss Layton, overjoyed at this expression of opinion, and secretly surprised at the interest taken by the barrister in the affair, for Hume had not as yet found time to tell her his friend's name.

"Quite sure, Miss Layton," he said, with the smile which made him such a prompt favourite with women. "I had nothing to do but observe the *mise-en-scéne*. The stage was quite clear for the chief actors. And now, may I make a suggestion? The longer we remain here the more likely are we to attract observation. Mr. Hume and I are going to call on Mrs. Eastham. May we expect you in an hour's time?"

"Can't you come in with us now?" exclaimed David eagerly.

She laughed excitedly, being yet flurried. The sudden appearance of her lover tried her nerves more than the Italian's passionate avowal.

"No, indeed," she cried. "I must go home. My father will forget all about his lunch otherwise, and I am afraid—I want to cry!"

Without another word she hurried off towards the rectory.

"My dear fellow," murmured Brett to the disconsolate Hume, "don't you understand? She cannot bear the constraint imposed by my presence at this moment, nor could she meet Mrs. Eastham with any degree of composure. Now, this afternoon she will return a mere iceberg. Mrs. Eastham, I am sure, has tact. I am going to the Hall. You two will be left alone for hours."

He turned aside to arrange with the groom concerning the care of the horse, as they would be detained sometime in the village. Then the two men approached Mrs. Eastham's residence.

That good person, a motherly old lady of over sixty, was not only surprised but delighted by the advent of David Hume.

"My dear boy," she cried, advancing to meet him with outstretched hands when he entered the morning-room. "What fortunate wind has blown you here?"

"I can hardly tell you, auntie," he said–both Helen and he adopted the pleasing fiction of a relationship that did not exist—"you must ask Mr. Brett."

Thus appealed to, the barrister set forth, in a few explicit words, the object of their visit.

"I hope and believe you will succeed," said Mrs. Eastham impulsively. "Providence has guided your steps here at this hour. You cannot imagine how miserable that man Capella makes me."

"Why?" cried Hume, darting a look of surprise at Brett.

"Because he is simply pestering Nellie with his attentions. There! I must speak plainly. He has gone to extremes that can no longer be misinterpreted. In our small community, Mr. Brett," she explained, "though we dearly love a little gossip, we are slow to believe that a man married to such a charming if somewhat unconventional woman as Margaret Hume-Frazer–I cannot train my tongue to call her Mrs. Capellawould deliberately neglect his wife and dare to demonstrate his unlawful affection for another woman, especially such a girl as Helen Layton."

"How long has this been going on?" inquired Brett, for Hume was too furious to speak.

"For some months, but it is only a fortnight ago since Helen first complained of it to me I promptly told Mr. Capella that I could not receive him again at my house. He discovered that Nellie came here a good deal, and managed to call about the same time as she did. Then he found that she was interested in Japanese art, and as he is really clever in that respect"

"Clever," interrupted the barrister. "Do you mean that he understands lacquer work, Satsuma ware, painting or inlaying? Is he a connoisseur or a student?"

"It is all Greek to me!" exclaimed the old lady, "but unquestionably the bits of china and queer carvings he often brought here were very beautiful. Nellie did not like him personally, but she could not deny his knowledge and enthusiasm. Margaret, too, used to invite her to the Hall, for Miss Layton has great taste as an amateur gardener, Mr. Brett. But this friendship suddenly ceased. Mr. Capella became very strange and gloomy in his manner. At last Nellie told me that the wretched man had dared to utter words of love to her, hinting that his wife could not live long, and that he would come in for her fortune. Now, as my poor girl has been the most faithful soul that ever lived, never for an instant doubting that someday the cloud would lift from Davie, you may imagine what a shock this was to her."

"Mrs. Eastham," said Brett, suddenly switching the conversation away from the Italian's fantasy, "you are well acquainted with all the circumstances connected with Sir Alan's murder. Have you formed any theory about the crime, its motive, or its possible author?"

"God forgive me if I do any man an injury, but in these last few days I have had my suspicions," she exclaimed.

"Tell me your reasons."

"It arose out of a chance remark by Nellie. She was discussing with me her inexplicable antipathy to Mr. Capella, even during the time when they were outwardly good friends. She said that once he showed her a Japanese sword, a most wonderful piece of workmanship, with veins of silver and gold let into the handle and part of the blade. To the upper part of the scabbard was attached a knife–a small dagger–similar"

"Yes, I understand. An implement like that used to kill Sir Alan Hume-Frazer."

"Exactly. Nellie at first hardly realised its significance. Then she hastily told Capella to take it away, but not before she noticed that he seemed to understand the dreadful thing. It is fastened in its sheath by a hidden spring, and he knew exactly how to open it. Any person not accustomed to such weapons would endeavour to pull it out by main force."

Brett did not press Mrs. Eastham to pursue her theory. It was plain that she regarded the Italian as a man who might conceivably be the murderer of his wife's brother. This was enough for feminine logic.

Hume, too, shared the same belief, and had not scrupled to express it openly.

There were, it was true, reasons in plenty, why Capella should have committed this terrible deed. He was, presumably, affianced to Margaret at the time. Apparently her father's will had contemplated the cutting down of her annual allowance. The young heir had, on the other hand, made up the deficit. But why did these artificial restrictions exist? Why were precautions taken by the father to diminish his daughter's income? She had been extravagant. Both father and brother quarrelled with her on this point. Indeed, there was a slight family disturbance with reference to it during Sir Alan's last visit to London. Was Capella mixed up with it?

At last there was a glimmering perception of motive for an otherwise fiendishly irrational act. Did it tend to incriminate the Italian?

A summons to luncheon dispelled the momentary gloom of their thoughts. Before the meal ended Miss Layton joined them.

Brett looked at his watch. "Fifty minutes!" he said.

Then they all laughed, except Mrs. Eastham, who marvelled at the coolness of the meeting between the girl and David. But the old lady was quick-witted.

"Have you met before?" she cried.

"Dearest," said the girl, kissing her; "do you mean to say they have not told you what happened in the park?"

"That will require a special sitting," said Brett gaily. "Meanwhile, I am going to the Hall. I suppose you do not care to accompany me, Hume?"

"I do not."

The reply was so emphatic that it created further merriment.

"Well, tell me quickly what this new secret is," exclaimed Mrs. Eastham, "because in five minutes I must have a long talk with my cook. She has to prepare pies and pastry sufficient to feed nearly a hundred school children next Monday, and it is a matter of much calculation."

Brett took his leave.

"I knew that good old soul would be tactful," he said to himself. "Now I wonder how Winter made such a colossal mistake as to imagine that Hume murdered his cousin. He was sure of the affections of a delightful girl; he could not succeed to the property; he has declined to take up the title. What reason could he have for committing such a crime?"

Then a man walked up the road—a man dressed like a farmer or grazier, rotund, strongly-built, cheerful-looking. He halted opposite Mrs. Eastham's house, where the barrister still stood drawing on his gloves on the doorstep.

"Yes," said Brett aloud, "you *are* an egregious ass, Winter."

"Why, Mr. Brett?" asked the unabashed detective. "Isn't the make-up good?"

"It is the make-up that always leads you astray. You never theorise above the level of the *Police Gazette*."

Mr. Winter yielded to not unnatural annoyance. With habitual caution, he glanced around to assure himself that no other person was within earshot; then he said vehemently:

"I tell you, Mr. Brett, that swine killed Sir Alan Hume-Frazer."

"You use strong language."

"Not stronger than he deserves."

"What are you doing here?"

"I heard he was in London, and watched him. I saw him go to your chambers and guessed what was up, so I came down here to see you and tell you what I know."

"Out of pure good-nature?"

"You can believe it or not, Mr. Brett. It is the truth."

"He has been tried and acquitted. He cannot be tried again. Does Scotland Yard"

"I'm on my holidays."

Brett laughed heartily.

"I see!" he cried. "A 'bus-driver's holiday! For how long?"

"Fourteen days."

"You are nothing if not professional. I suppose it was not your first offence, or they might have let you off with a fine."

The detective enjoyed this departmental joke. He grinned broadly.

"Anyhow, Mr. Brett," he said, "you and I have been engaged on too many smart bits of work for me to stand quietly by and let you be made a fool of."

The barrister came nearer, and said, in a low tone:

"Winter, you have never been more mistaken in your life. Now, attend to my words. If you help me you will, in the first place, be well paid for your services. Secondly, you will be able to place your hand on the true murderer of Sir Alan Hume-Frazer, or I will score my first failure. Thirdly, Scotland Yard will give you another holiday, and I can secure you some shooting in Scotland. What say you?"

The detective looked thoughtful. Long experience had taught him not to argue with Brett when the latter was in earnest.

"I will do anything in my power," he said, "but there is more in this business than perhaps you are aware of— more than ever transpired at the Assizes."

"Quite so, and a good deal that has transpired since. Now. Winter, don't argue, there's a good fellow. Go and engage the landlord of the local inn in a discussion on crops. I am off to Beechcroft Hall. Mr. Hume and I will call for you on our way back to Stowmarket. In our private sitting-room at the hotel there I will explain everything."

They parted. Brett was promptly admitted by Mrs. Crowe, and walked rapidly up the avenue.

Winter watched his retreating figure.

"He's smart, I know he's smart," mused the detective. "But he doesn't know everything about this affair. He doesn't know, I'll be bound, that David Hume-Frazer waited for his cousin that night outside the library. I didn't know it—worse luck!—until after he was acquitted. And he doesn't know that Miss Nellie Layton didn't reach home until 1.30 a.m., though she left the ball at 12.15, and her house is, so to speak, a minute's walk distant. And she was in a carriage. Oh, there's more in this case than meets the eye! I can't say which would please me most, to find out the real murderer, if Hume didn't do it, or prove Mr. Brett to be in the wrong!"

7
HUSBAND AND WIFE

Brett did not hurry on his way to the Hall. Already things were in a whirl, and the confusion was so great that he was momentarily unable to map out a definite line of action.

The relations between Capella and his wife were evidently strained almost to breaking point, and it was this very fact which caused him the greatest perplexity.

They had been married little more than six months. They were an extraordinarily handsome couple, apparently well suited to each other by temperament and mutual sympathies, whilst their means were ample enough to permit them to live under any conditions they might choose, and gratify personal hobbies to the fullest extent.

What, then, could have happened to divide them so completely?

Surely not Capella's new-born passion for Helen Layton. Not even a hot-blooded Southerner could be guilty of such deliberate rascality, such ineffable folly, during the first few months after his marriage to a beautiful and wealthy wife.

No, this hypothesis must be rejected. Margaret Capella had drifted apart from her husband almost as soon as they reached England on their return as man and wife. Capella, miserable and disillusioned, buried alive in a country place—for such must existence in Beechcroft mean to a man of his inclinations—had discovered a startling contrast between his passionate and moody spouse, and the bright, pleasant-mannered girl whose ill-fortune it was to create discord between the inmates of the Hall.

This theory did not wholly exonerate the Italian, but it explained a good deal. The barrister saw no cause as yet to suspect Capella of the young baronet's murder. Were he guilty of that ghastly crime, his motive must have been to secure for himself the position he was now deliberately imperiling–all for a girl's pretty face.

The explanation would not suffice. Brett had seen much that is hidden from public ken in the vagaries of criminals, but he had never yet met a man wholly bad, and at the same time in full possession of his senses.

To adopt the hasty judgment arrived at by Hume and Mrs. Eastham, Capella must be deemed capable of murdering his wife's brother, of bringing about the death of his wife after securing the reversion of her vast property to himself, and of falling in love with Helen–all in the same breath. This species of criminality was only met with in lunatics, and Capella impressed the barrister as an emotional personage, capable of supreme good as of supreme evil, but quite sane.

The question to be solved was this: Why did Capella and his wife quarrel in the first instance? Perhaps, that way, light might come.

He asked a footman if Mrs. Capella would receive him. The man glanced at his card.

"Yes, sir," he said at once. "Madam gave instructions that if either you or Mr. David called you were to be taken to her boudoir, where she awaits you."

The room was evidently on the first floor, for the servant led him up the magnificent oak staircase that climbed two sides of the reception hall.

But this was fated to be a day of interruptions. The barrister, when he reached the landing, was confronted by the Italian.

"A word with you, Mr. Brett," was the stiff greeting given to him.

"Certainly. But I am going to Mrs. Capella's room."

"She can wait. She does not know you are here. James, remain outside until Mr. Brett returns. Then conduct him to your mistress."

Capella's tone admitted of no argument, nor was it necessary to protest. Brett always liked people to talk in the way they deemed best suited to their own interests. Without any expostulation, therefore, he followed his limping host into a luxuriously furnished dressing-room.

Capella closed the door, and placed himself gently on a couch.

"Does your friend fight?" he said, fixing his dark eyes, blazing with anger, intently on the other.

"That is a matter on which your opinion would probably be more valuable than mine."

"Spare me your wit. You know well what I mean. Will he meet me on the Continent and settle our quarrel like a gentleman, not like a hired bravo?"

"What quarrel?"

"Mr. Brett, you are not so stupid. David Hume, notwithstanding his past, may still be deemed a man of honour in some respects. He treated me grossly this morning. Will he fight me, or must I treat him as a cur?"

Brett, without invitation, seated himself. He produced a cigarette and lit it, adding greatly to Capella's irritation by his provoking calmness.

"Really," he said at last, "you amuse me."

"Silence!" he cried imperatively, when the Italian would have broken out into a torrent of expostulations. "Listen to me, you vain fool!"

This method of address had the rare merit of achieving its object. Capella was reduced to a condition of speechless rage.

"You consider yourself the aggrieved person, I suppose," went on the Englishman, subsiding into a state of contemptuous placidity. "You neglect your wife, make love to an honourable and pure-minded girl, stoop to the use of unworthy taunts and even criminal innuendos, lose such control of your passion as to lay sacrilegious hands upon Helen Layton, and yet you resent the well-merited punishment administered to you by her affianced husband. Were I a surgeon, Mr. Capella, I might take an anatomical interest in your brain. As it is, I regard you as a psychological study in latter-day blackguardism. Do you understand me?"

"Perfectly. You have not yet answered my question. Will Hume fight?"

"I should say that nothing would give him greater pleasure."

"Then you will arrange this matter? I can send a friend to you?"

"And if you do I will send the police to you, thus possibly anticipating matters somewhat."

"What do you mean?"

"I mean that my sole purpose in life just now is to lay hands on the man who killed Sir Alan Hume-Frazer. Until that end is achieved, I will take good care that your crude ideas of honour are dealt with, as they were to-day, by the toe of a boot."

Capella was certainly a singular person. He listened unmoved to Brett's threats and insults. He gave that snarling smile of his, and toyed impatiently with his moustache.

"Your object in life does not concern me. Your courts tried their best to hang the man who was responsible for his cousin's death, and failed. I take it you decline this proffered duel?"

"Yes."

"Then I will fight David Hume in my own way. You have rejected the fair alternative on his behalf. Caramba! We shall see now who wins. He will never marry Helen."

"What did you mean just now when you said that he was 'responsible for his cousin's death'? Is that an Italian way of describing a cold-blooded murder?"

Capella leaned back and snarled silently again. It was a pity he had cultivated that trick. It spoilt an otherwise classically regular set of features.

"James!" he shouted.

The footman entered.

"Take this gentleman to your mistress. I have done with him."

"For the present, James," said Brett.

The astonished servant led him along a corridor and knocked at a door hidden by a silk curtain. Mrs. Capella rose to receive her visitor. She was very pale now, but quite calm and dignified in manner.

"Davie did not come with you?" she said when Brett was seated near to her in an alcove formed by an oriel window.

"No. He is with Miss Layton."

"Ah, I am not sorry, I prefer to talk with you alone."

"It is perhaps better. Your cousin is impulsive in some respects, though self-contained enough in others."

"It may be so. I like him, although we have not seen much of each other since we were children. I knew him this morning principally on account of his likeness to Alan. But you are his friend, Mr. Brett, and I can discuss with you matters I would not care to broach with him. He is with Helen Layton now, you say?"

"Yes, and let me add an explanation. Those two young people are devoted to each other. No power on earth could separate them."

"Why do you tell me that?"

"Because I think you wished to be assured of it?"

"You are clever, Mr. Brett. If you can interpret a criminal's designs as well as you can read a woman's heart you must be a terror to evil-doers."

A slight colour came into her cheeks. The barrister leaned forward, his hands clasped and arms resting on his knees.

"I have just seen your husband," he said.

She exhibited no marked sign of emotion but he thought he detected a frightened look in her eyes.

"Again I ask," she exclaimed, "why do you tell me?"

"The reason is obvious. You ought to know all that goes on. There was a quarrel this morning between him and David Hume. Your husband wished me to arrange a duel. I promised him a visit from the police if I heard any more of such nonsense."

"A duel! More bloodshed!" she almost whispered.

"Do not have any alarm for either of them. They are quite safe. I will guarantee so much, at any rate. But your husband is a somewhat curious person. He is prone to strong and sudden hatreds—and attachments."

Margaret pressed her hands to her face. She could no longer bear the torture of make-believe quiescence.

"Oh, what shall I do!" she wailed. "I am the most miserable woman in England to-day, and I might have been the happiest."

"Why are you miserable, Mrs. Capella?" asked Brett gently.

"I cannot tell you. Perhaps it is owing to my own folly. Are you sure that David and Helen intend to get married?"

"Yes."

"Then, for Heaven's sake, let the wedding take place. Let them leave Beechcroft and its associations forever."

"That cannot be until Hume's character is cleared from the odium attached to it."

"You mean my brother's death. But that has been settled by the courts. David was declared 'Not guilty.' Surely that will suffice! No good purpose can be gained by reopening an inquiry closed by the law."

"I think you are a little unjust to your cousin in this matter, Mrs. Capella. He and his future wife feel very grievously the slur cast upon his name. You know perfectly well that if half the people in this county were asked, 'Who killed Sir Alan Hume-Frazer?' they would say 'David Hume.' The other half would shake their heads in dubiety, and prefer not to be on visiting terms with David Hume and his wife. No; your brother was killed in a particularly foul way. He died needlessly, so far as we can learn. His death should be avenged, and this can only be done by tracking his murderer and ruthlessly bringing the wretch to justice. Are not these your own sentiments when divested of all conflicting desires?"

Brett's concluding sentence seemed to petrify his hearer.

"In what way can I help you?" she murmured, and the words appeared to come from a heart of stone.

"There are many items I want cleared up, but I do not wish to distress you unduly. Can you not refer me to your solicitors, for instance? I imagine they will be able to answer all my queries."

"No. I prefer to deal with the affair myself."

"Very well. I will commence with you personally. Why did you quarrel with your brother in London a few days before his death?"

"Because I was living extravagantly. Not only that, but he disapproved of my manner of life. In those days I was headstrong and wilful. I loved a Bohemian existence combined with absurd luxury, or rather, a wildly useless expenditure of money. No one who knows me now could picture me then. Yet now I am good and unhappy. Then I was wicked, in some people's eyes, and happy. Strange, is it not?"

"Not altogether so unusual as you may think. Was any other person interested in what I may term the result of the dispute between your brother and yourself?"

"That is a difficult question to answer. I was very careless in money matters, but it is clear that the curtailment of my rate of living from £15,000 to £5,000 per annum must make considerable difference to all connected with me."

"Had you been living at the former rate?"

"Yes, since my father's death. What annoyed Alan was the fact that I had borrowed from money-lenders."

"Who else knew of your disagreement with him besides these money-lenders and his solicitors?"

"All my friends. I used to laugh at his serious ways, when I, older and much more experienced in some respects, treated life as a tiresome joke. But none of my friends were commissioned to murder my brother so that I might obtain the estate, Mr. Brett."

"Not by you," he said thoughtfully.

He knew well that to endeavour to get Margaret to implicate her husband would merely render her an active opponent. She loved this Italian scamp. She was profoundly thankful that David Hume had come back to claim the hand of Helen Layton, the woman who had been the unwilling object of Capella's wayward affections. She would be only too glad to give half her property to the young couple if they would settle in New Zealand or Peru–far from Beechcroft.

Yet it was impossible to believe that she could love a man whom she suspected of murdering her brother. Why, then, had husband and wife drifted apart? Assuredly the pieces of the puzzle were inextricably mixed.

"Where did you marry Mr. Capella?" asked Brett suddenly.

"At Naples–a civil ceremony, before the Mayor, and registered by the British Consul."

"Had you been long acquainted"

"I met him, oddly enough, in Covent Garden Theatre, the night my brother was killed"

It was now Brett's turn to be startled.

"Are you quite certain of this?" he asked, his surprise at the turn taken by the conversation almost throwing him off his guard.

"Positive. Were you led to believe that Giovanni was the murderer?"

Her voice was cold, impassive, marvellously under control. It warned him, threw him back into the safe role of Hume's adviser and friend.

"I am led to believe nothing at present," he said slowly. "This inquiry is, as yet, only twenty-four hours old so far as I am concerned. I am seeking information. When I am gorged with facts I proceed to digest them."

"Well, what I tell you is true. There are no less than ten people, all living, I have no doubt, who can testify to its correctness. I had a box at the Fancy Dress Ball that New Year's Eve. I invited nine guests. One of them, an attaché at the Italian Embassy, brought Giovanni and introduced him to me. We were together from midnight until 4.30 a.m. Whilst poor Alan was lying here dead, I was revelling at a *bal masqué*. Do you think I am likely to forget the circumstances?"

The icy tones thrilled with pitiful remembrance. But the barrister's task required the unsparing use of the probe. He determined, once and for all, to end an unpleasant scene.

"Will you tell me why you and your husband have, shall we say, disagreed so soon after your marriage? You were formed by Providence and nature to be mated. What has driven you apart?"

The woman flushed scarlet under this direct inquiry.

"I cannot tell you," she said brokenly, "but the cause—in no way—concerns–either my brother's death–or David's innocence. It is personal–between Giovanni and myself. In God's good time, it may be put right."

Brett, singularly enough, was a man of quick impulse. He was moved now by a profound pity for the woman who thus bared her heart to him.

"Thank you for your candour, Mrs. Capella," he exclaimed, with a fervour that evidently touched her. "May I ask one more question, and I have done with a most unpleasant ordeal. Do you suspect any person of being your brother's assassin?"

"No," she said. "Indeed I do not."

8
REVELATIONS

Hume and Winter did not meet on terms that might be strictly described as cordial.

Brett, on quitting the Hall, had surrendered himself to a spell of vacant bewilderment. He haled the unwilling Hume from Helen's society, and picked up the detective at the Wheat Sheaf Inn. Then the barrister, from sheer need of mental relief, determined to have some fun with them.

"You two ought to know each other," he said good-humouredly. "At one time you took keen interest in matters of mutual concern. Allow me to introduce you. Hume—this is Mr. Winter, of Scotland Yard."

David was quite unprepared for the meeting.

"What?" he exclaimed, his upper lip stiffening, "the man who concocted all sorts of imaginary evidence against me!"

"'Concocted' is not the right word, nor imaginary' either," growled Winter.

"Quite right," said Brett. "Really, Hume, you should be more careful in your choice of language. Had Winter been as careless in his statements at the Assizes, he would certainly have hanged you."

Hume was too happy, after a prolonged *tête-à-tête* with his beloved, to harbour malice against any person.

"What are we supposed to do—shake hands?" he inquired blandly.

"It might be a good preliminary to a better understanding of one another. You think Winter is an unscrupulous ruffian. He described you to me as a swine not two hours ago. Now, you are both wrong. Winter is the best living police detective, and a most fair-minded one. He will be a valuable ally. Before many days are over you will be deeply in his debt in every sense of the word. On the other hand, you, Hume, are a much-wronged man, whom Winter must help to regain his rightful position. This is one of the occasions when Justice is compelled to take the bandage off her eyes. She may be impartial, but she is often blind. Now be friends, and let us start from that basis."

Silently the two men exchanged a hearty grip.

"Excellent!" cried the barrister. "Hume, take Winter with you in front. I will seat myself beside the groom, and please oblige me, both of you, by not addressing a word to me between here and Stowmarket."

Hume and the detective got along comfortably once the ice was broken. Naturally, they steered clear of all reference to the tragedy in the presence of the servant. Their talk dealt chiefly with sporting matters.

Brett, carried swiftly along the level road, kept his eyes fixed on Beechcroft and its contiguous hamlet until they vanished in the middle distance.

"This is the most curious inquiry I was ever engaged in," he communed. "Winter, of course, will fasten on to Capella like a horse leech when he knows the facts. Yet Capella is neither a coward nor an ordinary villain. For some ridiculous reason, I have a sneaking sympathy with him. Had he stormed and blustered when I pitched into him to-day I would have thought less of him. And his wife! What mysterious workings of Fate brought those two together and then disunited them? They become fascinated one with the other whilst the brother's corpse is still palpitating beneath that terrible stroke. They get married, with not unreasonable haste, but no sooner do they reach Beechcroft, a house of evil import if ever bricks and mortar had such a character, than they are driven asunder by some malign influence.

"And now, after eighteen months, I am asked to take up the tangled clues, if such may be said to exist. It is a difficult, perhaps an impossible, undertaking. Yet if I have done so much in a day, what may not happen in a fortnight!"

Long afterwards, recalling that soliloquy, he wondered whether or not, were he suddenly endowed with the gift of prophecy, he would, nevertheless, have pursued his quest. He never could tell.

Once securely entrenched in a private sitting-room of the Stowmarket Hotel, the three men began to discuss crime and tobacco.

Mr. Winter commenced by being confidential and professional.

"Now, Mr. Hume," he said, "as misunderstandings have been cleared, to some extent, by Mr. Brett's remarks, I will, with your permission, ask you a few questions."

"Fire away."

"In the first place, your counsel tried to prove–did prove, in fact–that you walked straight from the ball-room to the Hall, sat down in the library, and did not move from your chair until Fergusson, the butler, told you how he had found Sir Alan's body on the lawn."

"Exactly."

"So if a man comes forward now and swears that he watched you for nearly ten minutes standing in the shadow of the yews on the left of the house, he will not be telling the truth?"

"That is putting it mildly."

"Yet there is such a witness in existence, and I am certain he is not a liar in this matter."

"What!"

Brett and Hume ejaculated the word simultaneously; the one surprised, because he knew how careful Winter was in matters of fact, the other indignant at the seeming disbelief in his statement.

"Please, gentlemen," appealed the detective, secretly gratified by the sensation he caused, "wait until I have finished. If I did not fully accept Mr. Brett's views on this remarkable case, I would not be sitting here this minute. My conscience would not permit it"

"Be virtuous, Winter, but not too virtuous," broke in Brett drily.

"There you go again, sir, questioning my motives. But I am of a forgiving disposition. Now, there cannot be the slightest doubt that a poacher named John Wise, better known as 'Rabbit Jack,' who resides in this town, chose that New Year's Eve as an excellent time to net the meadows behind the Hall. He had heard about Mrs. Eastham's dance, and knew that on such a night the estate keepers would have more liking for fun with the coachmen and maids than for game-watching. He entered the park soon after midnight, and saw a gentleman walk up the avenue towards the house. He waited a few minutes, and crept quietly along the side of the hedge—in the park, of course. Being winter time, the trees and bushes were bare, and he was startled to see the same gentleman, with his coat buttoned up, standing in the shade of the yews close to the Hall. 'Rabbit Jack' naturally thought he had been spotted. He gripped his lurcher's collar and stood still for nearly ten minutes. Then it occurred to him that he was mistaken. He had not been seen, so he stole off towards the plantation and started operations. He is a first-rate poacher, and always works alone. About three o'clock he was alarmed by a policeman's lantern—the search of the grounds after the murder, you see—and made off. He entered Stowmarket on the far side of the town, and ran into a policeman's arms. They fought for twenty minutes. The P.C. won, and 'Rabbit Jack' got six months' hard labour for being in unlawful possession of game and assaulting the police. Consequently, he never heard a syllable about the 'Stowmarket Mystery,' as this affair was called by the Press, until long after Mr. Hume's second trial and acquittal. Yet the first thing 'Rabbit Jack' did after his release was to go straight to the police and tell them what he had seen. I think, Mr. Hume, that even you will admit a good deal depended on the result of the fight between the poacher and the bobby, for 'Rabbit Jack' described a man of your exact appearance and dressed as you were that night."

There was silence for a moment when Winter ended his recital.

"It is evident," said Brett, otherwise engaged in making smoke-rings, "that 'Rabbit Jack' saw the real murderer."

"A man like me—in evening dress! Who on earth could he be?" was Hume's natural exclamation.

"We must test this chap's story," said Brett.

"How?"

"Easily enough. There is a garden outside. Can you bring this human bunny here to-night?"

"I think so."

"Very well. Stage him about nine o'clock. Anything else?"

Mr. Winter pondered a little while; then he addressed Hume hesitatingly:

"Does Mr. Brett know everything that happened after the murder?"

"I think so. Yes."

"Everything! Say three-quarters of an hour afterwards?"

The effect of this remark on Hume was very pronounced. His habitual air of reserve gave place to a state of decided confusion.

"What are you hinting at?" he cried, striving hard to govern his voice.

"Well, it must out, sooner or later. Why did you go to meet Miss Helen Layton in the avenue about 1.30 a.m.— soon after Sir Alan's body had been examined by the doctor?'

"Oh, damn it, man, how did you ascertain that?" groaned Hume.

"I knew it all along, but I did not see that it was very material to the case, and I wanted to keep the poor young lady's name out of the affair as far as possible. I did not want to suggest that she was an accessory after the crime."

Hume was blushing like a schoolboy. He glanced miserably at Brett, but the barrister was still puffing artistic designs in big and little rings.

"Very well. My reason for concealment disappears now," he blurted out, for the young man was both vexed and ashamed. "That wretched night, after she returned home, Helen thought she had behaved foolishly in creating a scene. She put on a cloak, changed her shoes, and slipped back again to Mrs. Eastham's, where she met Alan just coming away. She implored him to make up the quarrel with me. He apologised for his conduct, and promised to do the same to me when we met. He explained that other matters had upset his temper that day, and he had momentarily yielded to an irritated belief that everything was against him. Helen watched him enter the park; she pretended that she was going in to Mrs. Eastham's. She could see the lighted windows of the library, and she wondered why he did not go inside, but imagined that at the distance she might easily be mistaken. At last she ran off to the rectory. Again she lingered in the garden, devoutly wishing that all might be well between Alan and me. Then she became conscious that something unusual had taken place, owing to the lights and commotion. For a long time she was at a loss to conjecture what could have happened. At last, yielding to curiosity, she came back to the lodge. The gates were wide open. Mrs. Eastham's dance was still in progress. She is not a timid girl, so she walked boldly up the avenue until she met Fergusson, the butler, who was then going to tell Mrs. Eastham. When she heard his story she was too shocked to credit it, and asked him to bring me. I came. By that time I was beginning to realise that I might be implicated in the affair, and I begged her to return home at once, alone. She did so. Subsequently she asked me not to refer to the escapade, for obvious reasons. It was a woman's little secret, Brett, and I was compelled to keep it."

"Anything else, Winter?" demanded the barrister, wrapped in a cloud of his own creation.

"That is all, sir, except the way in which I heard of Miss Layton's meeting with Mr. Hume."

"Not through Fergusson, eh?"

"Not a bit. The old chap is as close as wax. He seems to think that a Hume-Frazer must die a violent death outside that library window, and if the cause of the trouble is another Hume-Frazer, it is their own blooming business, and no other person's. Most extraordinary old chap. Have you met him?"

"No. Indeed, I am only just beginning to hear the correct details of the story."

Hume winced, but passed no remark.

"Well, my information came through an anonymous letter."

"You don't say so! How interesting! Have you got it?"

"I brought it with me, for a reason other than that which actuates me now, I must confess."

He produced a small envelope, frayed at the edges, and closely compressed. It bore the type-written address, "Police Office, Scotland Yard," and the postal stamp was "West Strand, January 18, 9 p.m."

Within, a small slip of paper, also typed, gave this message:

"About Stowmarket. David Hume Frazer killed cousin. Cousin talked girl in road. Girl waited wood. David Hume Frazer met girl in wood after 1 a.m."

Brett jumped up in instant excitement. Ha placed the two documents on a table near the window, where the afternoon sun fell directly on them.

"Written by the murderer!" he cried "The result of perusing the evening papers containing a report of the first proceedings before the magistrates! The production of an illiterate man, who knew neither the use of a hyphen nor the correct word to describe the avenue! Not wholly exact either, if your story be true, Hume."

"My story is true. Helen herself will tell it you, word for word."

"This is most important. Look at that broken small 'c,' and the bent capital 'D.' The letter 'a,' too, is out of gear, and does not register accurately. Do you note the irregular spacing in 'market,' 'Frazer,' 'talked'? You got that letter, Winter, and yet you did not test every Remington type-writer in London."

"Oh, of course it's my fault!"

Mr. Winter's *coup* has fallen on himself, and he knew it.

"Oh, Winter, Winter! Come to me twice a week from six to seven, Tuesdays and Fridays, and I will give you a night-school training. Now, I wonder if that type-writer has been repaired?"

The detective had seldom seen Brett so thoroughly roused. His eyes were brilliant, his nose dilated as if he could smell the very scent of the anonymous scribe.

"An illiterate man," he repeated, "in evening dress; the same height and appearance as Hume; in a village like Sleagill on a New Year's Eve; four miles from everywhere. Was ever clue so simple provided by a careless scoundrel! And eighteen months have elapsed. This is positively maddening!"

"Look here, old chap," said Hume, still smarting under the recollections of Brett's caustic utterance, "say you forgive me for keeping that thing back. There is nothing else, believe me. It was for Helen's sake."

"Rubbish!" cried the barrister. "The only wonder is that you are not long since assimilated in quicklime in a prison grave. You are all cracked, I think–living spooks, human March hares. As for you, Winter, I weep for you."

He strode rapidly to and fro along the length of the room, smoking prodigiously, with frowning brows and concentrated eyes. The others did not speak, but Winter treated Hume to an informing wink, as one might say.

"Now you will hear something."

9
THE KO-KATANA

Thinking aloud, rather than addressing his companions, Brett began again:

"The man must have had some place in which to change his clothes, for he would not court attention by walking about in evening dress by broad daylight He met and spoke with Alan Hume-Frazer that afternoon. The result was unsatisfactory. The stranger resolved to visit him again at night–the night of the ball. In a country village on such an occasion, a swallow-tailed coat was a *passe-partout*, as many gentry had come in from the surrounding district."

"Yes, that is so," broke in Hume.

Brett momentarily looked through him, and the detective shook his head to deprecate any further interruption.

"He could not enter Mrs. Eastham's house, for there everybody knew everybody else. He could not enter the library of the Hall, because the footman was on duty for several hours. Is not that so?"

He seemed to bite both men with the question.

"Yes," they answered.

"Then he was compelled to hang about the avenue, watching his opportunity–his opportunity for what? Not to commit a murder! He was unarmed, or, at any rate, his implement was a haphazard choice, selected on the spur of the moment. He saw David Hume leave the dance, and watched his brief talk with the butler. He correctly interpreted Hume's preparations to await his cousin's arrival. Did Hume's sleepiness suggest the crime, and its probable explanation? Perhaps. I cannot determine that point now. Assuredly it gave the opportunity to commit a

theft. Something was stolen from the secretaire. A bold
rascal, to force a drawer whilst another man was in the
room! Did he fear the consequences if he were caught? I
think not. He succeeded in his object, and went off, but
before he reached the gates he saw Miss Layton, whom he
did not know, talking to the baronet. He secreted himself
until the baronet entered the park alone. For some
reason, he made his presence known, and walked with Sir
Alan to the lawn outside the window, still retaining in his
hand the small knife used to prise open the lock. There
was a short and vehement dispute. Possibly the baronet
guessed the object of this unexpected appearance. There
may have been a struggle. Then the knife was sent home,
with such singular skill that the victim fell without a
word, a groan, to arouse attention. The murderer made
off down the avenue, but he was far too cold-blooded to
run away and encounter unforeseen dangers. No; he
waited among the trees to ascertain what would happen
when his victim was discovered, and frame his plans
accordingly. It was then that he saw Helen Layton and
David Hume. As soon as the news of the murder spread
abroad the dance broke up. Amidst the wondering crowd,
slowly dispersing in their carriages, he could easily slip
away unseen, for the police, of course, were sure that
David Hume killed his cousin. Don't you see, Winter?"

The inspector did not see.

"You are making up a fine tale, Mr. Brett," he said
doggedly, "but I'm blessed if I can follow your reasoning."

"No, of course not. Eighteen months of settled
conviction are not to be dispelled in an instant. But
accept my theory. This man, the guilty man, must have
resided in Stowmarket for some hours, if not days. Many
people saw him. He could not live in Sleagill, where even
the village dogs would suspect him. But the addle-headed
police, ready to handcuff David Hume, never thought of
inquiring about strangers who came and went at
Stowmarket in those days. Stowmarket is a metropolis, a
wilderness of changeful beings, to a country policeman. It

has a market-day, an occasional drunken man–life is a whirl in Stowmarket. Fortunately, people have memories. At that time you did not wear a beard, Hume."

"No," was the reply, "though I never told you that."

"Of course you told me, many times. Did not your acquaintances fail to recognise you? Had not Mrs. Capella to look twice at you before she knew you? Now, Winter, start out. Ascertain, in each hotel in the town, if they had any strange guests about the period of the murder. There is a remote chance that you may learn something. Describe Mr. Hume without a beard, and hint at a reward if information is forthcoming. Money quickens the agricultural intellect."

The detective, doubting much, obeyed. Hume, asking if there was any reason why he should not drive back to Sleagill for an hour before dinner, was sarcastically advised to go a good deal farther. Indeed, the sight of that tiny type-written slip had stirred Brett to volcanic activity.

He tramped backwards and forwards, enveloped in smoke. Once he halted and tore at the bell.

A waiter came.

"Go to my room, No. 11, and bring me a leather dressing-case, marked 'R.B.' Run! I give you twenty seconds. After that you lose sixpence a second out of your tip."

He pulled out his watch. The man dashed along the corridor, much to the amazement of a passing chamber-maid. He returned, bearing the bag in triumph.

"Seventeen seconds! By the law of equity you are entitled to eighteen pence."

Brett produced the money and led the gaping waiter out of the room, promptly shutting the door on him.

"He's a rum gentleman that," said the waiter to the girl.

"He must be, to make you hurry in such fashion. Why, you wouldn't have gone faster for a free pint."

"I consider that an impertinent observation." With tilted nose the man turned and cannoned against Hume.

"Here!" cried the latter. "Run to the stables and get me a horse and trap. If they are ready in two minutes I'll give you two shillings."

"Talk about makin' money!" gasped the waiter, as he flew downstairs, "this is coinin'. But, by gum, they *are* in a hurry."

Brett unlocked his bag and took from it the book of newspaper cuttings.

"Ah!" he said, after a rapid glance at his concluding notes. "I thought so. Here is what I wrote when the affair was fresh in my mind:

"'Why were no inquiries made at Stowmarket to learn what, if any, strangers were in the town on New Year's Eve?

"'Most minute investigations should be pursued with reference to Margaret Hume-Frazer's friends and associates.

"'Has Fergusson ever been asked if his master received any visitors on the day of the murder or during the preceding week? If so, who were they?

"What is the precise purpose of the knife attached to the Japanese sword? It appears to be too small to be used as a dagger. In any case, the sword scabbard would be an unsuitable place to carry an auxiliary weapon, to European ideas.'

"Now, I wonder if Fergusson is still at the Hall? The other matters must wait."

Winter returned about the same time as Hume. Brett and the latter dressed for dinner, and the adroit detective, not to be beaten, borrowed a dress-suit from the landlord, after telegraphing to London for his own clothes.

During the progress of the meal the little party scrupulously refrained from discussing business, an excellent habit always insisted on by Brett.

They had reached the stage of coffee and cigars when a waiter entered and whispered something to the police officer.

"'Rabbit Jack' is here," exclaimed Winter.

"Capital! Tell him to wait."

When the servant had left, Brett detailed his proposed test. He and Hume would go into the hotel garden, after donning overcoats and deer-stalker hats, for Hume told him that both his cousin and he himself had worn that style of headgear.

They would stand, with their faces hidden, beneath the trees, and Winter was to bring the poacher towards them, after asking him to pick out the man who most resembled the person he had seen standing in the avenue at Beechcroft.

The test was most successful. "Rabbit Jack" instantly selected Hume.

"It's either the chap hisself or his dead spit," was the poacher's dictum.

Then he was cautioned to keep his own counsel as to the incident, and he went away to get gloriously drunk on half-a-sovereign.

In the seclusion of the sitting-room, Winter related the outcome of his inquiries. They were negative.

Landlords and barmaids remembered a few commercial travellers by referring to old lodgers, but they one and all united in the opinion that New Year's Eve was a most unlikely time for the hotels to contain casual visitors.

"I was afraid it would be a wild-goose chase from the start," opined Winter.

"Obviously," replied Brett; "yet ten minutes ago you produced a man who actually watched the murderer for a considerable time that night."

Whilst Winter was searching his wits for a suitable argument, the barrister continued:

"Where is Fergusson now?"

"I can answer that," exclaimed Hume. "He is my father's butler. When Capella came to Beechcroft, the old man wrote and said he could not take orders from an Italian. It was like receiving instructions from a French cook. So my father brought him to Glen Tochan."

"Then your father must send him to London. He may be very useful. I understand he was very many years at Beechcroft?"

"Forty-six, man and boy, as he puts it."

"Write to-morrow and bring him to town. He can stay at your hotel. I will not keep him long; just one conversation—no more. Can you or your father tell me anything else about that sword?"

"I fear not. Admiral Cunningham"

"I guess I'm the authority there," broke in Winter. "I got to know all about it from Mr. Okasaki."

"And who, pray, is Mr. Okasaki?"

"A Japanese gentleman, who came to Ipswich to hear the first trial. He was interested in the case, owing to the curious fact that a murder in a little English village should be committed with such a weapon, so he came down to listen to the evidence. And, by the way, he took a barmaid back with him. There was rather a sensation."

"The Japs are very enterprising. What did he tell you about the sword?"

The detective produced a note-book.

"It is all here," he said, turning over the leaves. "A Japanese Samurai, or gentleman, in former days carried two swords, one long blade for use against his enemies, and a shorter one for committing suicide if he was beaten or disgraced. The sword Mr. Hume gave his cousin was a short one, and the knife which accompanied it is called the Ko-Katana, or little sword. As well as I could understand Mr. Okasaki, a Jap uses this as a pen-knife, and also as a queer sort of visiting-card. If he slays an enemy he sticks the Ko-Katana between the other fellow's ribs, or into his ear, and leaves it there."

"A P.P.C. card, in fact!"

"You always have some joke against the P.C.'s," growled the detective. "I never"

"You have just made a most excellent one yourself. Please continue, Winter. Your researches are valuable."

"That is all. Would you like to see the Ko-Katana that killed Sir Alan?"

"Yes. Where is it?"

"In the Black Museum at Scotland Yard. I will take you there."

"Thank you. By the way, concerning this man, Okasaki. Supposing we should want any further information from him on this curious topic, can you find him? You say he indulged in some liaison with an Ipswich girl, so I assume he has not gone back to Japan."

"The last I heard of him was at that time. Someone told me that he was an independent gentleman, noted for his art tastes. The disappearance of the girl created a rare old row in Ipswich."

"Make a note of him. We may need his skilled assistance. Was there any special design on the Ko-Katana?"

"It was ornamented in some way, but I forget the pattern."

"I can help you in that matter," said Hume. "I remember perfectly that the handle, of polished gun-metal, bore a beautiful embossed design in gold and silver of a setting sun surmounted by clouds and two birds."

"Correct, Mr. Hume, I recall it now," said the detective. "The same thing appears on the handle of the sword."

Brett ruminated silently on this fresh information. Like the other pieces in the puzzle, it seemed to have no sort of connection with the cause of the crime.

"Why do you say 'setting sun'? How does one distinguish it from the rising sun in embossed or inlaid work?" he asked Hume.

"I do not know. I only repeat Alan's remark. I gave the beastly thing to him because he became interested in Japanese arms during his Eastern tour, you will recollect."

"Ah, well. That is a nice point for Mr. Okasaki to settle if we chance to come across him. Don't forget, Winter, I want to see that Ko-Katana, Whom did you meet at Sleagill, Hume?"

The young man laughed. "Helen, of course."

"Any other person?"

"No. I told her I might chance to drive out in that direction about five o'clock, so"

"Dear me! You were not at all certain."

"By no means. I am at your orders."

"Excellent! Then my orders are that you shall meet the young lady on every possible occasion. You took her for a drive?"

"Well—er–yes, I did. You do not leave me much to tell."

"Did she say anything of importance–bearing upon our inquiry, I mean?"

"Nothing. She had not quitted the rectory since we came away. I asked her to pick up any village gossip about the people at the Hall, and let us know at the earliest moment if she regarded it as valuable in any way."

"That was thoughtful of you. A great deal may happen there at any moment."

A waiter knocked and entered. He handed a letter to Hume.

"From Nellie," said David hastily.

He opened the envelope and perused a short note, which he gave to Brett. It ran:

"DEAREST, I have just heard from Jane, our under-housemaid, that Mr. Capella is leaving the Hall for London by an early train to-morrow. Jane 'walks out' with Mr. Capella's valet, and is in tears. Tell Mr. Brett. I am going to help Mrs. Eastham to select prize books for the school treat to-morrow at eleven.

"With love, yours,

"NELLIE."

"Who brought this note?" inquired Hume from the waiter as he picked up pen and paper.

"A man from Sleagill, sir. Any reply?"

"Certainly. Tell him to wait in the tap-room at my expense." He commenced to write.

"Any message?" he asked Brett.

"Yes. Give Miss Layton my compliments, and say I regret to hear that Jane is in tears. Ask her—Miss Layton to get Jane to find out from the valet what train his master will travel by."

"Why?"

"Because I will go by an earlier one, if possible."

"But what about me! Confound it, I promised"

"To meet Miss Layton at eleven. Do so, my dear fellow. But come to town to-morrow evening. Winter and I may want you."

So the detective sent another telegram to detain that dress suit, and Hume seemed to have quickly conquered his disinclination to visit Stowmarket.

10
THE BLACK MUSEUM

Winter, who had never seen Capella, was so well posted by Brett as to his personal appearance that he experienced no difficulty in picking out the Italian when he alighted from the train at Liverpool Street Station next morning.

Capella did not conduct himself like a furtive villain. He jumped into a hansom. His valet followed in a four-wheeler with the luggage. In each instance the address given to the driver was that of a well-known West End hotel.

The detective's cab kept pace with Capella's through Old Broad Street, Queen Victoria Street, and along the Embankment. At the Mansion House, and again at Blackfriars, they halted side by side, and Winter noticed that his quarry was looking into space with sullen, vindictive eyes.

"He means mischief to somebody," was Winter's summing up. "I wonder if he intends to knife Hume?" for Brett had given his professional *confrère* a synopsis of all that happened before they met, and of his subsequent conversation with the "happy couple" in Beechcroft Hall.

He repeated this remark to the barrister when he reached Brett's chambers.

"Capella will do nothing so crude," was the comment. "He is no fool. I do not credit him with the murder of Sir Alan, but if I am mistaken in this respect, it is impossible to suppose that he can dream of clearing his path again by the same drastic method. Of course he means mischief, but he will stab reputations, not individuals."

"When will you come to the Black Museum?"

"At once, if you like. But before we set out I want to discuss Mr. Okasaki with you. What sort of person is he?"

"A genuine Jap, small, lively, and oval-faced. His eyes are like tiny slits in a water melon, and when he laughs his grin goes back to his ears."

"Really, Winter, I did not credit you with such a fund of picturesque imagery. Would you know him again?"

"I can't be certain. All Japs are very much alike, to my thinking, but if I heard him talk I would be almost sure. Why do you ask?"

"Because I have been looking up a little information with reference to the Ko-Katana and its uses. Now, Okasaki is the name of a Japanese town. Family names almost invariably have a topographical foundation, referring to some village, river, street, or mountain, and there may be thousands of Okasakis. Then, again, it was the custom some years ago for a man to be called one name at birth, another when he came of age, a third when he obtained some official position, and so on. For instance, you would be called Spring when you were born, Summer when you were twenty-one, Autumn when you became a policeman, and Winter when you reached your present rank."

"Oh, Christopher!" cried the detective. "And if I were made Chief Inspector?"

"Then your title would be 'Top Dog' or something of the sort."

Mr. Winter assimilated the foregoing information with a profound thankfulness that we in England do these things differently.

"Why are you so interested in Mr. Okasaki?" he inquired.

"I will answer your question by another. Why was he so interested in the Ko-Katana?"

"That is hardly what I told you, Mr. Brett. He professed to be interested in the crime itself. But now I come to think of it, he did ask me to let him see the thing."

"And did you?"

"Yes; I wanted all the information I could get."

"My position exactly. Let us go to Scotland Yard."

The famous Black Museum has so often been the subject of articles in the public press that no detailed description is needed here. It contains, in glass cases, or hanging on the walls, a weird collection of articles famous in the annals of crime. It is not open to the public, and Brett, who had not seen the place before, examined its relics with much curiosity.

The detective exhibited a pardonable pride in some of them, but his companion damped his enthusiasm by saying:

"This is a depressing sight."

"In what way?"

"British rogues are evidently of low intelligence in the average. A bludgeon and a halter make up their history."

"There's more than that in a good many cases."

"Ah, I forgot the handcuffs."

"Well, here is the Ko-Katana," said Winter shortly.

The barrister took the fateful weapon, not more deadly than a paper-knife in appearance, and scrutinised it closely.

"It has not been cleaned," he said.

"No, it was left untouched after the doctor withdrew it from the poor young fellow's breast."

Brett produced a magnifying glass. Beneath the rust on the blade he thought he could distinguish some Japanese characters in the quaint pictorial script adapted by that singular people from the Chinese system of writing.

He brought the knife nearer to the window and carefully focussed it. Then he produced a note-book and made a pencil drawing of the following inscription:

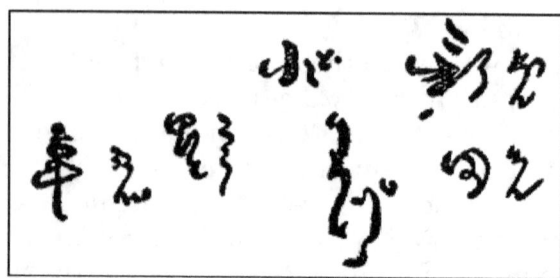

Winter watched him with quiet agony. He had never noticed the signs before.

"Mr. Okasaki did not tell you what these scratches meant?" inquired the barrister.

"No. He did not see them."

"Sure?"

"Quite positive. Of course, it is very smart on your part to hit upon them so quickly, but what possible purpose can it serve to find out the meaning of something carved in Japan more than fifty years ago, at the very least?"

"I do not know. It is very stupid of me, I admit, but I have not the faintest notion."

"Does it make the finding of Okasaki more important?"

"To a certain extent. We want to have everything explained. At present we have so little of what I regard as really definite evidence."

"May I ask what that little is?"

"Sir Alan Hume-Frazer was murdered with a knife produced by a man like David Hume, whom 'Rabbit Jack' saw standing beneath the yews. Not much, eh?"

Winter shook his head dubiously.

"If Sir Alan were shot instead of stabbed," went on the barrister, "the first thing you would endeavour to determine would be the calibre and nature of the bullet. Why not be equally particular about the knife?"

"But this weapon has been for fifty years in Glen Tochan. Its history is thoroughly established."

"Is it? Who made it? Whose crest does it bear? What does this motto signify? If you wanted to kill a man would you use this toy? Why was not the sword itself employed?"

"That string of questions leaves me out, Mr. Brett."

"I am equally uninformed. I can only answer the last one. The sword is intended for suicidal purposes, the Ko-Katana for an enemy. This is a case of murder, not suicide."

The detective wheeled sharply on his heels, thereby upsetting Charles Peace's telescopic ladder.

"You suspect Okasaki!" he cried.

"My dear fellow! Okasaki is, say, five feet nothing. The murderer is five feet ten inches in height. Japanese are clever people, but they are not—telescopes," and he picked up the ladder.

Winter grinned. "You always make capital out of my blunders," he said.

"Pooh! My banking account is limited. Let us go. The moral atmosphere in this room is vile."

Outside the Central Police Office they separated, Brett to pay some long-neglected calls, Winter to hunt up Capella's movements and initiate inquiries about Okasaki.

The detective came to Brett's chambers at five o'clock, in a great state of excitement.

"Thank goodness you are at home, sir." he cried, when Smith admitted him to the barrister's sanctum. "Capella is off to Naples."

Naples, the scene of his marriage! What did this journey portend? Naught but the gravest considerations would take him so far away from home when he knew that David and Helen were reunited.

"How did you discover this fact?" asked Brett, awaking out of a brown study.

"Easily enough, as it happened. Ninety-nine per cent. of gentlemen's valets are keen sports. Barbers and hotel-porters run them close. I do a bit that way myself"

The barrister groaned.

"Not often, sir, but this is holiday time, you see. Anyhow, I gave the hall-porter, whom I know, the wink to come to a neighbouring bar during his time off for tea. He actually brought Capella's man—William his name is—with him. I told them I had backed the first winner to-day, an eight to one chance, and that started them. I offered to put them on a certainty next week, and William's face fell. 'It's a beastly nuisance,' he said, 'I'm off to Naples with my boss to-morrow.' 'Well,' said I, 'if you're not going before the night train, perhaps I may be able' But that made him worse, because they leave by the 11 A.M., Victoria."

Brett began to pace the room. He could not make up his mind to visit Naples in person. For one thing, he did not speak Italian. But Capella must be followed. At last he decided upon a course of action.

"Winter," he said, "do you know a man we can trust, an Italian, or better still, an Italian-speaking Englishman, who can undertake this commission for us?"

"Would you mind ringing for Smith, sir?" replied the detective, who seemed to be mightily pleased with himself.

Smith appeared.

"At the foot of the stairs you will find a gentleman named Holden," said Winter. "Ask him to come up, please."

Holden appeared, a sallow personage, long-nosed and shrewd-looking. The detective explained that Mr. Holden was an ex-police sergeant, retained for many years at headquarters on account of his fluency in the language of Tasso. Winter did not mention Tasso. This is figurative.

An arrangement was quickly made. He was to start that evening and meet Capella on arrival at Naples; Winter would telegraph the fact of the Italian's departure according to programme. Holden was not to spare expense in employing local assistance if necessary. He was to report everything he could learn about Capella's movements.

Brett wanted to hand him £50, but found that all the money he had in his possession at the moment only totalled up to £35.

Winter produced a small bag.

"It was quite true what I said," he smirked. "I did back the first winner, and, what's more, I drew it–sixteen of the best."

"I had no idea the police force was so corrupt," sighed Brett, as he completed the financial transaction, and Mr. Holden took his departure. The detective also went off to search for Okasaki.

About nine o'clock Hume arrived.

"You will be glad to hear," he said, "that the rector invited me to lunch. He approves of my project, and will pray for my success. It has been a most pleasant day for me, I can assure you."

"The rector retired to his study immediately after lunch, I presume?"

"Yes," said David innocently. "Has anything important occurred in town?"

Brett gave him a resumé of events. A chance allusion to Sir Alan caused the young man to exclaim:

"By the way, you have never seen his photograph. He and I were very much alike, you know, and I have brought from my rooms a few pictures which may interest you."

He handed to Brett photographs of himself and his two cousins, and of the older Sir Alan and Lady Hume-Frazer, taken singly and in groups.

The barrister examined them minutely.

"Alan and I," pointed out his client, "were photographed during our last visit to London. Poor chap!

He never saw this picture. The proofs were not sent until after his death."

Something seemed to puzzle Brett very considerably. He compared the pictures one with the other, and paid heed to every detail.

"Let me understand," Brett said at last. "I think I have it in my notes that at the time of the murder you were twenty-seven, Sir Alan twenty-four, and Mrs. Capella twenty-six?"

"That is so, approximately. We were born respectively in January, October, and December. My twenty-seventh birthday fell on the 11th."

"Stated exactly, you were two years and nine months older than he?"

"Yes."

"You don't look it."

"I never did. We were always about the same size as boys, but he matured at an earlier age than I."

"It is odd. How old were you when this group was taken?"

The photograph depicted a family gathering on the lawn at Beechcroft. There were eight persons in it, three being elderly men.

David reflected.

"That was before I left Harrow, and Christmas time. Seventeen almost, within a couple of weeks."

"So your cousin Margaret was sixteen?"

"Yes."

"She was remarkably tall, well-developed for her age."

"That was a notable characteristic from an early age. We boys used to call her 'Mama,' when we wanted to vex her."

"The three old gentlemen are very much alike. This is the baronet. Who are the others?"

"My father and uncle."

"What! Do you mean to tell me there is another branch of the family?"

"Well, yes, in a sense. My uncle is dead. His son, my age or a little older, for the youngest of the three brothers was married first, was last heard of in Argentina."

Brett threw the photograph down with clatter.

"Good Heavens!" he vociferated, "when shall I begin to comprehend this business in its entirety? How many more uncles, and aunts, and cousins have you?"

Amazed by this outburst, Hume endeavoured to put matters right.

"I never thought" he commenced.

"You come to me to do the thinking, Hume. For goodness' sake switch your memory for five minutes from Miss Layton, and tell me all you know of your family history. Have you any other relations?"

"None whatever."

"And this newly-arrived cousin, what of him?"

"He was in the navy, and being of a quarrelsome disposition, was court-martialled for some small outbreak. He would not submit to discipline, and resigned the service. Then his father died, and Bob went off to South America. I have never heard of him since. I know very little about my younger uncle's household. Indeed, the occasion recorded by the photograph was the last time the old men met in friendship. There was a dispute about money matters. My Uncle Charles was in the city, the two estates being left by my grandfather to the two oldest sons. Charles Hume-Frazer died a poor man, having lost his fortune by speculation."

"Have you seen your cousin Robert? Did he resemble Alan and you?"

"We were all as like as peas. People say that our house is remarkable for the unchanging type of its male line. That is readily demonstrated by the family portraits. You have not been in the dining-room or picture-gallery at Beechcroft, or you must have noticed this instantly."

Brett flung himself into a chair.

"The Argentine!" he muttered. "A nice school for a 'quarrelsome' Hume-Frazer."

He had calmed sufficiently to reach for his cigarette-case when Smith entered with a note, delivered by a boy messenger.

It was from Winter:

"Have found Okasaki. His name is now Numagawa Jiro, so you were right, as usual. He and Mrs. Jiro live at 17 St. John's Mansions, Kensington."

11
MR. "OKASAKI"

In fifteen minutes Brett was bowling along Knightsbridge in a hansom, having left Hume with a strict injunction to rack his brains for any further undiscovered facts bearing upon the inquiry, and turn up promptly at ten o'clock next morning.

Although the hour was late for calling upon a complete stranger, the barrister could not rest until he had inspected the Jiro ménage. No. 17 was a long way from the ground level. Indeed, the cats of Kensington, if sufficiently enterprising, inhabitated the floor above.

He rang, and was surveyed with astonishment by a very small maid-servant.

"Is Mr. Numagawa Jiro at home?" he inquired.

"No, sir, but Mrs. Jiro is."

An infantine wail from one of the apartments showed that there was also a young Jiro.

The maid neither advanced nor retreated. She simply stood stock still, petrified by the sight of a well-dressed visitor.

Brett suggested that she should inform her mistress of his presence.

"Please, sir," whispered the girl, "are you from Ipswich?"

"No; from Victoria Street."

"I only asked, sir, because master is particular about people from Ipswich. They upset missus so."

She vanished into the interior, and came back to usher him into the drawing-room. The flat was expensively furnished, but very untidy. He at once perceived, however, that the "former" Mr. Okasaki was not romancing when he boasted of his artistic tastes. The

Japanese articles in the room were gems of faience and lacquer work.

The entrance of Mrs. Jiro drew the barrister's eyes from surrounding objects. He was momentarily stunned. The woman was almost a giantess, and amazingly stout. In a tiny flat, waited on by a diminutive servant, and married to a Japanese, she was grotesque.

Originally a very tall and fairly good-looking girl, she had evidently blossomed out like one of the gorgeous chrysanthemums of her husband's favoured land.

Assuredly she had acquired no Japanese traits either in manner or appearance. At first she seemed to be in a genuinely British bad temper, but Brett excelled in the art of smoothing the ruffled plumes of femininity.

"What is it?" she demanded, surveying him suspiciously.

"I wish to see Mr. Jiro," he said, "but permit me to apologise for making such an untimely call. As he is not at home, I must not trouble you beyond inquiring a likely hour to see him to-morrow."

He smiled so pleasantly that the lady became more complaisant.

"He may not be very long" she commenced, but the youthful Jiro's voice was again heard in fretful complaint.

"My baby is not well to-night," she explained.

"Poor little darling!" said Brett.

He was tempted to add: "What is its name?" but refrained.

"Won't you sit down?" said Mrs. Jiro. "As I was saying, my husband may not be very long"

She was fated not to complete that doubly accurate sentence, for at that moment a key rattled in the outer door.

"Here he is," she announced; and Mr. Jiro entered.

It was fortunate that the gravity of his errand, no less than his power of self-control, kept Brett from laughing. As it was, he smiled very broadly when he greeted the master of the flat, for the little man was small even for a Japanese.

The contrast between him and his helpmate was ludicrous. He could not possibly kiss her unless she stooped, nor would his arms encircle her shoulders.

"And how is my pretty *karasu*?" he asked, regarding his wife fondly.

"Don't call me that, Nummie!" she cried.

Turning to Brett she explained: "He calls me a crow, and says it is a compliment, but I don't like it."

"In Japan the clow speaks with the voice of love," grinned Jiro.

"Well, it sounds funny in London, so just attend to this gentleman. He has come to see you on business."

Mrs. Jiro forthwith seated herself to listen to the conclave. Brett, though warned by the maid's remark, could not help himself, so he went straight to the point.

"Over a year ago," he said, "you were in Ipswich."

Instantly a severe chill fell upon his hearers. The man shrank, the woman expanded, but before either could utter a word, the barrister continued:

"Personally, I know no one in Ipswich. I have only visited the town twice, during an Assize week. It has come to my knowledge that you gave the police some information with reference to a Japanese weapon which figured in a noted crime, and I have ventured to come here to ask you for additional details."

Mrs. Jiro heaved a great sigh of relief.

"My gracious!" she cried, "you did startle me. I can't bear to hear the name of Ipswich nowadays. I was married from there."

"Indeed!" said Brett, with polite interest.

"Yes; and my people are always hunting me up and making a row because I married Mr. Jiro. Sometimes they make me that ill that I feel half inclined to go with him to Japan. He is always worrying me to leave London, but the more I hear about Japan the less I fancy it."

"Ah, my own little *gan*" broke in her husband.

"There you go again," she snapped. "Calling me a *gana* goose, indeed! Now, Mr. Brett, how would you like to be called a wild goose?"

"I have often deserved it," he said.

"You do not understand," chirped Jiro. "In Japan the goose is beautiful, elegant. It flies fast like a white spilit."

His English was almost perfect, but in words containing a rolled "r" he often substituted an "l."

"I understand enough to keep away from Japan, a place where they have an earthquake every five minutes, and people live in paper houses. Besides, look at the size of your women-folk. Just imagine me, Mr. Brett, walking about among those little dolls, like a turkey among tom-tits."

"We give fat people much admilation," said Jiro.

"Nummie, I do hate that word fat. I can't help being tall and well developed; but it is only short women who become 'fat'."

She hissed the word venomously, as if she possessed the scorpion's fabled power to sting herself. Evidently Mrs. Jiro dreaded corpulence more than earthquakes.

Brett had never previously met such a strangely assorted couple. He would willingly have prolonged his visit for mere amusement, but he was compelled to return to the cause of his presence. Unless he asked direct questions he would make no progress. He took from his pocket-book the drawing made in the Black Museum, and handed it to the Japanese, saying:

"Would you mind telling me the meaning of that?"

Jiro screwed his queer little eyes upon the scrawling characters. The methods of writing in the Far East, being pictorial and inexact, require scrutiny of the context before a given sentence can be correctly interpreted.

The little man made no trouble about it, however.

"They are old chalacters," he said. "In Japan we joke a lot. Evely sign has sevelal meanings. This can be lead two ways. It is a plovelb, and says, 'A new field gives a small clop,' or 'Human life is but fifty years.' Where did you see it?"

"On the blade of the Ko-Katana that killed Sir Alan Hume-Frazer," answered Brett.

And now he experienced a fresh difficulty. The Japanese face is exceedingly expressive. When a native of the Island Empire smiles or scowls, exhibits surprise or fear, he apparently does these things with his whole soul. Such facial plasticity provides far more effective concealment of real emotions than the phlegmatic indifference of the Briton, who, in the words of Emerson, requires "pitchforks or the cry of 'fire!'" to arouse him.

It is possible to throw an Englishman off his guard by a shrewd thrust; but Mr. Numagawa Jiro was one of those persons whose lineaments would reveal the same amount of pain over a cut finger as a broken leg.

Nevertheless, Brett's reply did unquestionably make him jump, and even Mrs. Jiro's bulging features became anxious.

"Is that possible?" said the Japanese. "It is velly stlange the police gentleman did not tell me about it."

"He did not know of it until to-day," explained Brett, "and that is why I am here now. It is the motto of some important Japanese family, is it not?"

"It is a plovelb," repeated Jiro, who evidently intended to take thought.

"So I understand, but used in this way it represents a family, a clan?"

"I do not know."

"What! A man so interested in his country's art as to go to an out-of-the-way English provincial town merely to see a small knife, must surely be able to decide such a trivial matter as the use of mottoes on sword blades!"

Mr. Jiro's excellent knowledge of English seemed to fail him, but his wife took up the defence.

"My husband had more to think about in Ipswich than a small knife, Mr. Brett."

"Very much more, but it was the knife which brought him to the place. He carried the major attraction away with him."

Mrs. Jiro thought this sounded nice. She turned to her husband:

"Why don't you tell the gentleman all you know about it, Nummie?"

The little man looked at her curiously before he spoke to the barrister.

"I have nothing to tell," he said. "I told the police all that they asked me. That was a velly old Ko-Katana, a hundred yeals old. It was made by a famous altist. I have told you the meaning of the liting. That is all I know."

"Why did you give your name at Ipswich as Okasaki?" demanded Brett.

"Oh, that is vely easy. Okosaki is my family name. You English people say it quicker than Numaguwa Jiro, so I give it. But when I got mallied I used my light name. Japanese law does not pelmit the change of names now. My ploper name is Numagawa Jiro"—which he pronounced "Jilo."

"You told the detective at Ipswich that the device on the handle represented the setting sun. How did you know the sun was setting, and not rising?"

It was a haphazard shot. The description was Hume's, not Winter's.

Again the Japanese paused before answering.

"It was shown by the way in which the gold was used. Japanese altists have symbols for ideas. That is one."

"Thank you. I imagined you recognised the device, and could speak off-hand in the matter. By the way, do you use a type-writer?"

"Yes," said Mrs. Jiro. "My husband is clever at all that sort of thing, and when he found the people could not read his writing he bought a machine."

"I have sold it again," interfered Jiro, after a hasty glance round the room, "and I am going to buy another."

Mrs. Jiro rose to stir the fire unnecessarily.

"They are most useful," said Brett. "Which make do you prefer?"

"They are all vely much alike," answered the Japanese, "but I am going to buy a Yost or a Hammond."

"I am very much obliged to you for receiving me at this late hour," said the barrister, rising, "but before I go allow me to compliment you on your remarkable knowledge of English. I am sure you are indebted to your good lady for your idiomatic command of the language."

"I studied it for yeals in Japan" began Jiro, but in vain, for his very much better half resented the word "idiomatic."

"I don't know about that," she snorted. "He talked a lot of nonsense when we were married, but I've made him drop it, and he is teaching me Japanese."

"His task is a pleasant one. It is the tongue of poetry and love."

Again there was a pause. A minute later Brett was standing in the street trying to determine how best to act.

He was fully persuaded that Jiro had, in the first place, identified the crest as belonging to one of the many Samurai clans. But the motto was new to him, and its discovery had revealed the particular family which claimed its use.

Why did he refuse to impart his knowledge? There must be plenty of Japanese in London who would give this information readily.

Again, why did he lie about the type-writer, and endeavour to mislead him as to the make of the machine he used?

To-morrow, for a certainty, Jiro would dispose of the Remington which he now possessed. Well, he should meet with a ready purchaser, if a letter from Brett to every agency in London would expedite matters.

He did not credit Jiro with the death of Sir Alan Hume-Frazer, nor even with complicity in the crime. The Japanese had acted as the unwitting tool of a stronger personality, and the little man's brain was even at this moment considering fresh aspects of the affair not previously within his ken.

Moreover, how maddening the whole thing was! Beginning with Hume's fantastic dream, he reviewed the hitherto unknown elements in the case—Capella's fierce passion and queer behaviour, culminating in a sudden journey to Italy, Margaret's silent agony, the existence of an Argentine cousin, the evidence of "Rabbit Jack," the punning motto on the Ko-Katana, Jiro's perturbation and desire to prevent his wife's unconscious disclosures.

With the final item came the ludicrous remembrance of that ill-assorted couple. Laughing, Brett hailed a hansom.

12
WHAT THE STATIONMASTER SAW

The number of type-writer exchanges in London is not large. Impressing the services of Smith and his wife as amanuenses, Brett despatched the requisite letters before he retired for the night.

He was up betimes and out before breakfast, surprising the domestics of his club by an early visit to the library. The Etona contained a great many service members, and made a feature of its complete editions of Army and Navy lists.

In one of the latter, eight years old, Brett found, among the officers of the *Northumberland*, at that time in commission, "Robert Hume-Fraser, sub-lieutenant." A later volume recorded his retirement from the service.

Hume and Winter reached Brett's flat together.

"Any luck with the Jap, sir?" asked the detective cheerily.

Brett told them what had happened, and Winter sighed. Here, indeed, was a promising subject for an arrest. Why not lock him up, and seize the type-writer? But he knew the barrister by this time, and uttered no word.

"And now," said Brett, after a malicious pause to enable Winter to declare himself, "I am going back to Stowmarket. No, Hume, you are not coming with me. When does Fergusson arrive here?"

The question drove from David's face the disappointed look with which he received his friend's announcement.

"To-morrow evening," he replied. "My father thinks the old man should not risk an all-night journey. He has also sent me every detail he can get together, either from documents or recollection, bearing upon our family history."

He produced a formidable roll of manuscript. The old gentleman had evidently devoted many hours and some literary skill to the compilation.

"I will read that in the train," said Brett. "You must start at once for Portsmouth. I have here a list of all the officers serving with your cousin Robert on the *Northumberland* immediately prior to his quitting the Navy. Portsmouth, Devonport, Southsea, and the neighbourhood will almost certainly contain some of them. If not, people there will know where they are to be found. You must make yourself known to them, and endeavour to gain any sort of news concerning the ex-lieutenant. Naval men roam all over the world. Some of them may have met him in the Argentine, or in any of the South American ports where British warships are constantly calling. He was a sailor. He left the Navy under no cloud. Hence, the presence of a British man-o'-war would draw him like a magnet. Do not come back here until you bring news of him."

"Why is it so important? You cannot imagine"

"No; I endeavour to restrain my imagination. I want facts. You are the best person to obtain them. One relative inquiring for another is a natural proceeding. It will not arouse suspicions that you are a debt-collector."

"Suppose I obtain news of his whereabouts?"

"Telegraph to me and I will give you fresh instructions."

Hume walked to the door.

"Give my kind regards to Miss Layton," he said grimly.

"I will be delighted. Work hard. You will see her all the sooner."

"There goes a man in love," continued Brett, addressing the back of Winter's skull, though looking him straight in the face. "His career, his reputation, everything he values most in this world is at stake. He is a sensible, level-headed fellow, who has become embittered by unjust suspicion; yet he would unwillingly let a material item like his cousin's proceedings sink into oblivion just for the sake of telling a girl that she looks more charming to-day than she did yesterday, or some equally original remark peculiar to love-making. How do you account for it, Winter?"

"I give it up," sighed the detective. "We are all fools where women are concerned."

"You surprise me," said the barrister sternly. "Such a personal confession of weakness is unexpected–I may say distressing."

Winter shook his head.

"You're not married, Mr. Brett, or you wouldn't talk like that."

"Well, let it pass. I want you to make the acquaintance of that loving couple, Mr. and Mrs. Numagawa Jiro. You must disguise yourself. Jiro is to be shadowed constantly. Get any help you require, but do it. Be off, Winter, on the wings of the wind. Fasten on to Jiro. Batten on him. Become his invisible vampire. Above all else, discover his associates. Run now to the bank and cash this cheque. It repays the sum you advanced last night, and provides money for expenses."

"I must first see Capella off," gasped the detective.

"All the more reason that you should fly."

Left to himself, the barrister compiled memoranda for an hour or more. He read through what he had written.

"The web is spreading quickly," he murmured. "I wonder what sort of fly we shall catch! Is he buzzing about under our very noses, or will he be an unknown variety? As they say in the Argentine–*Quien sabe*?"

During the journey to Stowmarket he mastered the contents of the bulky document sent from Glen Tochan. It contained a great many irrelevant details, but he made the following notes:

After the duel in 1763, David Hume, the man who avenged with his sword the supposed injury inflicted upon his father by the first Sir Alan Hume-Frazer, escaped to the Netherlands, and was never heard of again.

There was a local tradition on the Scotch estate that five Hume-Frazers would meet with violent deaths in England. The reason for this singular belief was found in the recorded utterances of an old nurse, popularly credited with the gift of second sight, who prophesied, after the outlawry of the Humes in 1745, that there would be five long-lived generations of both families, and   that five Frazers would die in their boots.

"Curiously enough," commented the old gentleman who supplied this information, "Aunt Elspeth's prediction is capable of two interpretations, owing to the fact that the first Sir Alan Frazer assumed the additional surname of Hume, I have absolutely no knowledge of any distinct branch of the Hume family. David Hume's sister was married to my ancestor at the time of the duel."

Admiral Cunningham, the hardy old salt who brought from Japan the sword used by a Samurai to commit hari-kara, or suicide by disembowelling, commanded the British vessels of the combined squadron which sailed up the Bay of Yedo on July 6, 1853, to intimidate the Mikado.

He narrowly escaped assassination at the hands of a two-sword man, who was knocked down by a sailor and soundly kicked, after being disarmed.

The Admiral brought home the two weapons taken from his assailant, and the larger sword was still to be seen in the armoury at Glen Tochan.

The three brothers, of whom the writer alone survived, quarrelled over money matters about eight years before the murder of the fifth baronet. The youngest, Charles, had entangled himself in a disastrous speculation in the city, and bitterly reproached Alan and David (the narrator) because they would not come to his assistance.

The old gentleman laboured through many pages to explain the reasons which actuated this decision, but Brett skipped all of them.

Finally, he suspected no one of committing the crime itself, which was utterly inexplicable. At Stowmarket the barrister sought a few minutes' conversation with the stationmaster.

"Have you been long in charge of this station?" he asked, when the official ushered him into a private office.

"Nearly five years, sir," was the surprised answer.

"Ah, then you know nearly all the members of the Hume-Frazer family?"

"Yes, sir. I think so."

"Do you remember the New Year's Eve when the young baronet was killed?"

"Yes, generally speaking, I do remember it."

The stationmaster was evidently doubtful of the motives which actuated this cross-examination, and resolved not to commit himself to positive statements.

"You recollect, of course, that Mr. David Hume-Frazer was arrested and tried for the murder of his cousin?"

"Yes."

"Very well. Now I want you to search your memory well and tell me if you saw anyone belonging to the family in the station on that New Year's Eve. The terrible occurrence at Beechcroft the same night must have fixed the facts in your mind."

The stationmaster, a cautious man of kindly disposition, seemed to be troubled by the interrogatory.

"Do you mind if I ask you, sir, why you are seeking this information?" he inquired, after a thoughtful pause.

"A very proper question. Mr. David Hume-Frazer is a friend of mine, and he has sought my help to clear away the mystery attached to his cousin's death."

"But why do you come to me?"

"Because you are a very likely person to have some knowledge on the point I raised. You see every person who enters or leaves Stowmarket by train."

"That is true. We railway men see far more than people think," said the official, with a smile. "But it is very odd that you should be the first gentleman to think of talking to me in connection with the affair, though I can assure you certain things puzzled me a good deal at the time."

"And what were they?"

"You are the gentleman who came here three days ago with Mr. David, whom, by the way, I hardly recognised at first?"

"Exactly."

"Well, I suppose it is all right. I did not interfere because I could not see my way clear to voluntarily give evidence. Of course, were I summoned by the police, it would be a different matter. The incidents of that New Year's Eve fairly bewildered me."

"Indeed!"

"It was stated at the trial, sir, that Mr. David came from Scotland that morning, left Liverpool Street at 3.20 p.m., and reached Stowmarket at 5.22 p.m."

"Yes."

"Further, he was admittedly the second person to see his cousin's dead body, and remained at the Hall until arrested by the police on a warrant."

Brett nodded. The stationmaster's statement promised to be intensely interesting.

"Well, sir," continued the man excitedly, "I was mystified enough on New Year's Eve, but after the murder came out I thought I was fairly bewitched. That season is always a busy one for us, what between parcels, passengers, and bad weather. On the morning of December 31, I fancied I saw Mr. David leave the London train due here at 12.15 midday. I only caught a glimpse of him, because there was a crowd of people, and he was all muffled up. I didn't give the matter a second thought

until I saw him again step out of a first-class carriage at
2.20 p.m. I looked at him rather sharp that time. He was
differently dressed, and hurried off without any luggage.
He left the station quickly, so I imagined I had been
mistaken a couple of hours earlier. You could have
knocked me down with a feather when he appeared by
the 5.22 p.m. This time he had several leather trunks,
and a footman from the Hall was waiting for him on the
platform. Excuse me, sir, but it was a fair licker!"

"It must have been. I wonder you did not speak to
him!"

"I wish I had done so. Mr. David is usually a very
affable young gentleman, but, what between my surprise
and the bustle of getting the train away, I lost the
opportunity. However, the queerest part of my story is
coming. I'm blest if he didn't leave here again by the last
train at 5.58 p.m. I missed his entrance to the station, but
had a good look at him as the train went out. He showed
the ticket-examiner at Ipswich a return half to London,
because I asked by wire. Now what did it all mean?"

"If I could tell you, it would save me much trouble,"
said Brett gravely. "But why did you not mention these
incidents subsequently?"

"Perhaps I was wrong, sir. I did not know what to do
for the best. Everyone at the Hall, including Mr. David
himself, would have proved that I was a liar with respect
to his two earlier arrivals and his departure by the 5.58. I
did not see what I would accomplish except to arouse a
strong suspicion that I had been drinking."

"Which would be unjustifiable?"

The stationmaster regained his dignity.

"I have been a teetotaler, sir, for more than twenty
years."

"You are sure you are making no mistake?"

"Nothing of the kind, sir. I must have been very much
mistaken, but I did not think so at the time, and it
bothered me more than enough. If my evidence promised

to be of any service to Mr. David, no consideration would have kept me back. As it was"

"You thought it would damage him?"

"I'm afraid that was my idea."

"I agree with you. It is far better that it never came to the knowledge of the police. I am greatly obliged to you."

"May I ask, sir, if what I have told you will be useful in your inquiry?"

"Most decidedly. Some day soon Mr. David Hume-Frazer will thank you in person. I suppose you have no objection to placing your observations in written form for my private use, and sending the statement to me at the County Hotel?"

"Not the least, sir; good-day."

The barrister walked to the hotel, having despatched his bag by a porter.

"I suppose," he said to himself, "that when Winter came here he rushed straight to the police-station. How his round eyes will bulge out of their sockets when I tell him what I have just learnt."

13

Two Women

The surprising information given by the stationmaster impressed the barrister as so much unexpected trover which would assert its value in the progress of events. He certainly did not anticipate the discovery of three David Humes, though he had hoped to find traces of two.

Before he reached his hotel he experienced a spasm of doubt. Was his client telling the truth about his movements on that memorable Christmas Eve? David's story was fully corroborated by the railway official and the servants at the Hall, whose sworn evidence was in Brett's possession. But how about Hume's counterfeit presentments arriving by the earlier trains–coming from where and bound on what errands?

He resolutely closed down the trap-door opened by his imagination.

"The pit does not yawn for me," he communed, "but for the man who killed Sir Alan. Assuredly he will fall into it before many days. Nothing on earth can stop the meeting of two or more of the hidden channels now being opened up, and when they do meet there must be a dramatic outcome."

His chief purpose in revisiting Stowmarket was to seek further confidences from Mrs. Capella. He argued that the sudden journey of her husband to Naples would cause her much uneasiness, and she might now be inclined to reveal circumstances yet hidden.

He refused to take her at a disadvantage. From the hotel he sent a cyclist messenger with a note asking for an interview, and within an hour he received a cordial request to come at once.

Nevertheless, he was not a little astonished to find Helen Layton awaiting him in Margaret's boudoir.

The girl showed signs of recent agitation, but she explained her presence quietly enough.

"Mrs. Capella sent for me when your note reached her, Mr. Brett. She is greatly upset by recent events, and was actually on the point of telegraphing to Davie to ask him to bring you here at once when your message was handed to her. She will be here presently. Please do not press her too closely to reveal anything she wishes to withhold. She is so emotional and excited, poor thing, that I fear her health may be endangered."

Miss Layton's words were not well chosen. She was conscious of the fact, and blushed furiously when Brett received her request with a friendly nod of comprehension.

"I do not know what to say for the best," she went on desperately. "I am so sorry for Margaret, and it seems to me to be a terrible thing that my proposed marriage with her cousin should be the innocent cause of all this trouble."

"Is it the cause?" he asked.

"What else can it be? Certainly not Mr. Capella's foolish actions. If Davie and I were married, and far away from this neighbourhood, we would probably never see him again. I assure you I attach no serious significance to his mad fancy for me. The real reason for the present bother is Davie's desire to reopen the story of the murder. Of that I am convinced."

"Then what do you wish me to do?"

Helen's eyes became suspiciously moist.

"How am I to decide?" she said tremulously. "Naturally, I want the name of my future husband to be cleared of the odium attached to it, but it is hard that this cannot be done without driving a dear woman like Margaret to despair, perhaps to the grave."

"I do not see why the one course should involve the other."

"Nor do I; but the fact remains. Mr. Capella's decision to go to Naples is somehow bound up with it. Oh, dear! During the last two years a dozen or more girls have been happily married in this village without any one being killed, or running away, or dying of grief. Why should those things descend upon my poor little head?"

"Perhaps you are mistaken. Events have conspired to point to you as the unconscious source of a good deal that has happened. Personally, Miss Layton, I incline to the belief that you are no more responsible than David Hume-Frazer. If the mystery of Sir Alan's death is ever solved, I feel assured that its genesis will be found in circumstances not only beyond your control, but wholly independent, and likely to operate in the same way if both you and your fiancé had never either seen or heard of Beechcroft Hall."

"Oh, Mr. Brett," she cried impulsively, "I wish I could be certain of that!"

"Try and adopt my opinion," he answered, with a smile, for the girl's dubiety was not very flattering.

"I know I am saying the wrong thing. I cannot help it. Margaret's distress tried me sorely. Be gentle with her—that is all I ask."

The door opened, and Mrs. Capella entered. Helen's observations had prepared Brett to some extent, yet he was shocked to see the havoc wrought in Margaret's appearance by days of suffering and nights of sleepless agony.

Her face was drawn and ivory-white, her eyes unnaturally brilliant, her lips bloodless and pinched. She was again garbed in black, and the sombre effect of her dress supplied a startling contrast to the deathly pallor of her features.

She recognised Brett's presence by a silent bow, and sank on to a couch. She was not acting, but really ill, overwrought, inert, physically weak from want of food and sleep.

Helen ran to her side, and took her in a loving clasp.

"You poor darling!" she cried. "Why are you suffering so?"

Now there was nothing on earth Brett detested so thoroughly as a display of feminine sentiment, no matter how spontaneous or well-timed. At heart he was conscious of kindred emotions. A child's cry, a woman's sob, the groan of a despairing man, had power to move him so strangely that he had more than once allowed a long-sought opportunity to slip from his grasp rather than sear his own soul by displaying callous indifference to the sufferings of others.

The tears of these, two, however, set his teeth on edge. What were they whining about—the affections of a doll of a man whose antics had been rightly treated by David when he proved to Capella that there is nothing like leather.

For the barrister laboured under no delusions respecting either woman. Margaret, who secretly feared her husband, was only pining for his rekindled admiration, whilst Helen, though true as steel to David Hume, could not be expected to regard the Italian's misplaced passion as utterly outrageous. No woman can absolutely hate and despise a man for loving her, no matter how absurd or impossible his passion may be. She may proclaim, even feel, a vast amount of indignation, but in the secret recesses of her soul, hidden perhaps from her own scrutiny, she can find excuses for him.

Brett regarded Capella as an impressionable scamp, endowed with a too vivid imagination, and he determined forthwith to stir his hearers into revolt, defiance—anything but languishing regret and condolence.

Margaret soon gave him an opportunity. Recovering her self-possession with an effort, she said:

"I am glad you are here, Mr. Brett. Helen has probably told you that we need your presence—not that I have much to say to you, but I must have the advice of a wiser and clearer head than my own in the present position of affairs."

"Exactly so," replied the barrister cheerily. "As a preliminary to a pleasant chat, may I suggest a cup of tea for each of us?"

The ladies were manifestly astonished. Tea! When broken hearts were scattered around! The suggestion was pure bathos.

Margaret, with a touch of severity, permitted Brett to ring, and coldly agreed with Helen's declaration that she could not think of touching any species of refreshment at such a moment.

"Then," said Brett, advancing and holding out his hand, "I will save your servants from needless trouble, Mrs. Capella. I am equally emphatic in my insistence on food and drink as primary necessities. For instance, a cup of good tea just now is much more important in my eyes than your husband's vagaries."

"Surely you will not desert me?" appealed Margaret.

"Mr. Brett, how can you be so heartless?" cried Helen.

"Your words cut me to the bone," he answered, with an easy smile, "but in this matter I must be adamant. My dear ladies, pray consider. What a world we should live in if people went without their meals because they were worried. Three days of such treatment would end the South African War, give Ireland Home Rule, bring even the American Senate to reason. A week of it would extinguish the human race. If the system has such potentialities, is it unreasonable to ask whether or not any single individual—even Mr. Capellais worth the loss of a cup of tea because he chooses to go to Naples?"

A servant entered.

"Is it to be for three, or none?" inquired Brett, compelling Margaret to meet his gaze.

"James, bring tea at once," said Mrs. Capella.

The barrister accepted this partial surrender. He looked out over the park.

"What lovely weather!" Brett exclaimed. "How delightful it must be at the sea-side just now! Really, I am greatly tempted to run up to Whitby for a few days. Have you ever been there, Mrs. Capella? Or you, Miss Layton? No! Well, let me recommend the north-east coast of Yorkshire as a cure for all ills. Do you know that, within the next fortnight, you can, if energetic enough, see from the cliffs at Whitby the sun rise and set in the sea? It is the one place in England where such a sight is possible. And the breeze there! When it blows from the north, it comes straight from the Polar Sea. There is no land intervening. Naples—evil-smelling, dirty Naples! Pah! Who but a lunatic would prefer Naples to Whitby in July!"

Margaret was now incensed, Helen surprised, and even slightly amused.

Brett rattled on, demanding and receiving occasional curt replies. The tea came.

Whatever the failings of Beechcroft might be, they had not reached the kitchen. Delightful little rolls of thin bread and butter, sandwiches of cucumber and *paté de foie gras*, tempting morsels of pastry, home-made jam, and crisp biscuits showed that the housekeeper had unconsciously adopted Brett's view of her mistress's needs.

Margaret, hardly knowing what she did, toyed at first with these delicacies, until she yielded to the demands of her stimulated appetite. Helen and Brett were unfeignedly hungry, and when Brett rose to ring for more cucumber sandwiches, they all laughed.

"The first time I met you," said Margaret, whose cheeks began to exhibit a faint trace of colour, "I told you that you could read a woman's heart. I did not know you were also qualified to act as her physician."

"If the first part of my treatment is deemed successful, then I hope you will adopt the second. I am quite in earnest concerning Whitby, or Cromer, if you do not care to go far north."

"But, Mr. Brett, how can I possibly leave Beechcroft now?"

"Did Mr. Capella consult you when he went to Naples? Are you not mistress here? Take my advice. Give the majority of your servants a holiday. Close your house, or, better still, have every room dismantled on the pretence of a thorough renovation. Leave it to paperhangers, plasterers, and caretakers. The rector may be persuaded to allow Miss Layton to come with you to London, where you should visit your dressmaker, for you can now dispense with mourning. When your husband returns from Naples, let him rage to the top of his bent. By that time I may be able to spare Mr. Hume to look after both of you for a week or so. Permit your husband to join you when he humbly seeks permission—not before. Believe me, Mrs. Capella, if you have strength of will to adopt my programme in its entirety, the trip to Naples may have results wholly unexpected by the runaway."

"Really, Margaret, Mr. Brett's advice seems to me to be very sensible. It happens, too, that my father needs a change of air, and I think we could both persuade him to come with us to the coast."

Helen, like all well regulated young Englishwomen, quickly took a reasonable view of the problem. Already Capella's heroics and his wife's lamentations began to appear ridiculous.

Margaret looked wistfully at both of them.

"You do not understand why my husband has gone to Naples," she said slowly, seemingly revolving something in her mind.

"I think I can guess his motive," said the barrister.

"Tell me your explanation of the riddle," she answered lightly, though a shadow of fear crossed her eyes.

"Soon after your marriage he imagined that he discovered certain facts connected with your family—possibly relative to your brother's death—which served to estrange him from you. Whatever they may be, whether existent or fanciful, you are in no way responsible. He has gone to Naples to obtain proofs of his suspicions, or knowledge. He will come back to terrorise you, perhaps to seek revenge for imaginary wrongs. Therefore, I say, do not meet him half-way by sitting here, blanched and fearful, until it pleases him to return. Compel him to seek you. Let him find you at least outwardly happy and contented, careless of his neglect, and more pleased than otherwise by his absence. Tell him to try Algiers in August and Calcutta in September."

Margaret's eyes were widely distended. Her mobile features expressed both astonishment and anxiety. She covered her face with her hands, in an attitude of deep perplexity.

They knew she was wrestling with the impulse to take them wholly into confidence.

At last she spoke:

"I cannot tell you," she said, "how comforting your words are. If you, a stranger, can estimate the truth so nearly, why should I torture myself because my husband is outrageously unjust? I will follow your counsel, Mr. Brett. If possible, Nellie and I will leave here to-morrow. Perhaps Mrs. Eastham may be able to come with us to town. Will you order my carriage? A drive will do me good. Come with Nellie and me, and stay here to dinner. For to-day we may dispense with ceremony."

She left the room, walking with a firm and confident step.

Brett turned to Miss Layton.

"Capella is in for trouble," he said, with a laugh. "He will be forced to make love to his wife a second time."

14

MARGARET SPEAKS OUT

During the drive the presence of servants rendered conversation impossible on the one topic that engrossed their thoughts.

The barrister, therefore, had an opportunity to display the other side of his engaging personality, his singular knowledge of the world, his acquaintance with the latest developments in literature and the arts, and so much of London's *vie intime* as was suited to the ears of polite society.

Once he amused the ladies greatly by a trivial instance of his faculty for deducing a definite fact from seemingly inadequate signs.

He was sitting with his back to the horses. They passed a field in which some people were working. Neither of the women paid attention to the scene. Brett, from mere force of habit, took in all details.

A little farther on he said: "Are we approaching a village?"

"Yes," answered Miss Layton, "a small place named Needham."

"Then it will not surprise me if, during the next two minutes, we meet a horse and cart with a load of potatoes. The driver is a young man in his shirt sleeves. Sitting by his side is a brown-eyed maid in a poke bonnet. Probably his left arm follows the line of her apron string."

His hearers could not help being surprised by this prediction. Helen leaned over the side and looked ahead.

"You are wrong this time, Mr. Brett," she laughed merrily. "The only vehicle between us and a turn in the road is a dog-cart coming this way."

"That merely shows the necessity of carefully choosing one's words. I should have said 'overtake,' not 'meet.'"

The carriage sped swiftly along. Helen craned her head to catch the first glimpse of the yet hidden stretch of road beyond the turning.

"Good gracious!" she cried suddenly.

Even Margaret was stimulated to curiosity. She bent over the opposite side.

"What an extraordinary thing!" she exclaimed.

Brett sat unmoved, anything in front being, of course, quite invisible to him. On the box the coachman nudged the footman, as if to say:

"Did you ever! Well, s'elp me!"

For, in the next few strides, the horses had to be pulled to one side to avoid a cart laden with potatoes, driven by a coatless youth who had one arm thrown gracefully around the waist of a girl in a huge bonnet.

Nellie turned and stared at them in most unladylike manner, much to their discomfiture.

"I do declare," she cried, "the girl has brown eyes! Mr. Brett, do tell us how you did it."

"I will," he replied gaily. "Those labourers in a field half a mile away were digging potatoes. Among the women sorters was a girl who was gazing anxiously in this direction, and who resumed work in a very bad temper when another woman spoke to her in a chaffing way. The gate was left open, and there were fresh wheel-tracks in this direction. The men were all coatless, so I argued a young man driving and a girl by his side, hence the annoyance of the watcher in the field, owing particularly to the position of his arm. The presence on the road of several potatoes, with the earth still damp on them, added certainty to my convictions. It is very easy, you see."

"Yes, but how about the colour of the girl's eyes?"

"That was hazardous, to an extent. But five out of every six women in this county have brown eyes."

"Well, you may think it easy; to me it is marvellous."

"It is positively startling," said Margaret seriously; and if the barrister indulged in a fresh series of deductions he remained silent on the topic.

He tried to lead the conversation to Naples, but was foiled by Mrs. Capella's positive disinclination to discuss Italy on any pretext, and Miss Layton's natural desire not to embarrass her friend.

Indeed, so little headway did he make, so fully was Margaret's mind taken up with the new departure he had suggested, that when the carriage stopped at the rectory to drop Helen–who wished to tell her father about the dinner and to change her costume–he was strongly tempted to wriggle out of the engagement.

Inclination pulled him to his quiet sitting-room in the County Hotel; impulse bade him remain and make the most of the meagre opportunities offered by the drift of conversation.

"I hope," said Helen, at parting, "that I may persuade you to come here and dine with my father some evening when Mrs. Capella and I are in town. If you take any interest in old coins he will entertain you for hours."

"Then I depend on you to bring an invitation to the Hall this evening. I expect to be in Stowmarket next week."

"Are you leaving to-morrow?" inquired Mrs. Capella.

"I think so."

"Would you care to walk to the house with me now?"

"I will be delighted."

So the carriage was sent off, and the two followed on foot. Brett thought that impulse had led him aright.

Once past the lodge gates, Margaret looked at him suddenly, with a quick, searching glance. Hume was not in error when he spoke of her "Continental tricks of manner."

"You wonder," she said, "why I do not trust you fully? You know that I am keeping something back from you?

You imagine that you can guess a good deal of what I am endeavouring to hide?"

"To all those questions, I may generally answer 'Yes.'"

"Of course. You observe the small things of life. The larger events are built from them. Well, I can be candid with you. My husband believes that I not only deceived him in regard to my marriage, but he is, or was, very jealous of me."

She paused, apparently unable to frame her words satisfactorily.

"Having said so much," put in the barrister gently, "you might be more specific."

His cool, even voice reassured her.

"I hardly know how best to express myself," she cried. "Question me. I will reply so far as I am able."

"Thank you. You have told me that you first met Mr. Capella on New Year's Eve two years ago, at Covent Garden?"

"That is so."

"Had you ever heard of him before?"

"Never. He was brought to my party by an Italian friend."

"Did the acquaintance ripen rapidly?"

"Yes. We found that our tastes were identical in many respects. I did not know of my brother's death until the 2nd of January. No one in Beechcroft had my address, and my solicitor's office was closed on the holiday. Mr. Capella called on me, by request, the day after the ball, and already I became aware of his admiration. Italians are quick to fall in love."

"And afterwards?"

"When poor Alan's murder appeared in the press, Giovanni was among the first to write me a sympathetic letter. Later on we met several times in London. I did not come to reside in the Hall until all legal formalities were settled. A year passed. I went to Naples. He came from his estate in Calabria, and we renewed our friendship.

You do not know, perhaps, that he is a count in his own country, but we decided not to use the title here."

"Then Mr. Capella is not a poor man?"

"By no means. He is far from rich as we understand the word. He is worth, I believe, £1,500 a-year. Why do you ask? Had you the impression that he married me for my money?"

"There might well be other reasons," thought Brett, glancing at the beautiful and stately woman by his side. But it was no moment for idle compliments.

"Such things have been done," he said drily.

"Then disabuse your mind of the idea. He is a very proud man. His estates are involved, and in our first few days of happiness we did indeed discuss the means of freeing them, whilst our marriage contract stipulates that in the event of either of us predeceasing the other, and there being no children, the survivor inherits. But all at once a cloud came between us, and Giovanni has curtly declined any assistance by me in discharging his family debt."

Brett could not help remembering Capella's passionate declaration to Helen, but Margaret's words read a new meaning into it. Possibly the Italian was only making a forlorn hope attack on a country maiden's natural desire to shine amidst her friends. Well, time would tell.

Meanwhile, Mrs. Capella's outburst of confidence was valuable.

"A cloud!" he said. "What sort of a cloud?"

"Giovanni suddenly discovered that his father and mine were deadly enemies. It was a cruel whim of Fate that brought us together. Poor fellow! He was very fond of his father, and it seems that a legacy of revenge was bequeathed to him against an Englishman named Beechcroft. I remembered, too late, that he once asked me how our house came to be so named, and I explained its English meaning to him. I joked about it, and said the

place should rightly be called Yewcroft. During our
honeymoon at Naples he learnt that my father, for some
reason, had travelled over a large part of Italy in an
assumed name"

"How did he learn this?" broke in Brett.

"I cannot tell you. The affair happened like a flash of
lightning. We had been to Capri one afternoon, and I was
tired. I went to my room to rest for a couple of hours, fell
asleep, and awoke to find Giovanni staring at me in the
most terrifying manner. There was a fierce scene. We are
both hot-tempered, and when he accused me of a
ridiculous endeavour to hoodwink him in some
indefinable way I became very indignant. We patched up
a sort of truce, but I may honestly say that we have not
had a moment's happiness since."

"But you spoke of jealousy also?"

"That is really too absurd. My cousin Robert"

"What, the gentleman from the Argentine?"

"Yes; I suppose David told you about him?"

"He did," said the barrister grimly.

"Robert is poor, you may know. He is also very good-
looking."

"A family trait," Brett could not avoid saying.

"It has not been an advantage to us," she replied
mournfully.

They were standing now opposite the library, almost
on the spot where her brother fell. They turned and
strolled back towards the lodge.

"Robert came to see me," she resumed. "He paid a
visit in unconventional manner—waylaid me, in fact, in
this very avenue, and asked me to help him. He declined
to meet my husband, and was very bitter about my
marriage to a foreigner. However, I forgave him, for my
own heart was sore in me, and he also had been
unfortunate in a different way. We had a long talk, and I
kissed him at parting. I afterwards found that Giovanni
had seen us from his bedroom. He thought Robert was
David. I do not think he believed me, even when I showed

him the counterfoil of my cheque-book, and the amount of a remittance I sent to Robert next day."

"How much was the sum?"

"Five hundred pounds."

"And where did you send it?"

"To the Hotel Victoria."

"In his own name?"

"Certainly."

"Have you ever met him since?"

"Yes, unfortunately. I was in London, driving through Regent Street in a hansom, when I saw him on the pavement. I stopped the cab, and asked him to come to luncheon. We have no town house, so I was staying at the Carlton alone. Yet how stupidly compromising circumstances can occasionally become! I returned to Beechcroft. I did not mention my meeting with Robert because, indeed, Giovanni and I were hardly on speaking terms. One day, in the library, I was sorting a number of accounts, when I was summoned elsewhere for a few minutes. On top of the pile was my receipted hotel bill. My husband came in, glanced at the paper, and saw a charge for a guest. When I returned he asked me whom I had been entertaining. I told him, and could not help blushing, the affair being so flagrantly absurd."

"Is that all?"

"I declare to you, Mr. Brett, that you are now as well informed as I am myself concerning our estrangement."

"There is, I take it, no objection on your part to the inquiry I have undertaken—the fixing of responsibility for your brother's death, I mean?"

Margaret was silent for a few seconds before she said, in a low and steady voice:

"We are a strange race, we Hume-Frazers. Somehow I felt, when I first saw you and Davie together, that you would be bound up with a crisis in my life. I dread crises. They have ever been unfortunate for me. I cannot explain myself further. I know I am approaching an eventful epoch. Well, I am prepared. Go on with your work, in God's name. I cannot become more unhappy than I am."

15
AN UNEXPECTED VISITOR

A clock in the church tower chimed the half-hour.

"We dine at seven," said Mrs. Capella. "Let us return to the house. I told the housekeeper to prepare a room for you. Would you care to remain for the night? One of the grooms can bring from Stowmarket any articles you may need."

Brett declined the invitation, pleading a certain amount of work to be done before he retired to rest, and his expectation of finding letters or telegrams at the hotel.

They walked more rapidly up the avenue, and the barrister noted the graceful ease of Margaret's movements.

"Is it a fact" he asked, "that you suffer from heart disease?"

She laughed, and said, with a certain charming hesitation:

"You are both doctor and lawyer, Mr. Brett. My heart is quite sound. I have been foolish enough to seek relief from my troubles in morphia. Do not be alarmed. I am not a morphinée. I promised Nellie yesterday to stop it, and I am quite certain to succeed."

The dinner passed uneventfully.

As Brett was unable to change his clothes, neither of the ladies, of course, appeared in elaborate costumes.

Helen wore a simple white muslin dress, with pale blue ribbons. Margaret, mindful of the barrister's hint concerning her attire, now appeared in pale grey crêpe de chine, trimmed with cerise panne velvet.

When she entered the drawing-room she almost startled the others, so strong was the contrast between her present effective garments and the black raiment she had affected constantly since her return to Beechcroft after her marriage.

"The reform has commenced," she cried gaily, seeing how they looked at her. "My maid is in ecstasies about the proposed visit to my dressmaker's. She insisted on showing me a study for an Ascot frock in the *Queen*."

"Ah, she is a Frenchwoman?" said Brett.

"Yes; and pray what mystery have you elucidated now?"

"Not a mystery, but a sober fact. A Frenchwoman must be in the mode. Anybody else would have told you to copy yourself. Fashions are a sealed book to me, but I do claim a certain taste in colour effect, and you have gratified it."

"And have you nothing nice to say to me, Mr. Brett?" pouted Helen.

"So much that I must remain dumb. I have a vivid recollection of Mr. Hume's tragic air when he asked me to give you 'his kind regards.'"

"The dear boy! You have not yet told us why you left him in London."

In view of Mrs. Capella's outspokenness concerning her cousin, this was a poser. Brett fenced with the query, and the announcement of dinner stopped all personal references. The barrister's eyes wandered round the dining-room. The shaded candles on the table did not permit much light to fall on the walls, but such portraits as were visible showed that David was right when he said the "Hume-Frazers were all alike." They were a handsome, determined-looking race, strong, dour, inflexible.

The night was beautifully fine. The day seemed loth to die, and the twilight lingering on the pleasant landscape tempted them outside, after the butler had handed Brett a box of excellent cigars.

They went through the conservatory into the park, and sauntered over the springy pastureland, whilst Brett amused the ladies by a carefully edited account of his visit to the Jiro family.

An hour passed in pleasant chat. Then Miss Layton thought it was time she went home, and Brett proposed to escort her to the Rectory, subsequently picking up his conveyance at the inn.

They walked obliquely across the park towards the house, regaining it through a clump of laurels and the conservatory.

It chanced that for a moment they were silent. Margaret led the way. Helen followed. Brett came close behind.

When the mistress of Beechcroft Hall stepped on to the turf in front of the library, a man who was standing under the yews a little way down the avenue moved forward to accost her.

She uttered a little cry of alarm and retreated quickly.

"Why, Davie," cried Helen, "surely it cannot be you!"

The stranger made no reply, but paused irresolutely. Even in the dim light Brett needed no second glance to reveal to him the astounding coincidence that this mysterious prowler was Robert Hume-Frazer.

"Good evening," he said politely. "Do you wish to see your cousin?"

"And who the devil may you be?" was the uncompromising answer.

"A friend of Mrs. Capella's."

"H'm! I'm glad to hear it. I thought you could not be that beastly Italian."

"You are candour itself; but you have not answered me?"

"About seeing my cousin? No. I will call when she is less engaged."

He turned to go, but Brett caught him by the shoulder.

"Will you come quietly," he said, "or by the scruff of the neck?"

The other man wheeled round again. That he feared no personal violence was evident. Indeed, it was possible Brett had over-estimated his own strength in suggesting the alternative.

The Argentine cousin laughed boisterously.

"By the Lord Harry," he cried, "I like your style! I will come in, if only to have a good look at you."

They approached the two frightened women. Margaret had recognised his voice, and now advanced with outstretched hand.

"I am glad to see you, Robert," she said in tones that vibrated somewhat. "Why did you not let me know you were coming?"

"Because I did not know myself until an hour before I left London. Moreover, you might have wired and told me to stop away, so I sailed without orders."

The position was awkward. The new-comer had evidently walked from Stowmarket. He had the appearance of a gentleman, soiled and a trifle truculent, perhaps, but a man of birth and good breeding.

Helen was gazing at him in sheer wonderment He was so extremely like David that, at a distance, it was easy to confuse the one with the other.

Brett, too, examined him curiously. He recalled "Rabbit Jack's" pronouncement"—either the chap hisself or his dead spit."

But it behoved him to rescue the ladies from an *impasse*.

"When you reached Stowmarket did the stationmaster exhibit any marked interest in you?" he inquired.

"Well, now, that beats the band," cried Robert. "He looked at me as though I had seven heads and horns to match. But how did you know that?"

"Merely on account of your marked resemblance to David Hume-Frazer. It puzzled the stationmaster some time ago. By the way, you appear to like the shade of the yew trees outside. Do you always approach Beechcroft Hall in the same way?"

The ex-sailor's bold eyes did not fall before the barrister's penetrating glance.

"What the deuce has it got to do with you?" he replied fiercely. "Who has appointed you grand inquisitor to the family, I should like to know? Margaret, I beg your pardon, but this chap"

"Is my friend, Mr. Reginald Brett. He is engaged in unravelling the manner and cause of poor Alan's death. He has my full sanction, Robert, and was brought here, in the first instance, by David. I hope, therefore, you will treat him more civilly."

"I will treat him as he treats me. I owe him nothing, at any rate."

They were talking in the ill-fated library, having entered the house through the centre window. The unbidden guest faced the others, and although the cloud of suspicion hung heavily upon him, the barrister was far too shrewd an observer of human nature to attribute his present defiant attitude to other than its true origin—a feeling of humiliated pride.

Brett understood that to question him further was to risk a scene—a thing to be avoided at all costs.

"No doubt," he said, "you wish to speak privately to Mrs. Capella. I was on the point of escorting Miss Layton to her house. Shall I return and drive you back to Stowmarket? I will be here in fifteen minutes."

"It would be better than walking," replied Robert wearily, settling into a chair with the air of a man physically tired and mentally perturbed.

Again there was a dramatic pause. Helen, more alarmed than she wished to admit, gave Margaret a questioning look, and received a strained but reassuring smile.

"Then I will go now" she began, but instantly stopped. Like the others, she heard the quick trot of a horse, and the sound of rapid wheels approaching from the lodge.

"Who on earth can this be?" cried Margaret, blanching visibly. The vehicle, a dog-cart, drew nearer. They all went to the window. Even the indifferent Robert rose and joined them.

Helen startled them by running out to the side of the drive.

"This time I am not mistaken," she cried hysterically. "It is Davie!"

The proceedings of the gentleman who jumped from the dog-cart left no doubt on the point. He brazenly kissed her, and in her excitement she seemed to like it.

She evidently whispered something to him, for his first words to Brett were:

"How did you find out"

But the barrister was not anxious to let the cousin from Argentina into the secret of the search for him.

"I have found out nothing," he interrupted. "I have been at Beechcroft all the afternoon and evening. Meanwhile, you must be surprised to meet Mr. Robert Hume-Frazer here so unexpectedly."

David luckily grasped his friend's intention. Such information as he possessed must wait until they were alone. "How d'ye do, Bob?" he said, frankly holding out his hand. "Why have you left us alone all those years, to turn up at last in this queer way?"

The young man's kind greeting, his manly attitude, had an unlooked-for effect.

Robert ignored the proffered hand. He reached for his hat.

"I feel like a beastly interloper," he growled huskily. "Accept my apologies, Margaret, and you, Miss Layton. I will call in the morning. Mr. Brett, if you still hold to your offer, I will await you at the lodge, or any other place you care to name."

With blazing eyes, and mouth firmly set, he endeavoured to reach the open window. Brett barred his way.

"Sit down, man," he said sternly. "Why are you such a fool as to resist the kindness offered to you? I tried to make matters easy for you. Now I must speak plainly. You are weak with hunger."

He had seen what the others had missed. The colour in Robert's face was due to exposure, but he was otherwise drawn and haggard. His clothes were shabby. He had walked from Stowmarket because he could not afford to hire any means of conveyance.

The abject confession compelled by Brett's words was too much for him. He again collapsed into a chair and covered his face with his hands.

16
THE COUSINS

Brett was the only person present who kept his senses. Margaret was too shocked, the lovers too amazed, to speak coherently.

"Mr. Hume-Frazer has allowed himself to become run down," said the barrister, with the nonchalance of one who discussed the prospects of to-morrow's weather. "What he needs at the moment is some soup and a few biscuits. You, Mrs. Capella, might procure these without bringing the servants here, especially if Miss Layton were to help you."

Without a word, the two ladies quitted the room.

Robert looked up.

"You ring like good metal," he said to the barrister. "Is there any liquor in the dining-room? I feel a trifle hollow about the belt. A drink would do me good."

"Not until you have eaten something first," was the firm answer. "Are you so hard up that you could not buy food?"

"Well, the fact is, I have been on my beam ends during the past week. To-day I pawned a silver watch, but unfortunately returned to my lodgings, where my landlady made such a fiendish row about the bill that I gave her every penny. Then I pawned my overcoat, raising the exact fare to Stowmarket. I could not even pay for a 'bus from Gower Street to Liverpool Street. All I have eaten to-day was a humble breakfast at 8.30 a.m., and I suppose the sun and the journey wore me out. Still, you must be jolly sharp to see what was the matter. I thought I kept my end up pretty well."

David sat down by his side.

"Forgive me, old chap," continued Robert. "It broke me up to see that you were happy after all your troubles. You are engaged to a nice girl; Alan is dead; I am the only unlucky member of the family."

The man was talking quite sincerely. He even envied his murdered cousin. Nothing in his words, his suspicious mode of announcing his presence, the vague doubts that shadowed his past career, puzzled Brett so greatly as that chance phrase.

The ladies came back, laden with good things from the kitchen, which they insisted on carrying themselves, much to the astonishment of the servants.

All women are born actresses. Their behaviour before the domestics left the impression that some huge joke was toward in the library.

The tactful barrister drew Hume and Helen outside to discuss immediate arrangements. David promised faithfully to return from the rectory in fifteen minutes, and Brett re-entered the library.

Robert Hume-Frazer gave evidence of his semi-starvation. He tried to disguise his eagerness, but in vain. Biscuits, sandwiches, and soup vanished rapidly, until Margaret suggested a further supply.

"No, Rita," said her cousin; "I have fasted too often on the Pampas not to know the folly of eating too heartily. I will be all right now, especially when Mr. Brett produces the whisky he spoke about."

The barrister brought a decanter from the dining-room. The stranger was still an enigma. He placed bottle and glass on the table, wondering to what extent the man would help himself.

The quantity was small and well diluted. So this member of the family was not a drunkard.

"How did you come to be in such a state?" asked Margaret nervously. "It is hardly six months since I sent you £500; not a very large sum, I admit, but all you asked me for, and more than enough to live on for a much longer period."

Robert laughed pleasantly. It was the first token of returning confidence. He reached for a cigar, and sought Margaret's permission to smoke.

"My dear girl," he answered, "I am really a very unfortunate person. I own a hundred thousand acres of the best land in South America, and I have been in England nearly two years trying to raise capital to develop it. If I owned a salted reef or an American brewery I could have got the money for the asking. Because my stock-raising proposition is a sound paying concern, requiring a delay of at least three years before a penny of profit can be realised, I have worn my boots out in climbing up and down office stairs to no purpose. Out of your £500, nearly £400 went out at once to pay arrears of Government taxation to save my property. Of the remaining hundred I spent fifty in a fortnight on dinners and suppers given to a gang of top-hatted scoundrels, who, I found subsequently, were not worth a red cent. They hoped to fleece me in some way, and their very association discredited me in the eyes of one or two honest men. Oh, I have had a bad time of it, I can assure you!"

"Why did you not write to me again?"

He looked at her steadily before he explained:

"Because you are a woman."

"What has that got to do with it? I am your relative, and rich. How much do you want? If your scheme is really sound, I imagine my solicitors might sanction my co-operation."

Again he hesitated.

"Thank you, Rita. You are a good sort. But I am not here on a matter of high finance. I want you to lend me, say, £250. I will return to the Argentine, and take twenty years to accomplish what I could do in five with the necessary capital."

"Come and see me in the morning. The sum you name is absurdly small, in any case. Perhaps Mr. Brett will accompany you. His advice will be useful to both of us. Come early. I leave here to-morrow."

"Going away! Where to?"

"To Whitby, in Yorkshire."

"Well, that is curious," said Robert, who clearly did not like to question her about her husband.

"Mr. Capella is in Naples," she added. "I cannot say when he will return."

Her cousin's look was eloquent of his thoughts. He did not like the Italian, for some inexplicable reason, for to Margaret's knowledge they had never met.

The barrister naturally did not interfere in this family conclave. He listened intently, and had already drawn several inferences from the man's words. For the life of him he could not classify Robert Hume-Frazer. The man was either a consummate scoundrel, the cold-blooded murderer of Margaret's brother, or a maligned and ill-used man.

Within a few minutes he would be called upon to treat him in one category or the other. A few questions might elucidate matters considerably.

The hiatus in the conversation created by the mention of Capella gave him an opportunity.

"Did you endeavour to raise the requisite capital for your estate in London only?" he inquired.

"No; I tried elsewhere," was the quick rejoinder.

"Here, for instance, on the New Year's Eve before last?"

"Now, how the blazes did you learn that?" came the fierce demand, the speaker's excitement rendering him careless of the words he used.

"It is true, then?"

"Yes, but"

"Robert!" Margaret's voice was choking, and her face was woefully white once more—"were you—here–when Alan–was killed?"

"No, not exactly. This thing bewilders me. Let me explain. I saw him that afternoon. We had a furious quarrel. I never told you about it, Rita. It was a family matter. I do not hold you responsible. I"

"Hold me responsible! What do you mean? Did you kill my brother?"

She rose to her feet. Her eyes seemed to peer into his soul. He, too, rose and faced her.

"By God," he cried, "this is too much! Why didn't you ask your husband that question?"

"Because my husband, with all his faults, is innocent of that crime. He was with me in London the night that Alan met his death."

"And I, too, was in London. I left Stowmarket at six o'clock."

"Having reached the place at 2.20?" interposed Brett.

The other turned to him with eager pleading.

"In Heaven's name, Mr. Brett, if you know all about my movements that day, disabuse Margaret's mind of the terrible idea that prompted her question."

"Why did you come here on that occasion?"

"The truth must out now. My two uncles swindled my father—that is, Margaret, your father led my Uncle David with him in a most unjust proceeding. My father took up some risky business in City finance, on the verbal understanding with his brothers that they would share profits or bear losses equally. The speculation failed, and your father basely withdrew from the compact, persuading the other brother to follow his lead. Perhaps there may have been some justification for his action, but my poor old dad was very bitter about it. The affair killed him. I made my own way in the world, and came here to ask Alan to undo the wrong done years ago, and help me to get on my feet. He was not in the best of tempers, and we fell out badly, using silly recriminations. I went back to London, and next day travelled to Monte Carlo, where I lost more money than I could afford. Believe me, I never even knew of Alan's death until I saw the reports of Davie's trial."

"Why did you not come forward then?"

"Why? No man could have better reasons. First, it seemed to me that Davie had killed him. Then, when the second trial ended, I came to the conclusion—Lord help my wits—that there was some underhanded work about the succession to the property, and my doubts appeared to receive confirmation by the news of Margaret's marriage. In any case, if I turned up to give evidence, I could only have helped to hang one of my own relatives."

"It never occurred to you that you might be suspected?"

"Never, on my honour! The suggestion is preposterous. You seem to know everything. Tell Margaret that I did leave Stowmarket by the train I named, that I stayed in the Hotel Victoria the same night, and left for the Riviera at 11 a.m. next day. Margaret, don't you believe me? You and I were sweethearts as children. Can you think I murdered your brother? Why, dear girl, I refrained from seeing your husband lest I should wound you by revealing my thoughts."

He placed his hands on her shoulders, and looked at her with such genuine emotion that she lifted her swimming eyes to his, and faltered:

"Forgive me, Robert, though I can never forgive myself. Your words shocked me. I am sorry. I am not mistaken now. You are innocent as I am."

"You have also convinced me, Mr. Frazer," said Brett quietly.

Robert gazed quickly from one to the other. Then he laughed constrainedly.

"I have been accused of several offences in my time," he said, "but this notion that got into your heads licks creation."

"What is the matter now?" said David Hume, entering through the window.

17
"CHERCHEZ LA FEMME"

The three men drove to Stowmarket in the same vehicle, the grooms returning in the second dog-cart.

On the way Robert Frazer—who may be designated by his second surname to distinguish him from his cousin—was anxious to learn what had caused the present recrudescence of inquiry into Alan's death. This was easily explained by David, and Brett took care to confine the conversation to general details.

Frazer was naturally keen to discover how the barrister came to be so well posted in his movements, and David listened eagerly whilst Brett related enough of the stationmaster's story to clear up that point.

Hume broke in with a laugh:

"That shows why he was so unusually attentive when I arrived this evening. He spotted me getting out of the train, and would not leave me until I was clear of the station. He was evidently determined to ascertain my exact identity without any mistake, for he began by asking if I were not Mr. David Hume-Frazer, laying stress on my Christian name. It surprised me a little, because I thought the old chap knew me well."

"Are you both absolutely certain that there are no other members of your family in existence?" asked Brett.

"It depends on how many of our precious collection you are acquainted with," said Robert.

"The only person Mr. Brett is not acquainted with is my father," exclaimed David stiffly.

"I was not alluding to him, of course. Indeed, I had no individual specially in my mind."

"Surely you had some motive for your remark?"
questioned David. "The only remaining relative is Mrs.
Capella."

"There again—how do you define the word 'relative.' I
suppose, Mr. Brett, you are fairly well posted in the
history of our house?"

"Yes."

"Well, has it never struck you that there was
something queer about the manner of my Uncle Alan's
marriage—Margaret's father, I mean?"

"Perhaps. What do you know about it?"

"Nothing definite. When I was a mid-shipman on
board the *Northumberland* I have a lively recollection of a
fiendish row between a man named Somers and another
officer who passed some chaffing remark about my
respected uncle's goings on in Italy. The officer in
question had forgotten, or never knew, that Sir Alan
married Somers's sister—they were Bristol people, I
think—but he stuck to it that Sir Alan had an Italian wife.
He had seen her."

Brett was driving, Frazer sitting by his side, and
David leaning over the rail from the back seat. Had a
bombshell dropped in their midst the two others could not
have been more startled than by Robert's chance
observation.

"Good Heavens!" cried Hume, "why has Capella gone
to Italy?"

"That question may soon be answered," said Brett.

"Was that one of the other reasons you hinted at in
the library when telling us why you did not volunteer
evidence at the trial?" he asked Robert.

"It was. The cat is out of the bag now. I did not know
where the affair might end, so I held my tongue. It also
accounts for my unwillingness to meet Capella. I am very
fond of Margaret. She is straight as a die, and I would not
do anything to cause her suffering. In a word, I let
sleeping dogs lie. If you can manage your matrimonial

affairs without all this fuss, Davie, I should advise you to do the same."

"What are you hinting at? What new mystery is this?" cried Hume.

"Let us keep to solid fact for the present," interposed the barrister. "I wish I had met you sooner, Mr. Frazer. I would be nearing Naples now, instead of entering Stowmarket Have you any further information?"

"None whatever. Even what I have told you is the recollection of a boy who did not understand what the row was about. Where does it lead us, anyhow? What is known about Capella?"

"Very little. Unless I am much mistaken, he will soon tell us a good deal himself. I am beginning to credit him with the possession of more brains and powers of malice than I was at first inclined to admit. He is a dangerous customer."

"Look here," exclaimed Robert angrily. "If that wretched little Italian annoys Margaret in any way I will crack his doll's head."

They reached the hotel, where a room was obtained for Frazer, and David undertook to equip him out of his portmanteau. Brett left the cousins to arrange matters, and hurried to his sitting-room, where a number of telegrams awaited him.

Those from Hume he barely glanced at. David could tell his own story.

There were three from Winter. The first, despatched at 1.10 p.m., read:

"Capella and valet left by club train. Nothing doing Japanese."

The second was timed 4.30 p.m.:

"Jap, accompanied by tall, fat man, left home 2.45. They separated Piccadilly Circus. Followed Jap–("Oh, Winter!" groaned Brett)–and saw him enter British Museum. Four o'clock he met fat man again outside Tottenham Court Road Tube Station. They drove west in

hansom. Heard address given. Am wiring before going same place."

This telegram had been handed in at an Oxford Street office.

The third, 7.30., p.m.:

"Nothing important. All quiet. Wiring before your local office closes."

The facetious Winter had signed these messages *"Snow."*

Brett promptly wrote a telegram to the detective's private address:

"Your signature should have been 'Frost.' If that fat man turns up again follow him. Call on Jap and endeavour to see his wife. You may be sadder but wiser. Meet me Victoria Street, 5 p.m. to-day."

He called a waiter and gave instructions that this message should be sent off early next morning. Then he lit a cigar to soothe his disappointment.

"I cannot emulate the House of Commons bird," he mused, "or at this moment I would be close to Jiro's flat in Kensington, and at the same time crossing Lombardy in an express. What an ass Winter is, to be sure, whenever a subtle stroke requires an ingenious guard. Jiro dresses his wife in male attire and sends her on an errand he dare not perform himself. The fact that they depart together from their residence is diplomatic in itself. If they are followed, the watcher is sure to shadow Jiro and leave his unknown friend. Just imagine Winter dodging Jiro around the Rosetta Stone or the Phoebus Apollo, whilst the woman is visiting someone or some place of infinite value to our search. It is positively maddening."

Perhaps, in his heart, Brett felt that Winter was not so greatly to blame. The sudden appearance on the scene of a portly and respectable stranger was disconcerting, but could hardly serve as an excuse for leaving Jiro's trail at the point of bifurcation.

Moreover, it is difficult to suspect stout people of criminal tendencies. Winter had the best of negative evidence that they are not adapted for "treasons, spoils, and stratagems." Even a convicted rogue, if corpulent, demands sympathy.

But Brett was very sore. He stamped about the room and kicked unoffending chairs out of the way. His unfailing instinct told him that a rare opportunity had been lost. It was well for Winter that he was beyond reach of the barrister's tongue. A valid defence would have availed him naught.

David entered.

"I just seized an opportunity" he commenced eagerly, but Brett levelled his cigar at him as if it were a revolver.

"You want to tell me," he cried, "that before you were two hours in Portsmouth you ascertained Frazer's address from an old friend. You caught the next train for London, went to his lodgings, encountered a nagging landlady, and found that your cousin had taken his overcoat to the pawnbroker's to raise money for his fair to Stowmarket You drove frantically to Liverpool Street, interviewed a smart platform inspector, and he told you"

"That all I had to do was to ask Brett, and he would not only give me a detailed history of my own actions, but produce the very man he sent me in search of," interrupted David, laughing. Nothing the barrister said or did could astonish him now.

"What has upset you?" he went on. "I hope I made no mistakes."

"None. Your conduct has been irreproachable. But you erred greatly in the choice of your parents. There are far too many Hume-Frazers in existence."

"Please tell me what is the matter?"

"Read those." Brett tossed the detective's telegrams across the table.

Hume puzzled over them.

"I think we ought to know who that fat man was," he said.

"We do know. She is a fat woman, the ex-barmaid from Ipswich. Next time, they will send out the youthful Jiro in a perambulator."

"But why are you so furious about it?" demanded Hume. "Was it so important to ascertain what she did during that hour and a quarter?"

"Important! It is the only real clue given us since 'Rabbit Jack' saw a man like you standing motionless in the avenue."

18
FURTHER COMPLICATIONS

Brett devoted half an hour to Frazer's business affairs next morning. David was present, and the result of the conclave is shown by the following excerpt from a letter the barrister sent by them to Mrs. Capella, incidentally excusing his personal attendance at the Hall:

"In my opinion, your cousin David and you should guarantee the payment of the land-tax on Mr. Frazer's estate—£650 per annum—for five years. You should give him a reasonable sum to rehabilitate his wardrobe and pay the few small debts he has contracted, besides allowing him a weekly stipend to enable him to live properly for another year. I will place him in touch with sound financial people, who will exploit his estate if they think the prospects are good, and you can co-operate in the scheme, if you are so advised by your solicitors, with whom the financiers I recommend will carry weight. Failing support in England, Mr. Frazer says he can make his own way in the Argentine if helped in the manner I suggest."

He explained to the two young men that his movements that day would be uncertain. If the ladies still adhered to their resolve to proceed to London forthwith, the whole party would stay at the same hotel. In that event they should send a telegram to his Victoria Street chambers, and he would dine with them. Otherwise they must advise him of their whereabouts.

Left to himself, he curled up in an arm-chair, knotting legs and arms in the most uncomfortable manner, and rendering it necessary to crane his neck before he could remove a cigar from his lips.

In such posture, alternated with rapid walking about the room, he could think best.

The waiter, not knowing that the barrister had remained in the hotel, came in to see what trifles might be strewed about table or mantelpiece in the shape of loose "smokes" or broken hundreds of cigarettes.

Like most people, his eyes could only observe the expected, the normal. No one was standing or sitting in the usual way—therefore the room was empty.

A box of Brett's Turkish cigarettes was lying temptingly open. He advanced.

"Touch those, and I slay you," snapped Brett. "Your miserable life is not worth one of them."

The man jumped as if he had been fired at. The barrister, coiled up like a boa-constrictor, glared at him in mock fury.

"I beg pardon, sir," he blurted out, "I didn't know you was in."

"Evidently. A more expert scoundrel would have stolen them under my very nose. You are a bungler."

"I really wasn't goin' to take any, sir—just put them away, that is all."

"In that packet," said Brett, "there are eighty-seven cigarettes. I count them, because each one is an epoch. I don't count the cigars in the sideboard."

"I prefer cigars," grinned the waiter.

"So I see. You have two of the landlord's best 'sixpences' in the left pocket of your waistcoat at this moment."

"Well, if you ain't a fair scorcher," the man gasped.

"What, you rascal, would you call me names?"

Brett writhed convulsively, and the waiter backed towards the door.

"No, sir, I was callin' no names. We don't get too many perks—we waiters don't, sir. I was out of bed until one o'clock and up again at six. That's wot I call hard work, sir."

"It is outrageous. Take five cigars."

"Thank you kindly, sir."

"What kept you up till one o'clock?"

"Gossip, sir—just silly gossip. All about Mrs. Capella, an' Beechcroft, an' I don't know wot"

"Indeed, and who was so interested in these topics as to spoil your beauty sleep?"

"The new gentleman, who is so like Mr. David."

"How very interesting," said the barrister, who certainly did not expect this revelation.

"It seemed to be interesting to 'im, sir. You see, the 'ouse is pretty full, and when you brought 'im 'ere last night, sir, the bookkeeper gev' 'im the room next to mine. Last thing, I fetched the gentleman a Scotch an' soda an' a cigar. 'E said 'e couldn't sleep, and 'e was lookin' at a fotygraf. I caught a squint at it, an' I sez, 'Beg parding, sir, but ain't that Mrs. CapellaMiss Margaret as used to be?' That started 'im."

"You surprise me."

"And the gentleman surprised me," confided the waiter, whose greatest conversational effects were produced by quickly adapting remarks made to him. "P'r'aps you are not aware, sir, that the lady's Eye-talian 'usbin' ain't no good?"

"I have heard something of the sort."

"Then you've heard something right, sir. They do say as 'ow 'e beats her."

"The scoundrel!"

"Scoundrel! You should 'ave seen No. 18 last night when I tole 'im that. My conscience! 'E went on awful, 'e did. 'E seemed to be mad about Mrs. Capella."

"He is her cousin."

"Cousin! That won't wash, sir, beggin' your pardon. You an' me knows better than that"

"I tell you again he is her cousin."

The waiter absent-mindedly dusted the back of a chair.

"Well, sir, it isn't for the likes of me to be contradictious, but I've got two sisters an' 'arf-a-dozen cousins, an' I don't go kissin' their pictures an' swearin' to 'ave it out with their 'usbin's."

"Oh, come now. You are romancing."

"Not a bit, sir. When I went to my room Ier'eard 'im."

"Is there a wooden partition between No. 18 and your room?"

"Yes, sir."

"And cracks–large ones?"

"Yes, sir. But why you shouldoh, I see! Excuse me, sir; I thought I 'eard a bell."

The waiter hurried off, and Brett unwound himself.

"So Robert is in love with Margaret," he said, laughing unmirthfully. "Was there ever such a tangle! If I indulge in a violent flirtation with Miss Layton, and I persuade Winter to ogle Mrs. Jiro, the affair should be artistically complete."

The conceit brought Ipswich to his mind. He was convinced that the main line of inquiry lay in the direction of Mr. Numagawa Jiro and the curious masquerading of his colossal spouse.

He had vaguely intended to visit the local police. Now he made up his mind to go to Ipswich and thence to London. Further delay at Stowmarket was useless.

Before his train quitted the station he made matters right with the stationmaster by explaining to him the identity of the two men who had attracted his attention the previous evening. Somehow, the barrister imagined that the third visitant of that fateful New Year's Eve two years ago would not trouble the neighbourhood again. Herein he was mistaken.

At the county town he experienced little difficulty in learning the antecedents of Mrs. Numagawa Jiro.

In the first hotel he entered he found a young lady behind the bar who was not only well acquainted with Mrs. Jiro, but remembered the circumstances of the courtship.

"The fact is," she explained, "there are a lot of silly girls about who think every man with a dark skin is a prince in his own country if only he wears a silk hat and patent leather boots."

"Is that all?" said Brett.

"All what?" cried the girl. "Oh, don't be stupid! I mean when they are well dressed. Princess, indeed! Catch me marrying a nigger."

"But Japanese are not niggers."

"Well, they're not my sort, anyhow. And fancy a great gawk like Flossie Bird taking on with a little man who doesn't reach up to her elbow. It was simply ridiculous. What did you say her name is now?"

He gave the required information, and went on:

"Had Mr. Jiro any other friends in Ipswich to your knowledge?"

"He didn't know a soul. He was here for the Assizes, about some case, I think. Oh, I remember–the 'Stowmarket Mystery'–and he stayed at the hotel where Flossie was engaged. How she ever came to take notice of him, I can't imagine. She was a queer sort of girl–used to wear bloomers, and get off her bike to clout the small boys who chi-iked at her."

"Do her people live here?"

"Yes, and a rare old row they made about her marriage–for she is married, I will say that for her. But why are you so interested in her?"

The fair Hebe glanced in a mirror to confirm her personal opinion that there were much nicer girls than Flossie Bird left in Ipswich.

"Not in her," said Brett; "in the example she set."

"What do you mean?"

"If a little Japanese can come to this town and carry off a lady of her size and appearance, what may not a six-foot Englishman hope to accomplish?"

"Oh, go on!"

He took her advice, and went on to the hotel patronised by Mr. Jiro during his visit to Ipswich. The landlord readily showed him the register for the Assize week. Most of the guests were barristers and solicitors, many of them known personally to Brett. None of the other names struck him as important, though he noted a few who arrived on the same day as the Japanese, "Mr. Okasaki."

He took the next train to London, and reached Victoria Street, to find Mr. Winter awaiting him, and carefully nursing a brown paper parcel.

"I got your wire, Mr. Brett," he explained, "and this morning after Mr. Jiro went out alone"

"Where did he go to?"

"The British Museum."

"What on earth was he doing there?"

"Examining manuscripts, my assistant told me. He was particularly interested inlet me see—it is written on a bit of paper. Here it is, the 'Nihon Guai Shi,' the 'External History of Japan,' compiled by Rai Sanyo, between 1806 and 1827, containing a history of each of the military families. That is all Greek to me, but my man got the librarian to jot it down for him."

"Your man has brains. What were you going to say when I interrupted you?"

"Only this. No fat companion appeared to day, so I called at No. 17 St. John's Mansions in my favourite character as an old clo' man."

The barrister expressed extravagant admiration in dumb show, but this did not deceive the detective, who, for some reason, was downcast.

"I saw Mrs. Jiro, and knew in an instant that she was the stout gentleman who left her husband at Piccadilly Circus yesterday. I was that annoyed I could hardly do a deal. However, here they are."

He began to unfasten the string which fastened the brown paper parcel.

"Here are what?" cried Brett.

"Mrs. Jiro's coat, and trousers, and waistcoat," replied Winter desperately. "She doesn't want 'em any more; sold 'em for a songglad to be rid of 'em, in fact."

He unfolded a suit of huge dimensions, surveying each garment ruefully, as though reproaching it personally for the manner in which it had deceived him.

Then Brett sat down and enjoyed a burst of Homeric laughter.

19
THE THIRD MAN APPEARS

The Rev. Wilberforce Layton raised no objection to his daughter's excursion to London with Mrs. Capella. Indeed, he promised to meet them in Whitby a week later, and remain there during August. Mrs. Eastham pleaded age and the school treat.

It was, therefore, a comparatively youthful party which Brett joined at dinner in one of the great hotels in Northumberland Avenue.

Someone had exercised rare discretion in ordering a special meal; the wines were good, and two at least of the company merry as emancipated school children.

The barrister soon received ample confirmation of the discovery made by the Stowmarket waiter.

Robert Hume-Frazer was undoubtedly in love with his cousin, or, to speak correctly, for the ex-sailor was a gentleman, he had been in love with her as a boy, and now secretly grieved over a hopeless passion.

Whether Margaret was conscious of this devotion or not Brett was unable to decide. By neither word nor look was Robert indiscreet. When she was present he was lively and talkative, entertaining the others with snatches of strange memories drawn from an adventurous career.

It was only when she quitted their little circle that Brett detected the mask of angry despair that settled for a moment on the young man's face, and rendered him indifferent to other influences until he resolutely aroused himself.

Yet, on the whole, a great improvement was visible in Frazer. Attired in one of David's evening dress suits, carefully groomed and trimmed, he no sooner donned the garments which gave him the outward semblance of an aristocrat than he dropped the curt, somewhat coarse, mannerisms which hitherto distinguished him from his cousin.

Beyond a more cosmopolitan style of speech, he was singularly like David in person and deportment. They resembled twins rather than first cousins. They were both remarkably fine-looking men, tall, wiry, and in splendid condition. It was only the slightly more attenuated features of Robert that made it possible, even for Brett, to distinguish one from the other at a little distance.

Helen was pleased to be facetious on the point.

"Really, Davie," she said, "now that your cousin has come amongst us, you must remove your beard at once."

"Why?" he asked.

"Because you are so alike that some evening, in these dark corridors, I shall mistake Mr. Frazer for you."

"That won't be half bad," laughed Robert.

Nellie blushed, and endeavoured to evade the consequences of her own remark.

"I meant," she exclaimed, "that you would be sure to laugh at me if I treated you as Davie."

"Not at all. I would consider it a cousinly duty to make you believe I was David, and not myself."

"Then," she cried, "I will guard against any possibility of error by treating both of you as Mr. Robert Hume-Frazer until I am quite sure."

"Waiter!" said David, "where is the barber's shop?"

Helen became redder than ever, but they enjoyed the joke at her expense. The waiter politely informed his questioner that the barber would not be on duty until the morning at 8 a.m.

"Then book the first chair for me!" said David.

"And the second for me!" joined in Robert.

"Mr. Brett," said Margaret, "don't you consider this competition perfectly disgraceful?"

"I am overjoyed," he replied. "It appears to me that the result must be personally most satisfactory."

"In what way?"

"It is obvious that you have no resource but to accept my willing slavery, Miss Layton having monopolised the attentions of your two cousins."

"Hello!" cried Frazer. "This is an unexpected attack. Miss Layton, I resign. Have no fear. In the darkest corridor I will warn you that my name is 'Robert.'"

Though the words were carelessly good-humoured, they were just a trifle emphatic. The incident passed, but they recalled it subsequently under very different circumstances.

Brett went home about ten o'clock. Next day at noon he was arranging for the immediate delivery of a typewriter machine, sold by Mr. Numagawa Jiro to a West End exchange, when a telegram reached him:

"Come at once. Urgent.–HUME."

He drove to the hotel, where David and Helen were sitting in the foyer awaiting his arrival.

Hume had kept his promise anent the barber. He no longer desired to alter his appearance in any way, and had only grown a beard on account of his sensitiveness regarding his two trials at the Assizes.

But the fun of the affair had quite gone.

Helen was pale, David greatly perturbed.

"A terrible thing has happened," he said, in a low voice, when he grasped the barrister's hand. "Someone tried to kill Bob an hour ago."

The blank amazement on Brett's face caused him to add hurriedly:

"It is quite true. He had the narrowest escape. He is in bed now. The doctor is examining him. We have secured the next room to his, and Margaret is there with a nurse."

The barrister made no reply, but accompanied them to Frazer's apartment. In the adjoining room they found Margaret, terribly scared, but listening eagerly to the doctor's cheery optimism.

"It is nothing," he was saying, "a severe squeeze, some slight abrasions, and a great nervous shock, quite serious in its nature, although your friend makes light of it, and wishes to get up at once. I think, however"

A nurse entered.

"The patient insists upon my leaving the room," she cried angrily. "He is dressing."

They heard Robert's voice:

"Confound it, I have been rolled on three times in one day by a bucking broncho, and thought nothing of it. I absolutely refuse to stop in bed!"

The doctor resigned professional responsibility; and the nature of Margaret's cheque caused him to admit that, to a man accustomed to South American ponies, unbroken, the nervous shock might not amount to much.

Indeed, Robert appeared almost immediately, and in a bad temper.

"I lost my wind," he explained, "when that horse fell on me, and everyone promptly imagined I was killed. I hope, Margaret, the needless excitement of my appearance on a stretcher did not alarm you. They were going to whip me off to the hospital when I managed to gurgle out the name of the hotel."

"What happened?" said Brett.

"The most extraordinary thing. Have you told him, Davie?"

"No, I attributed your first words to me as being due to delirium. I had no idea you were in earnest."

"Well, Mr. Brett," said Frazer, sitting down, for notwithstanding his protests, he was somewhat shaky, "it began to rain after breakfast."

"Excellent!" cried the barrister, "An Englishman, in his sound mind, always starts with the state of the weather."

"I am sound enough, thank goodness, but I had a very close shave. Don't laugh, Davie. My ribs are sore. As the ladies decided not to go out until the weather took up, Davie said he would keep them company whilst I seized the opportunity to visit a tailor. I left the hotel and walked quickly to the corner of Whitehall. It was hardly worth while taking a cab to Bond Street, and I intended to cross in front of King Charles's statue. It is an awkward place, and a lot of 'buses, cabs, and vans were bowling along downhill from the Strand and St. Martin's Church. I waited a moment on the kerbstone, watching for a favourable opportunity, when suddenly I was pitched head foremost in front of a passing 'bus. My escape from instant death was solely due to the splendid way in which the driver handled his horses and applied his brake. The near horse was swung round so sharp that he fell and landed almost, not quite, on the top of me. I could feel his hot, reeking body against my face, and although the greater part of his impact was borne by the road, I got enough to knock the breath out of me. You will see by the state of my clothes in the other room how I was flattened in the mud. By the way, Davie, it is your suit."

Helen choked back something she was going to say, and Frazer continued:

"A policeman pulled me from under the horse, and I kept my senses sufficiently to note how the near front wheel had gouged a channel in the mud within an inch or so of my head. It went over my hat. Where is it?"

Hume ran into the bedroom, and returned with a bowler hat torn to shreds.

"There you are," said Robert coolly, "Fancy my head in that condition."

"You used the word 'pitched.' Do you mean that someone cannoned against you?"

"Not a bit of it. It was no accident of a hurrying man blindly following an umbrella. I have been a sailor, Mr. Brett, and am accustomed to maintaining my balance in a sudden lurch. I do it intuitively. It is as much a part of my second self as using my eyes or ears with unconscious accuracy. Some mana big, powerful man—designedly threw me down, and did so very scientifically, first pressing his knee against the tendons of my left leg, and then using his elbow. Not one in a thousand Londoners would know the trick."

"You are a first-rate witness. Pray go on," said Brett.

"Being a sailor, however, I did manage to twist round slightly as I fell, and I'm blessed if I didn't think it was Davie here who did it."

The barrister's keen face lighted curiously. The others, closely watching him, afterwards agreed that he reminded them of a greyhound straining after a luckless hare.

"That seems to interest you, Mr. Brett," said Frazer. "I assure you the momentary impression was very distinct. My assailant was dressed like Davie, too, in dark blue serge, and wore a beard. For the moment I forgot that Davie had visited the barber this morning, and I blurted out something when he met me being carried in through the hall."

"Yes," exclaimed Hume. "You said: 'Davie, why did you try to murder me?' I was sure you were delirious, as I had not left Nellie and Margaret for an instant since you went out."

"That is so," cried Helen.

Margaret uttered no word. She sat, with hands clasped, and pale, set face, watching her cousin as if his story had a mesmeric effect.

"I'm awfully sorry," said Frazer penitently. "I knew at once I was a fool, but you see, old chap, I remembered you best as I had seen you during the previous twenty-four hours, and not as you looked at breakfast this morning. Do forgive me."

But Brett broke in impatiently:

"My dear fellow, your natural mistake is the most important thing that has happened since your cousin Alan met his death. The man who attacked you mistook you, in turn, for David. He will try again. I wonder if your accident will be reported in the papers?"

"Yes," said Hume. "A youngster came to me, inquired all about Robert, and seemed to be quite sorry he was not mangled."

"Then it will be your affair next time. Keep a close look-out whenever you are alone. If anyone resembling yourself lays a hand on you, try and detain him at all costs."

"Mr. Brett!" shrieked Helen, "you surely cannot mean it."

His enthusiasm had caused him to ignore her presence. For the next five minutes he was earnestly engaged in explaining away his uncanny request.

20
The Trail

Standing on the steps of the hotel, Brett cast a searching glance along the line of waiting hansoms. He wanted a strong, sure-footed horse, one of those marvellous animals, found only in the streets of London, which trots like a dog, slides down Savoy Street on its hind legs, slips in and out among the traffic like an eel, and covers a steady eight miles an hour for a seemingly indefinite period.

"Shall I whistle for a cab, sir?" said the hall-porter.

"No. You whistle without discrimination," replied the barrister.

He found the stamp of gee-gee he needed fourth on the rank.

"How long has your horse been out of the stable?" he asked the driver.

"I've just driven him here, sir."

"Is he up to a hard day's work?"

"The best tit in London, sir."

"Pull him up to the pavement."

The man obeyed. Instantly his three predecessors on the rank began a chorus:

"'Ere! Wot th'"

"All right, Jimmy. Wait till"

"Well, I'm"

"What is the matter?" inquired Brett, "You fellows always squeal before you are hurt. Here is a fare each for you," and he solemnly gave them a shilling a-piece.

Even then they were not satisfied. They all objurgated Jimmy for his luck as he drove off.

It was an easy matter to find the constable who had been on point duty at the crossing when the "accident" happened. This man produced his note-book containing the number of the Road Car Company's Camden Town and Victoria 'bus, the driver of which had so cleverly avoided a catastrophe. The policeman knew nothing of events prior to the falling of the horse. There was the usual crowd of hurrying people; the scream of a startled woman; a rush of sightseers; and the rescue of Frazer from beneath the prostrate animal.

"Did you chance to notice the destination of the omnibus immediately preceding the Road Car vehicle?" said Brett.

"Yes, sir. It was an Atlas."

"Have you noted the exact time the accident occurred?"

"Here it is, sir10.45 a.m."

At Victoria he was lucky in hitting upon the Camden Town 'bus itself, drawn up outside the District Railway Station, waiting its turn to enter the enclosure.

The driver was a sharp fellow, and disinclined to answer questions. Brett might be an emissary of the enemy. But a handsome tip and the assurance that a very substantial present would be forwarded to his address by the friends of the gentleman whose life he saved unloosed his tongue.

"I never did see anything like it, sir," he confided. "The road was quite clear, an' I was bowlin' along to get the inside berth from a General just behind, when this yer gent was chucked under the 'osses' 'eds. Bli-me, I would ha' thort 'e was a suicide if I 'adn't seed a bloke shove 'im orf the kerb."

"Oh, you saw that, did you?"

"Couldn't 'elp it, sir. I was lookin' aht for fares. Jack, my mate, sawr it too."

The conductor thus appealed to confirmed the statement. They both described the assailant as very like his would-be victim in size, appearance, and garments.

Jack said he could do nothing, because the sudden swerving of the 'bus, the fall of the horse, and the instant gathering of a crowd, prevented him from making the attempt to grab the other man, who vanished, he believed, down Whitehall.

"You did not tell the police about the assault?" inquired Brett.

"Not me, guv'nor," said the driver. "The poor chap in the road was not much 'urt. I knew that, though the mob thort 'e was a dead 'un. An' wot does it mean? A day lost in the polis-court, an' a day lost on my pay-sheet, too."

"Well," said Brett, "the twist you gave to the reins this morning meant several days added to your pay-sheet. Would either of you know the man again if you saw him?"

This needed reflection.

"I wouldn't swear to 'im," was the driver's dictum, "but I would swear to any man bein' like 'im."

"Same 'ere," said the conductor.

The barrister understood their meaning, which had not the general application implied by the words. He obtained the addresses of both men and left them.

His next visit was to an Atlas terminus. Here he had to wait a full hour before the 'bus arrived that had passed Trafalgar Square on a south journey at 10.45.

The conductor remembered the sudden stoppage of the Road Car vehicle.

"Ran over a man, sir, didn't it?" he inquired.

"Nearly, not quite. Now, I want you to fix your thoughts on the passengers who entered your 'bus at that point. Can you describe them?"

The man smiled.

"It's rather a large order, sir," he said. "I've been past there twice since. If it's anybody you know particular, and you tell me what he was like, I may be able to help you."

Brett would have preferred the conductor's own unaided statement, but seeing no help for it, he gave the man a detailed description of David Hume, plus the beard.

"Has he got black, snaky eyes and high cheek-bones?" the conductor inquired thoughtfully.

The barrister had described a fair man, with brown hair; and the question in no way indicated the colour of the Hume-Frazer eyes. Yet the odd combination caught his attention.

"Yes," he said, "that may be the man."

"Well, sir, I didn't pick him up there, but I dropped him there at nine o'clock. I picked him up at the Elephant, and noticed him particular because he didn't pay the fare for the whole journey, but took penn'orths."

"I am greatly obliged to you. Would you know him again?"

"Among a thousand! He had a funny look, and never spoke. Just shoved a penny out whenever I came on top. Twice I had to refuse it."

"Was he a foreigner?"

"Not to my idea. He looked like a Scotchman. Don't you know him, sir?"

"Not yet. I hope to make his acquaintance. Can you remember the 'bus which was in front of you at Whitehall at 10.45?"

"Yes; I can tell you that. It was a Monster, Pimlico. The conductor is a friend of mine, named Tomkins. That is the only time I have seen him to-day."

At the Monster, Pimlico, after another delay, Tomkins was produced. Again Brett described David Hume, adorned now with "black, snaky eyes and high cheek-bones."

"Of course," said Tomkins. "I've spotted 'im. 'E came aboard wiv a run just arter a hoss fell in front of the statoo. Gimme a penny, 'e did, an' jumped orf at the 'Orse Guards without a ticket afore we 'ad gone a 'undred yards. I thort 'e was frightened or dotty, I did. Know 'im agin? Rather. Eyes like gimlets, 'e 'ad."

The barrister regained the seclusion of the hansom.

"St John's Mansions, Kensington," he said to the driver, and then he curled up on the seat in the most uncomfortable attitude permitted by the construction of the vehicle.

On nearing his destination he stopped the cab at a convenient corner.

"I want you to wait here for my return," he told the driver.

"How long will you be, sir?"

"Not more than fifteen minutes."

"I only asked, sir, because I wanted to know if I had time to give the horse a feed."

Cabby was evidently quite convinced that his eccentric fare was not a bilker.

Brett glanced around. In the neighbouring street was a public-house, which possessed what the agents call "a good pull-up trade." He pointed to it.

"I think," he said, "if you wait there it will be more comfortable for you and equally good for the horse."

The cabby pocketed an interim tip with a grin.

"I've struck it rich to-day," he murmured, as he disappeared through a swing door bearing the legend, "Tap," in huge letters.

Meanwhile, Brett sauntered past St. John's Mansions. Across the road a man was leaning against the railings of a large garden, being deeply immersed in the columns of a sporting paper.

The barrister caught his eye and walked on. A minute later Mr. Winter overtook him.

"Not a move here all day," he said in disgust, "except Mrs. Jiro's appearance with the perambulator. She led me all round Kensington Gardens, and her only business was to air the baby and cram it with sponge-cakes."

"Where is her husband?"

"In the house. He hasn't stirred out since yesterday's visit to the Museum."

"Who is looking after the place in your absence?"

"One of my men has taken a room over the paper shop opposite. He has special charge of the Jap. My second assistant is scraping and varnishing the door of No. 16 flat. He sees everyone who enters and leaves the place during the day. If Mrs. Jiro comes out he has to follow her until he sees that I am on the job."

"Good! I want to talk matters over with you. I have a cab waiting in a side street."

"Why, sir, has anything special happened?"

A newsboy came running along shouting the late edition of the *Evening News*. The barrister bought a paper and rapidly glanced through its contents.

"Here you are," he said. "Someone in that office has a good memory."

The item which Brett pointed out to the detective read as follows:

> *"ACCIDENT IN WHITEHALL.*
>
> *"Mr. Robert Hume-Frazer, residing in one of the great hotels in Northumberland Avenue, was knocked down and nearly run over by an omnibus in Whitehall this morning. The skill of the driver averted a very serious accident. It is supposed that Mr. Hume-Frazer slipped whilst attempting to cross before the policeman on duty at that point stopped the traffic.*
>
> *"The injured gentleman was carried to his hotel, where he is staying with his cousin, Mr. David Hume-Frazer, whose name will be recalled in connection with the famous 'Stowmarket Mystery' of last year."*

"What does it all mean?" inquired Winter.

"It means that you must listen carefully to what I am going to tell you. Here is my cab. Jump in. Driver, I am surprised that a man of your intelligence should waste your money on a public-house cigar. Throw it away. Here is a better one. And now, Victoria Street, sharp."

Winter's ears were pricked to receive Brett's intelligence. Beyond a sigh of professional admiration at the result of Brett's pertinacity with regard to the omnibuses passing through Whitehall at 10.45, he did not interrupt until the barrister had ended.

Even then he was silent, so Brett looked at him in surprise, "Well, Winter, what do you think of it?" he said.

"Think! I wish I had half your luck, Mr. Brett," he answered sadly.

"How now, you green-eyed monster?"

"No. I'm not jealous. You beat me at my own game; I admit it. I would never have thought of going for the 'buses. I suppose you would have interviewed the driver and conductor of every vehicle on that route before you gave in. You didn't trouble about the hansoms. Hailing a cab was a slow business, and risked subsequent identification. To jump on to a moving 'bus was just the thing. Yes, there is no denying that you are smart."

"Winter, your unreasonable jealousy is making you vulgar."

"Wouldn't any man swear, sir? Why did I let such a handful as Mrs. Jiro slip through my fingers the other day? Clue! Why, it was a perfect bale of cotton. If I had only followed her instead of that little rat, her husband, we would now know where the third man lives, and have the murderer of Sir Alan under our thumb. It is all my fault, though sometimes I feel inclined to blame the police system—a system that won't even give us telephones between one station and another. Never mind. Wait till I tackle the next job for the Yard. I'll show 'em a trick or two."

21
CONCERNING CHICKENS, AND MOTIVES

The detective cooled off by the time they reached Brett's flat. On the dining-room tables they found two telegrams and a Remington type-writer.

The messages were from Holden, Naples.

The first: *"Johnson arrived here this morning."*

The second: *"Johnson's proceedings refer to poorhouse and church registers."*

"Johnson is Capella," explained Winter. "I forgot to tell you we had arranged that."

Brett surveyed the second telegram so intently that the detective inquired:

"How do you read that, sir?"

"Capella is securing copies of certificates—marriages, births, or deaths; perhaps all three. He is also getting hold of living witnesses."

"Of what?"

"He will tell us himself. He is preparing a bombshell of sorts. It will explode here. Goodness only knows who will be blown up by it."

He took the cover off the type-writer, seized a sheet of paper, and began to manipulate the keyboard with the methodical carefulness of one unaccustomed to its use.

He wrote:

"About Stowmarket. David Hume Frazer
killed cousin. Cousin talked girl in road.
Girl waited wood. David Hume Frazer met
girl in wood after 1 a.m."

"Do you mean to say," cried the detective, "that you can remember the anonymous letter word for word? You have only seen it once, and that was several days ago."

"Not only word for word, but the spacing, the number of words in a line, the lines between which creases appear. Look, Winter. Here is the small broken 'c,' the bent capital 'D,' the letter 'a' out of register. Where is the original?"

"Here, in my pocket-book."

They silently compared the two typed sheets. It needed no expert to note that they had been written by the same machine.

"It would take a clever counsel to upset that piece of evidence," said Winter. "I wish I had hold of the writer."

"You have spoken to him several times."

"Surely you cannot mean Jiro!"

"Who else? Jiro is but the tool of a superior scoundrel. He is just beginning to suspect the fact, and trying to use it for his own benefit. I wish I was in Naples with your friend Holden."

"But, Mr. Brett, the murderer is in London! What about this morning's attempt"

"My dear fellow, you are already constructing the gallows. Leave that to the gaol officials. What we do not yet know is the motive. The key to the mystery is in Naples, probably in Capella's hands at this moment. If I were there it would be in mine, too. Do not question me, Winter. I am not inspired. I can only indulge in vague imaginings. Capella will bring the reality to London."

"Then what are we to do meanwhile?"

"Await events patiently. Watch Jiro with the calm persistence of a cat watching a hole into which a mouse has disappeared. At this moment, eat something."

He rang for Smith, and told him to attend to the wants of the waiting cabman, whilst Mrs. Smith made the speediest arrangements for an immediate dinner.

The two men sat down, and Winter could not help asking another question.

"Why are you keeping the cab, Mr. Brett?"

"Because I am superstitious."

The detective opened wide his eyes at this unlooked-for statement.

"I mean it," said the barrister. "Look at all I have learnt to-day whilst darting about London in that particular hansom, which, mind you, I carefully selected from a rank of twenty. Abandon it until I am dropped at my starting-point! Never!"

Winter sighed.

"I never feel that way about anything on wheels," he said. "Do you really think you will be able to clear up this affair, sir? It seems to me to be a bigger muddle now than when I left it after the second trial. Don't laugh at me. That is awkwardly put, I know. But then we had a straightforward crime to deal with. Now, goodness knows where we have landed."

Smith entered, and commenced laying the table. Brett did not reply to the detective's spoken reverie. Both men idly watched the deft servant's preparations.

"Smith," suddenly cried the master of the household, "what sort of chicken have we for dinner?"

"Cold chicken, sir."

"Thank you. As you seem to demand Miltonic precision in phrase, I amend my words. What breed of chicken have we for dinner?"

"A dorking, sir."

"And how do you know it is a dorking?"

"Oh, there's lots of ways of knowin' that, sir. You can tell by the size, by its head and feet, and by the tuft of feathers left on its neck."

"Q.E.D."

"Beg pardon, sir!"

"I was only saying, 'Right you are!'"

Smith went out, and Brett turned to his companion:

"Did you note Smith's philosophy in the matter of dorkings?" he inquired.

"Yes."

"Does it convey no moral to you? I fear not. Now mark me, Winter. Just as the breed of the chicken is indelibly stamped on it in the eyes of a man skilled in chickens, so is the murder we are investigating marked by characteristics so plain that a child of ten, properly trained to use his eyes, might discern them. What you and I suffer from are defects implanted by idle nursemaids and doting mothers. Let us, for the moment, adopt the policy of the theosophists and sit in consultation apart from our astral bodies. Who killed Sir Alan Hume-Frazer? I answer, a relative. What relative? Someone we do not know, whom he did not know, or who committed murder because he was known. What sort of person is the murderer? A man physically like either David or Robert, so like that 'Rabbit Jack' would swear to the identity of either of them as readily as to the person of the real murderer. Why did he use such a weird instrument as the Ko-Katana? Because he found it under his hand and recognised its sinister purpose, to be left implanted in the breast or brain of an enemy's lifeless body. Where is the man now? In London, perhaps outside this building, perhaps watching the Northumberland Avenue Hotel, waiting quietly for another chance to take the life of the person who caused us to reopen this inquiry. To sum up, Winter, let us find such an individual, a Hume-Frazer with black, deadly eyes, with a cold, calculating, remorseless brain, with a knowledge of trick and fence not generally an attribute of the Anglo-Saxon race—let us lay hands on him, I say, and you can book him for kingdom come, via the Old Bailey."

"Yes, sir!" broke in Winter excitedly. "But the motive!"

"Et tu, Brute! Would the disciple rend his master? Have I not told you that Capella will bring that knowledge with him from Naples? I have hopes even of your long-nosed friend, Holden, giving us all the details we need."

"What did the murderer steal from Sir Alan's writing-desk, from the drawer broken open before the blow was struck?"

Smith entered, bearing a chicken.

"The motive, Winter! The motive!" laughed Brett, and in pursuance of his invariable practice, he refused to say another word about the crime or its perpetrator during the meal.

22
THE SECOND ATTACK

Mrs. Smith was accustomed to her master's occasional freaks in the matter of dinner. Her husband, aided by long experience, knew whether Brett's "immediately" meant one minute, or five, or even fifteen.

This time he gave his wife the longest limit, so, in addition to the chicken, a bird whose unhappy attribute is a facility for being devoured with the utmost speed, a mixed grill of cutlets, bacon, and French sausages appeared on the table.

The diners were hungry and the good things were appreciated. It was well that they wasted no time on mere words. They were still intent on the feast when a boy messenger brought a note. It was from Helen, written in pencil:

"David was coming to see you when he was attacked. Can you come to us at once?

"H.L.

"P.S.–David is all right–only shaken and covered with mud. It occurred five minutes ago."

"Dear me!" said Brett. "Dear me!"

There was such a hiss of concentrated fury in his voice that Winter was puzzled to account for the harmless expression the barrister had twice used. The detective knew that his distinguished friend never, by any chance, indulged in strong language, yet something had annoyed him so greatly that a more powerful expletive would have had a very natural sound.

Brett glared at him.

"It is evident," he said, "that you do not know the meaning of 'Dear me.' It is simply the English form of the

Italian 'O Dio mio!' and a literal translation would shock you."

"It doesn't appear that much damage has been done to your client," gasped Winter, for Brett had unceremoniously dragged him from his chair with the intention of rushing downstairs forthwith.

They hurried out together, and dashed into the waiting hansom.

"Think of it, Winter," groaned the barrister. "Whilst we were seduced by a dorking and a French sausage—an unholy alliance—the very man we wanted was waiting in Northumberland Avenue. You are avenged! All my jibes and sneers at Scotland Yard recoil on my own head. I might have known that such a desperate scoundrel would soon make another attempt, and next time upon the right person. You followed Mrs. Jiro. I am led astray by a cooked fowl. Oh, Winter, Winter, who could suspect such depravity in a roasted chicken!"

"I'm dashed if I can guess what you're driving at," growled the detective.

"No; I understand. The blood has left your brain and gone to your stomach. You will not be able to think for hours."

Raving thus, in disjointed sentences that Winter could not make head or tail of, Brett refused to be explicit until they reached the hotel, when he discharged the cabman with a payment that caused the gentleman on the perch to spit on the palm of his hand in great glee, whilst he promptly wheeled the horse in the direction of his livery stables.

They were met by David himself, seated in the foyer by the side of Helen, who looked white and frightened.

"This chap is a terror," began Hume, once they were safe in the privacy of their sitting-room. "I would never have believed such things were possible in London if they had not actually happened to Robert and me to-day. We had dinner rather early, and dined in private, as Robert is feeling stiff now after this morning's adventure. Margaret suggested"

"Where is Mrs. Capella?" interrupted the barrister.

Miss Layton answered:

"She is with Mr. Frazer. They have found a quiet corner of the ladies' smoking-room—I mean the smoking-room where ladies go—and we have not told them yet what has happened to Davie."

"Well," resumed Hume, "Margaret's idea is that we should all leave here for the North to-morrow. She wanted you to approve of the arrangement, so I got into a hansom and started for your chambers. It was raining a little, and the street was full of traffic. The driver asked if I would like the window closed, but I would sooner face a tiger than drive through London in a boxed-up hansom, so I refused. The middle of the road, you know, has a long line of waiting cabs, broken by occasional crossing-places. The horse was just getting into a trot when a man, wrapped in a mackintosh, ran alongside, caught the off rein in the crook of his stick, swung the poor beast right round through one of the gaps in the rank, and down we went—horse, cab, driver, and myself—in front of a brewer's dray. Luckily for me and the driver, we were flung right over the smash into the gutter, for the big, heavy van ran into the fallen hansom, crushed it like a matchbox, and killed the horse. Had the window been closed—well, it wasn't, so there is no need for romancing."

Poor Nellie clung to her lover as if to assure herself that he was really uninjured.

"Did you see your assailant clearly?"

"Unfortunately, no. The side windows were blurred with rain, and I was trying to strike a match. The first thing I was conscious of was a violent swerve. I looked up, saw a tall, cloaked figure wrenching at the reins with a crooked stick, and over we went. I fell into a bed of mud. It absolutely blinded me. I jumped up, and fancying that the blackguard ran up Northumberland Street I dashed after him. I cannoned against some passer-by and we both fell. A news-runner, who witnessed the affair, did go after the cause of it, and received such a knock-out blow on the jaw that he was hardly able to speak when found by a policeman."

"Where is this man now?"

"With the cabman in a small hotel across the road. I had not the nerve to bring them here. If we have any more adventures, the management will turn us out. I fancy they think our behaviour is hardly respectable. The instant Robert or I endeavour to leave the door we are used to clean up a portion of the roadway."

"Miss Layton, would you mind joining the others for a few minutes. Mr. Hume is going out with Mr. Winter and myself."

The barrister's request took Helen by surprise.

"Is there any need for further risk?" she faltered. "Moreover, Margaret will see at once that something has gone wrong. I am a poor hand at deception where—where Davie is concerned."

"Have no fear. Tell them everything. Mr. Hume will be very seriously injured—in to-morrow morning's papers. This expert in street accidents must be led to believe he has succeeded. In any case, aided by a miserable fowl, he is far enough from here at this moment. We will return in twenty minutes."

The girl was so agitated that she hardly noticed Brett's words. But their purport reassured her, and she left them.

The three men passed out into the drizzling rain. Owing to the Strand being "up," a continuous stream of traffic flowed through the Avenue. Hume pointed out the gap through which the horse was forced, and then they darted across the roadway.

"I fell here," he said, indicating a muddy flood of road scrapings, in which were embedded many splinters from the wreckage of the hansom.

Brett, careless of the amazement he caused to hurrying pedestrians, waded through the bed of mud, kicking up any objects encountered by his feet.

He uttered an exclamation of triumph when he produced a stick from the depths.

"I thought I should find it," he said. "When the horse fell it was a hundred to one against the stick being extricated from the reins, and its owner could not wait an instant. You and the stick, my dear Hume, lay close together."

A small crowd was gathering. The barrister laughed.

"Gentleman," he said, "why are you so surprised? Which of you would not dirty his boots to recover such a valuable article as this?"

Some people grinned sympathetically. They all moved away.

In an upper room of the neighbouring public-house were a suffering "runner" and a disconsolate "cabby." The "runner" could tell them nothing tangible concerning the man he pursued.

"I sawr 'im bring the hoss dahn like a bullick," he whispered, for the poor fellow had received a terrible blow. "I went arter 'im, dodged rahnd the fust corner, an', bli-me, 'e gev me a punch that would 'ave 'arted Corbett."

"What withhis fist?" inquired Brett.

"Nah, guv'nor'is 'eel, blawst 'im. I could 'ave dodged a square blow. I can use my dukes a bit myself."

"What was the value of the punch?"

The youth tried to smile, though the effort tortured him. "It was worth 'arf a thick 'un at least, guv'nor."

Hume gave him two sovereigns, and the runner could not have been more taken aback had the donor "landed him" on the sound jaw.

"And now, you," said Brett to the cabman. "What did you see?"

"Me!" with a snort of indignation. "Little over an hour ago I sawr a smawt keb an' a tidy little nag wot I gev thirty quid fer at Ward's in the Edgware Road a fortnight larst Toosday. And wot do I see now? Marylebone Work'us fer me an' the missis an' the kids. My keb gone, my best hoss killed, an' a pore old crock left, worth abart enough to pay the week's stablin'. I see a lot, I do."

The man was telling the truth. He was blear-eyed with misery. Brett looked at Hume, and the latter rang a bell. He asked the waiter for a pen and ink.

"How much did your cab cost?" he said to the driver, who was so downcast that he actually failed to correctly interpret David's action. The question had to be repeated before an answer came.

"It wasn't a new 'un, mister. I was just makin' a stawt. I gev fifty-five pound fer it, an' three pun ten to 'ave it done up. But there! What's the use of talkin'? I'm orf 'ome, I am, to fice the missis."

"Wait just a little while," said David kindly. "You hardly understand this business. The madman who attacked us meant to injure me, not you. Here is a cheque for £100, which will not only replace your horse and cab, but leave you a little over for the loss of your time."

Winter caught the dazed cabman by the shoulder.

"Billy," he said, "you know me. Are you going home, or going to get drunk?"

Billy hesitated.

"Goin' 'ome," he vociferated. "S'elp me"

"One moment," said Brett. "Surely you have some idea of the appearance of the rascal who pulled your horse over?"

The man was alternately surveying the cheque and looking into the face of his benefactor.

"I dunno," he cried, after a pause. "I feel a bit mixed. This gentleman 'ere 'as acted as square as ever man did. 'E comes of a good stock, 'e does, an' yet—I 'umbly ax yer pawdon, sir—but the feller who tried to kill you an' me might ha' bin yer own brother."

23
MARGARET'S SECRET

The waiter managed to remove the most obvious traces of Brett's escapade in the gutter, and incidentally cleaned the stick.

It was a light, tough ashplant, with a silver band around the handle. The barrister held it under a gas jet and examined it closely. Nothing escaped him. After scrutinising the band for some time, he looked at the ferrule, and roughly estimated that the owner had used it two or three years. Finally, when quite satisfied, he handed it to Winter.

"Do you recognise those scratches?" he said, with a smile, pointing out a rough design bitten into the silver by the application of aqua regia and beeswax.

The detective at once uttered an exclamation of supreme astonishment.

"The very thing!" he cried. "The same Japanese motto as that on the Ko-Katana!"

Hume now drew near.

"So," he growled savagely, "the hand that struck down Alan was the same that sought my life an hour ago!"

"And your cousin's this morning," said Brett

"The cowardly brute! If he has a grudge against my family, why doesn't he come out into the open? He need not have feared detection, even a week ago. I could be found easily enough. Why didn't he meet me face to face? I have never yet run away from trouble or danger."

"You are slightly in error regarding him," observed Brett. "This man may be a fiend incarnate, but he Is no coward. He means to kill, to work some terrible purpose, and he takes the best means towards that end. To his mind the idea of giving a victim fair play is sheer nonsense. It never even occurs to him. But a coward! no. Think of the nerve required to commit robbery and murder under the conditions that obtained at Beechcroft on New Year's Eve. Think of the skill, the ready resource, which made so promptly available the conditions of the two assaults to-day. Our quarry is a genius, a Poe among criminals. Look to it, Winter, that your handcuffs are well fixed when you arrest him, or he will slip from your grasp at the very gates of Scotland Yard."

"If I had my fingers round his windpipe" began David.

"You would be a dead man a few seconds later," said the barrister. "If we three, unarmed, had him in this room now, equally defenceless, I should regard the issue as doubtful."

"There would be a terrible dust-up," smirked Winter.

"Possibly; but it would be a fight for life or death. No half measures. A matter of decanters, fire-irons, chairs. Let us return to the hotel."

Whilst Hume went to summon the others, Brett seated himself at a table and wrote:

"A curious chapter of accidents happened in Northumberland Avenue yesterday. Early in the morning, Mr. Robert Hume-Frazer quitted his hotel for a stroll in the West End, and narrowly escaped being   run over in Whitehall. About 8 p.m. his cousin, Mr. David   Hume-Frazer, was driving through the Avenue in a hansom, when the vehicle upset, and the young gentleman was thrown out. He was picked up in a terrible condition, and is reported to be in danger of his life."

The barrister read the paragraph aloud.

"It is casuistic," he commented, "but that defect is pardonable. After all, it is not absolutely mendacious, like a War Office telegram. Winter, go and bring joy to the heart of some penny-a-liner by giving him that item. The 'coincidence' will ensure its acceptance by every morning paper in London, and you can safely leave the reporter himself to add details about Mr. Hume's connection with the Stowmarket affair."

The detective rose.

"Will you be here when I come back, sir?" he asked.

"I expect so. In any case, you must follow on to my chambers. To-night we will concert our plan of campaign."

Margaret entered, with Helen and the two men. Robert limped somewhat.

"How d'ye do, Brett?" he cried cheerily. "That beggar hurt me more than I imagined at the time. He struck a tendon in my left leg so hard that it is quite painful now."

Brett gave an answering smile, but his thoughts did not find utterance. How strange it was that two men, so widely dissimilar as Robert and the vendor of newspapers, should insist on the skill, the unerring certainty, of their opponent.

"Mrs. Capella," he said, wheeling round upon the lady, "when you lived in London or on the Continent did you ever include any Japanese in the circle of your acquaintances?"

"Yes," was the reply.

Margaret was white, her lips tense, the brilliancy of her large eyes almost unnatural.

"Tell me about them."

"What can I tell you? They were bright, lively little men. They amused my friends by their quaint ideas, and interested us at times by recounting incidents of life in the East."

"Were they all 'little'? Was one of them a man of unusual stature?"

"No," said Margaret

The barrister knew that she was profoundly distressed.

"If she would be candid with me," he mused, "I would tear the heart from this mystery to-night."

One other among those present caught the hidden drift of this small colloquy. Robert Frazer looked sadly at his cousin. Natures that are closely allied have an electric sympathy. He could not even darkly discern the truth, but he connected Brett's words in some remote way with Capella. How he loathed the despicable Italian who left his wife to bear alone the trouble that oppressed her—who only went away in order to concoct some villainy against her.

Margaret could not face the barrister's thoughtful, searching gaze. She stood up—like the others of her race when danger threatened. She even laughed harshly.

"I have decided," she said, "to leave here to-morrow morning. Helen says she does not object Our united wardrobes will serve all needs of the seaside. Robert's tailor visited him to-day, and assured him that the result would be satisfactory without any preliminary 'trying on.' Do you approve, Mr. Brett?"

"Most heartily. I can hardly believe that our hidden foe will make a further attack until he learns that he has been foiled again. Yet you will all be happier, and unquestionably safer, away from London. Does anyone here know where you are going?"

"No one. I have not told my maid or footman. It was not necessary, as we intended to remain here a week."

"Admirable! When you leave the hotel in the morning give Yarmouth as your destination. Not until you reach King's Cross need you inform your servants that you are really going to Whitby. Would you object to—ah, well that is perhaps, difficult. I was about to suggest an assumed name, but Miss Layton's father would object, no doubt."

"If he did not, I would," said Robert impetuously. "Who has Margaret to fear, and what do David and I care for all the anonymous scoundrels in creation?"

"Is there really so much danger that such a proceeding is advisable?" inquired the trembling Nellie.

"To-day's circumstances speak for themselves, Miss Layton," replied Brett. "Neither you nor Mrs. Capella run the least risk. I will not be answerable for the others. Grave difficulties must be surmounted before the power for further injury is taken from the man we seek. In my professional capacity, I say act openly, advertise your destination, make it known that Mr. Hume escaped from the wreck of the hansom unhurt. Should the would-be murderer follow you to Whitby he cannot escape me. Here in London he is one among five millions. But speaking as a friend, I advise the utmost vigilance unless another Hume-Frazer is to die in his boots."

It was not Helen but Margaret who wailed in agony:

"Do you really mean what you say? Have matters reached that stage?"

"Yes, they have."

His voice was cold, almost stern.

"Kindly telegraph your Whitby address to me," he said to Hume. Then he walked to the door, leaving them brusquely.

For once in his career he was deeply annoyed.

"Confound all women!" he muttered in anger. "They nurse some petty little secret, some childish love affair, and deem its preservation more important than their own happiness, or the lives of their best friends. They are all alike—duchess or scullery-maid. Their fluttering hearts are all the world to them, and everything else chaos. If that woman only chose"

"Mr. Brett!" came a clear voice along the corridor.

It was Margaret. She came to him hastily

"Why do you suspect me?" she exclaimed brokenly. "I am the most miserable woman on earth. Suffering and death environ me, and overwhelm those nearest and dearest. Yet what have I done that you should think me capable of concealing from you material facts which would be of use to you?"

The barrister was tempted to retort that what she believed to be "material" might indeed be of very slight service to him, but the contrary proposition held good, too.

Then he saw the anguish in her face, and it moved him to say gently:

"Go back to your friends, Mrs. Capella. I am not the keeper of your conscience. I am almost sure you are worrying yourself about trifles. Whatever they may be, you are not responsible. Rest assured of this, in a few days much that is now dim and troublous will be cleared up. I ask you nothing further. I would prefer not to hear anything you wish to say to me. It might fetter my hands Good-bye!"

24
THE MEETING

"There!" he said to himself, as he passed downstairs, "I am just as big a fool as she is. She followed me to make a clean breast of everything, and I send her back with a request to keep her lips sealed. Yet I am angry with her for the risk she is taking!"

He reached the hall and was about to cross the foyer when he caught the words, "Gentleman thrown out of a cab," uttered by a handsome girl, cheaply but gaudily attired, who was making some inquiry at the bureau.

He stopped and searched for a match. Then he became interested in the latest news, pinned in strips on the baize-covered board of a "ticker."

The girl explained to an official that she had witnessed an accident that evening. She was told that a gentleman who lived in the hotel was hurt. Was he seriously injured?

The hotel man, from long practice, was enabled to sum up such inquirers rapidly.

"Do you know the gentleman?" he inquired.

"No—that is, slightly."

"Well, madam, if you give me your card I will send it to his friends. They will give you all necessary information."

She became confused. She was not accustomed to the quiet elegance of a great hotel. The men in evening dress, the gorgeously attired ladies passing to elevator or drawing-room, seemed to be listening to her. Why did the bureau keeper speak so loudly? Then the assurance of the Cockney came to her aid.

"I don't see why there should be such a fuss about nothing," she said. "I don't know his people. I saw the gentleman pitched out of a cab and was sorry for him, so I just called to ask how he was."

She angrily tossed her head, and stared insolently at an old lady who came to inquire if there were any letters for the Countess of Skerry and Ness.

"No letters, your ladyship," said the man. "And you, miss, must either send a personal message or see the manager."

The young woman bounced out in a fury, and Brett followed her, silently thanking the favouring planets which had sent him down the stairs at the very moment when the girl was proffering her request to the clerk.

Fortunately, the weather was better now. There was a clear sky overhead, and the streets looked quite cheerful after the steady downpour, London's myriad lamps being reflected in glistening zigzags across the wet pavement.

The girl did not head towards the busy Strand, but walked direct to Charing Cross station on the District Railway.

The barrister thought she intended to go somewhere by train. He quickened his pace in order to be able to rapidly obtain a ticket and thus keep up with her. Herein he was lucky. To his surprise, she passed out of the station on the embankment side.

He followed, and nowhere could he see her. Then he remembered the steps leading to the footpath along the Hungerford Bridge. Running up these steps he soon caught sight of the young woman, who was walking rapidly towards Waterloo.

A man of the artisan class stared at her as she passed, and said something to her. She turned fiercely.

"Do you want a swipe on the jaw?" she demanded.

No, he did not. What had he done, he would like to know.

"You mind your own business," she said. "Where am I goin', indeed. What's it got to do with you?"

The episode was valuable to the listening barrister. It classified the anxious inquirer after Hume's health.

Her abashed admirer hung back, and the girl resumed her onward progress. The man was conscious that the gentleman behind him must have heard what passed. He endeavoured to justify himself.

"She's pretty O.T., she is," he grinned.

"Do you know her?" said Brett.

"I know her by sight. Seen her in the York now an' then."

"She can evidently take care of herself."

"Rather. Don't you so much as look at her, mister, or off goes your topper into the river. She's in a bad temper to-night."

Brett laughed and walked ahead. On reaching the Surrey side the girl made for the Waterloo Road. There she mounted on top of a 'bus. The barrister went inside. He thought of the "man with black, snaky eyes," who "took penn'orths" all the way from the Elephant to Whitehall.

And now he, Brett, took a penn'orth to the Elephant. The 'bus reached that famous centre of humanity, passing thence through Newington Butts to the Kennington Park Road.

In the latter thoroughfare the girl skipped down from the roof, and disdaining the conductor's offer to stop, swung herself lightly to the ground. The barrister followed, and soon found himself tracking her along a curved street of dingy houses.

Into one of these she vanished. It chanced to be opposite a gas-lamp, and as he walked past he made out the number37.

Externally it was exactly like its neighbours, dull, soiled, pinched, old curtains, worn blinds, blistered paint. He knew that if he walked inside he would tread on a strip of oilcloth, once gay in red and yellow squares, but now worn to a dirty grey uniformity. In the "hall" he would encounter a rickety hat-stand faced by an ancient print entitled "Idle Hours," and depicting two ladies, reclining on rocks, attired in tremendous skirts, tight jackets, and diminutive straw hats perched between their forehead and chignonsin the middle distance a fat urchin, all hat and frills, staring stupidly at the ocean.

In the front sitting-room he would encounter horsehair chairs, frayed carpet, and more early Victorian prints; in the back sitting-room more frayed carpet, more prints, and possibly a bed.

Nothing very mysterious or awe-inspiring about 37 Middle Street, yet the barrister was loth to leave the place. The scent of the chase was in his nostrils. He had "found."

He was tempted to boldly approach and frame some excuse—a hunt for lodgings, an inquiry for a missing friend, anything to gain admittance and learn something, however meagre in result, of the occupants.

He reviewed the facts calmly. To attempt, at such an hour, to glean information from the sharp-tongued young person who had just admitted herself with a latchkey, was to court failure and suspicion. He must bide his time. Winter was an adept in ferreting out facts concerning these localities and their denizens. To Winter the inquiry must be left.

He stopped at the further end of the street, lit a cigar, and walked back.

He had again passed No. 37, giving a casual glance to the second floor front window, in which a light illumined the blind, when he became aware that a man was approaching from the Kennington Park Road. Otherwise the street was empty.

The lamp opposite No. 37 did not throw its beams far into the gloom, but the advancing figure instantly enlisted Brett's attention.

The man was tall and strongly built. He moved with the ease of an athlete. He walked with a long, swinging stride, yet carried himself erect He was attired in a navy blue serge suit and a bowler hat.

The two were rapidly nearing each other.

At ten yards' distance Brett knew that the other man was he whom he sought, the murderer of Sir Alan Hume-Frazer, the human ogre whose mission on earth seemed to be the extinction of all who bore that fated name.

It is idle to deny that Brett was startled by this unexpected rencontre. Not until he made the discovery did he remember that he was carrying the stick rescued from the mud of Northumberland Avenue.

The knowledge gave him an additional thrill. Though he could be cool enough in exciting circumstances, though his quiet courage had more than once saved his life in moments of extreme peril, though physically he was more than able to hold his own with, say, the average professional boxer, he fully understood that the individual now about to pass within a stride could kill him with ridiculous ease.

Would this dangerous personage recognise his own stick?–That was the question.

If he did, Brett could already see himself describing a parabola in the air, could hear his skull crashing against the pavement. He even went so far as to sit with the coroner's jury and bring in a verdict of "Accidental Death."

In no sense did Brett exaggerate the risk he encountered. The individual who could stab Sir Alan to death with a knife like a toy, hurl a stalwart sailor into the middle of a street without perceptible effort, and bring down a horse and cab at the precise instant and in the exact spot determined upon after a second's thought, was no ordinary opponent.

Their eyes met.

Truly a fiendish-looking Hume-Frazer, a Satanic impersonation of a fine human type. For the first and only time in his life Brett regretted that he did not carry a revolver when engaged in his semi-professional affairs.

The barrister, be it stated, wore the conventional frock-coat and tall hat of society. His was a face once seen not easily forgotten, the outlines classic and finely chiselled, the habitual expression thoughtful, preoccupied, the prevalent idea conveyed being tenacious strength. Quite an unusual person in Middle Street, Kennington.

They passed.

Brett swung the stick carelessly in his left hand, but not so carelessly that on the least sign of a hostile movement he would be unable to dash it viciously at his possible adversary's eyes.

He remembered the advice of an old cavalry officer: "Always give 'em the point between the eyes. They come head first, and you reach 'em at the earliest moment."

Nevertheless, he experienced a quick quiver down his spine when the other man deliberately stopped and looked after him. He did not turn his head, but he could "feel" that vicious glance travelling over him, could hear the unspoken question: "Now, I wonder who *you* are, and what you want here?"

He staggered slightly, recovered his balance, and went on. It was a masterpiece of suggestiveness, not overdone, a mere wink of intoxication, as it were.

It sufficed. Such an explanation accounts for many things in London.

The watcher resumed his interrupted progress. Brett crossed the street and deliberately knocked at the door of a house in which the ground floor was illuminated.

Someone peeped through a blind, the door opened as far as a rattling chain would permit.

"Good evening," said Brett.

"What do you want?" demanded a suspicious woman.

"Mr. Smith–Mr. Horatio Smith."

"He doesn't live here."

"Dear me! Isn't this 76 Middle Street?"

"Yes; all the same, there's no Smiths here."

The door slammed; but the barrister had attained his object. The other man had entered No. 37.

25
WHERE DID MARGARET GO?

In the Kennington Park Road he hailed hansom and drove home. Winter awaited him, for Smith now admitted the detective without demur should his master be absent.

The barrister walked to a sideboard, produced a decanter of brandy, and helped himself to a stiff dose.

"Ah," he said pleasantly, "our American cousins call it a 'corpse reviver,' but a corpse could not do that, could he, Winter?"

"I know a few corpses that would like to try. But what is up, sir? I have not often seen you in need of stimulants."

"I am most unfeignedly glad to give you the opportunity. Winter, suppose, sometime to-morrow, you were told that the body of Reginald Brett, Esq., barrister-at-law, and a well-known amateur investigator of crime, had been picked up shortly after midnight in the Kennington district, whilst the medical evidence showed that death was caused by a fractured skull, the result of a fall, there being no other marks of violence on the person, what would you have thought?"

"It all depends upon the additional facts that came to light."

"I will tell them to you. You were aware that I had quitted the hotel, because you called there?"

"Yes."

"Whom did you see?"

"Mr. David. He said that you were angry with Mrs. Capella, for no earthly reason that he could make out. He further informed me that she had followed you when you left the room, and had not returned, being presumably in her own apartment."

"Anything further?"

"Mr. Hume asked Miss Layton to go and see if Mrs. Capella had retired for the night. Miss Layton came back, looking rather scared, with the information that Mrs. Capella had dressed and gone out. After a little further talk we came to the conclusion that you were both together. Was that so?"

Brett had commenced his cross-examination with the intention of humorously proving to Winter that he (the detective) would suspect the wrong person of committing the imagined murder. Now he straightened himself, and continued in deadly earnest:

"When did you leave the hotel?"

"About 10.15."

"Had not Mrs. Capella returned?"

"Not a sign of her. Miss Layton was alarmed, both the men furious, Mr. Robert particularly so. I did not see any use in remaining there; thought, in fact, I ought to obey orders and await you here, so here I am."

The barrister scribbled on a card: "Is Mrs. C. at home?" He rang for Smith, and said:

"Take a cab to Mr. Hume's hotel. Give him that card, and bring me the answer. If you and the cabman must have a drink together, kindly defer the function until after your return."

Smith took such jibes in good part. He knew full well that to attempt to argue with his master would produce a list of previous convictions.

Then Brett proceeded to amaze Winter in his turn, giving him a full, true, and complete history of events since his parting from Mrs. Capella in the corridor.

He had barely finished the recital when Smith returned with a note:

"Yes; she came in at 10.45, and has since retired for the night. She says that her head ached, that she wanted to be alone, and went for a long walk. Seemed rather to

resent our anxiety. Helen and I will be glad when we are all safely away from London. D.H."

The barrister pondered over this communication for a long time.

"I fear," he said at last, "that I came away from Middle Street a few minutes too soon. To tell the truth, I was in an abject state of fear. Next time I meet Mr. Frazer the Third I will be ready for him."

"Is he really so like the others that he might be mistaken for one of them?"

"In a sense, yes. He has the same figure, general conformation, and features. But in other respects he is utterly different. Have you ever seen a great actor in the role of Mephistopheles?"

"I don't remember. My favourite villain was Barry Sullivan as Richard III."

Brett laughed hysterically.

"Let me speak more plainly. You have, no doubt, a vague picture in your mind of a certain gentleman of the highest descent who is popularly credited with the possession of horns, hoofs, and a barbed tail?"

"I've heard of him."

"Very well. You will see someone very like him, minus the adornments aforesaid, when you set eyes on the principal occupant of 37 Middle Street."

Winter slowly assimilated this description. Then he inquired:

"Why did you say just now that you came away from Middle Street a few minutes too soon?"

"Where did Mrs. Capella go when she left the hotel?"

"If she went to visit the man you met, then she is acting in collision with her brother's murderer, and she knows it."

"That is a hard thing to say, Winter."

"It is a harder thing to credit, sir; but one cannot reject all evidence, merely because It happens to be straightforward and not hypothetical."

"Winter, you are sneering at me."

"No; I am only trying to make you admit the tendency of facts discovered by yourself. There is a period in all criminal investigation when deductive reasoning becomes inductive."

"Now I have got you," cried Brett "I thought I recognised the source of your new-born philosophy in the first postulate. The second convinces me. You have been reading 'The Murders in the Rue Morgue.'"

"The book is in my pocket," admitted Winter.

"I recommend you to transfer it to your head. It should be issued departmentally as a supplement to the Police Code. But let us waste no more time. To-morrow we have much to accomplish."

"I am all attention."

"In the first place, Mrs. Capella is leaving London for the North. She must not be regarded in our operations. The woman is weighted with a secret. I am sorry for her. I prefer to allow events as supplied by others to unravel the skein. Secondly, Jiro and his wife, and all who visit them, or whom they visit, must be watched incessantly. Get all the force required for this operation in its fullest sense. You, with one trusted associate, must keep a close eye on No. 37 Middle Street. On no account obtrude yourself personally into affairs there. Rather miss twenty opportunities than scare that man by one false move. Do you understand me thoroughly?"

"I am to see and not be seen. If I cannot do the one without the other, I must do neither."

"Exactly. What a holiday you are having! You will return to the Yard with an expanded brain. When you buy a new hat you will be astounded and gratified. But beware of the fate of the frog in the fable. He inflated himself until he emulated the size of the bull."

"And then?"

"Oh, then he burst."

The detective changed the conversation abruptly.

"What do you propose doing, Mr. Brett?"

"I purpose reading a chapter in 'The Stowmarket Mystery,' written by your friend, Mr. Holden."

They heard a loud rat-tat on the outer door.

"Probably," continued Brett, "this is its title."

Smith entered with a telegram. It was in the typed capitals usually associated with Continental messages. It read:

"Johnson leaves Naples to-night with others, I travel same train.–HOLDEN."

The barrister surveyed the simple words with an intensity that indicated his desire to wrest from their context its hidden significance.

Winter, more subject to the influences of the hour, puffed his cigar furiously.

"You arrange your words to suit the next act for all the world like an Adelphi play," he growled.

"I see that Holden has the same gift. What does he mean by 'others'? Who is Capella bringing with him?"

"Witnesses," volunteered Winter.

"Just so; but witnesses in what cause?"

"How the–how can I tell?"

"By applying your borrowed logic. Try the deductive reasoning you flung at me a while ago."

"I don't quite know what 'deductive' means," was the sulky admission.

"That is the first step towards wisdom. You admit ignorance. Deduction, in this sense, is the process of deriving consequences from admitted facts. Now, mark you. Capella wishes to be rid of his wife, by death or legal separation. He thinks he wants to marry Miss Layton. He is convinced that something within his power, if done effectively, will bring about both events. He can shunt Mrs. Capella, and so disgust Miss Layton with the Hume-Frazers that she will turn to the next ardent and sympathetic wooer that presents himself. He knew the points of his case, and went to Naples to procure proofs. He has obtained them. They are chiefly living persons. He is bringing them to England, and their testimony will convict Mrs. Capella of some wrong-doing, either voluntary or involuntary. Holden knows what Capella has accomplished, and thinks it is unnecessary to remain longer in Naples. He is right. I tell you, Winter, I like Holden."

"And I tell you, Mr. Brett, that if I swallowed the whole of Mr. Poe's stories, I couldn't make out Holden's telegram in that fashion. So I must stick to my own methods, and I've put away a few wrong 'uns in my time. When shall I see you next?"

Brett took out his watch.

"At seven p.m., the day after to-morrow," he said coolly. "Until then my address is 'Hotel Metropole, Brighton.'"

26
MR. OOMA

He kept his word. Early next morning, after despatching a message to David Hume, and receiving an answer—an acknowledgment of his address in case of need—he took train to London-by-the-Sea, and for thirty-six hours flung mysteries and intrigues to the winds.

He came back prepared for the approaching climax. In such matters he was a human barometer. The affairs of the family in whose interests he had become so suddenly involved were rapidly reaching an acute stage. Something must happen soon, and that something would probably have tremendous and far-reaching consequences.

Capella and his companions, known and unknown, would reach London at 7.30 p.m. It pleased Brett to time his homeward journey so that he would speed in the same direction, but arrive before them.

In these trivial matters he owned to a boyish enthusiasm. It stimulated him to "beat the other man," even if he only called upon the London, Brighton, and South Coast line to conquer a weak opponent like the South-Eastern.

At his flat were several letters and telegrams. Mrs. Capella wrote:

"I have seriously considered your last words to me. It is hard for a woman, the victim of circumstances, and deprived of her husband's support at a most trying and critical period, to know how to act for the best. You said you wished your hands to be left unfettered. Well, be it so. You will encounter no hindrance from me. I pray for your success, and can only hope that in bringing happiness to others you will secure peace for me."

"Poor woman!" he murmured. "She still trusts to chance to save her. Whom does she dread? Not her husband. Each day that passes she must despise him the more. Does she know that Robert loves her? Is she afraid that he will despise her? Really, a collision in which Capella was the only victim would be a perfect godsend."

David telegraphed the safe arrival of the party at a Whitby hotel. "We have seen nothing more of our Northumberland Avenue acquaintance," he added.

Holden, too, cabled from Paris, announcing progress. The remainder of the correspondence referred to other matters and social engagements, all which latter fixtures the barrister had summarily broken.

Winter was announced. His face heralded important tidings.

"Well, how goes the ratiocinative process?' was Brett's greeting.

"I don't know him," said the detective. "But I do happen to know most of the private inquiry agents in London, and one of 'em is going strong in Middle Street. He's watching Mr. Ooma for all he's worth."

"Mr. Whom-a?"

"I'm not joking, Mr. Brett. That is the name of the mysterious gent in No. 37Ooma, no initials. Anyhow, that is the name he gives to the landlady, and her daughter–the girl you followed from the hotel–tells all her friends that when he gets his rights he will marry her and make her a princess."

"Oomaa princess," repeated Brett.

"Such is the yarn in Kennington circles. I obeyed orders absolutely. I and my mate took turn about in the lodgings we hired, where we are supposed to be inventors. My pal has a mechanical twist. He puts together a small electric machine during his spell, and I take it to pieces in mine. Yesterday my landlady was in the room, and Ooma looked out of the opposite window. Then she told me the whole story."

"Go ondo!"

"Mr. Ooma is evidently puzzled to learn what has become of the Hume-Frazers and Mrs. Capella."

"Why do you bring in her name?"

"Because it leads to the second part of my story. Someone–Capella or his solicitors, I expect–instructed Messrs. Matchem and Smith, private detectives, to keep a close eye on the lady. Their man is an ex-police constable, a former subordinate of mine who was fined for taking a drink when he ought not to. Of course, I knew him and he knew me, so I hadn't much trouble in getting it out of him."

The speaker paused with due dramatic effect.

"Got what out of him?" cried Brett impatiently. "And don't puff your cheeks in that way. Remember the terrible fate of the frog who would be a bull."

"There's neither frogs nor bulls in this business," retorted Winter, calm in the consciousness of his coming revelation. "Mrs. Capella did go to Middle Street that night. She drove there in a hansom, had a long talk with Ooma, and nearly drove Miss Dew crazy with jealousy."

"We guessed that already. Miss Dew is the prospective princess, I presume?"

"Yes. She has been twice to the hotel since, trying to find out where the party went to."

"Next?"

"Ooma has plenty of money, and now for my prize packet–he is a Jap!"

"Impossible!"

"This time you are wrong, Mr. Brett. You have only seen him once. You were full of his remarkable likeness to the Hume-Frazers. It is startling, I admit, and at night-time no man living could avoid the mistake. But I tell you he is a Jap. He met Jiro yesterday, and they walked in Kensington Palace Gardens. They talked Japanese all the time. My mate heard them. He distinctly caught the word 'Okasaki' more than once. He managed to shadow them very neatly by hiring a bath-chair and telling the attendant to come near to the pair every time there was a chance. More than that, when you know it, you can see the Japanese eyes, skin, and mouth. It is the grafting of the Jap on the European model that gives him the likeness towell, to the party you mentioned the other day."

"The devil!" exclaimed Brett.

"That's him!"

It was useless to explain that the exclamation was one of amazement.

The barrister began to roam about the apartment, frowning with the intensity of his thoughts. Once he confronted Winter.

"Are you sure of this?" he demanded.

"So sure that were it not for your positive instructions, Mr. Ooma would now be in Holloway, awaiting his trial on a charge of murder. Look at the facts. 'Rabbit Jack' can identify him. He knew how to use the Ko-Katana. He knew the Japanese tricks of wrestling, which enabled him to make those two clever attacks on the two cousins. He has some power over Mrs. Capella, which brings her to him at eleven at night in a distant quarter of London. He made Jiro write the typed letter in my possession. He sent Jiro to Ipswich to attend Mr. David's second trial when the first missed fire. I can string Mr. Ooma on that little lot."

"Winter," said Brett sternly, "you make me tired. Have all these stunning items of intelligence invaded your intellect only since you went to Middle Street?"

"No, not exactly, Mr. Brett. I must admit that each one of them is your discovery, except the fact that he is a Jap–always excepting that–but yesterday I strung them together, so to speak."

"Ending your task by stringing Ooma, in imagination. I allow you full credit for your sensational development– always excepting this, that I sent you to Middle Street. Why did he kill Sir Alan? How does his Japanese nationality elucidate an utterly useless and purposeless murder?"

"I don't know, Mr. Brett."

"Unless I am much mistaken, you will learn to-night. Holden is nearly due."

The barrister resumed his stalk round the room. In another minute he stopped to glance at his watch.

"Half-past seven," he murmured. "Just time to get a message through to Whitby, and perhaps a reply."

He wrote a telegram to Hume: "Where is Fergusson? I want to see him."

"What has Fergusson got to do with the business?" asked the detective.

"Probably nothing. But he is the oldest available repository of the family secrets. His master has told him to be explicit with me. By questioning him, I may solve the riddle presented by Mr. Ooma. Does the name suggest nothing to you, Winter?"

"It has a Japanese ring about it."

"Nothing Scotch? Isn't it like Hume, for instance?"

"By Jove! I never thought of that. Well, there, I give in. Ooma! Dash my buttons, that beats cock-fighting!"

The barrister paid no heed to Winter's fall from self-importance. He pondered deeply on the queer twist given to events by the detective's statement. At last he took a volume from his book-case.

"Do you remember what I told you about Japanese names?" he said. "I described to you, for instance, what strange mutations your surname would undergo were you born in the Far East."

"Yes; I would be called Spring, Summer, etc, according to my growth."

"Then listen to this," and he read the following extract from that excellent work, "The Mikado's Empire," by W.E. Griffis:

"It has, until recently, in Japan been the custom for every Samurai to be named differently in babyhood, boyhood, manhood, or promotion, change of life, or residence, in commemoration of certain events, or on account of a vow, or from mere whim."

"What a place for aliases!" interpolated the professional.

"At the birth of a famous warrior," went on Brett, "his mother, having dreamed that she conceived by the sun, called him Hiyoshi Maro (good sun). Others dubbed him Ko Chiku (small boy), and afterward Saru Watsu (monkey-pine)."

He closed the volume.

"This gentleman has twenty other names," he added; "but the foregoing list will suffice. Doesn't it strike you as odd that the man who struck down the fifth Hume-Frazer baronet on the spot so fatal to his four predecessors, should bring from a country given to such name-changes a cognomen that irresistibly recalls the original enemy of the family, David Hume?"

"It is odd," asserted Winter.

Someone rang, and was admitted.

"Mr. Holden," announced Smith.

27
HOLDEN'S STORY

The long-nosed ex-sergeant entered. His sallow face was browned after his long journeys and exposure to the Italian sun in midsummer. He was soiled and travel-stained.

"Excuse my appearance," he said. "I have had no time for even a wash since this morning. On board the boat I thought it best to keep a constant watch on Capella and his companions."

"Who are they?" demanded Brett.

Mr. Holden looked at the barrister with an injured air.

"I am a man of few words, sir," he said, "and if you do not mind, I will tell my story in my own way."

Winter was secretly delighted to hear the "Old 'Un," as they called him in the Yard, take a rise out of Brett in this manner.

"Perhaps," exclaimed the barrister, "your few words will come more easily if you wet your whistle."

"Well, I must admit that Italian wine"

"Is not equal to Scotch; or is it Irish?"

"Irish, sir, if you please."

Mr. Holden's utterance having been cleared of cinders, he made a fresh start.

"As I was saying, gentlemen, I kept an observant eye on Capella and his companions, and at the same time occupied myself in the fashioning of certain little models with which to illustrate my subsequent remarks."

He produced a map of Naples, which he carefully smoothed out on the table, pressing the creases with his fingers until Brett itched to tweak his long nose.

The man was evidently a Belfast Irishman, and the barrister forced himself to find amusement in speculating how such an individual came to speak Italian fluently. Speculation on this abstruse problem, however, yielded to keen interest in Mr. Holden's proceedings.

On the face of the map he located a number of small wooden carvings, which were really very ingenious. They represented churches, an hotel, a mansion, three ordinary houses, a rambling building like a public institution, and a nondescript structure difficult to classify.

"I find," said Mr. Holden, when the *mise-en-scène* was quite to his liking, "that a good map, and a few realistic models of the principal buildings dealt with in my discourse, give a lucidity and a coherence otherwise foreign to the narrative."

Even Winter became restive under this style of address. Brett caught his eye, and moved by common impulse, they lessened the whisky-mark in a decanter of Antiquary.

"Allow me to remark," interpolated Brett, "that your telegrams were admirably terse and to the point."

"Thank you, sir. Many eminent judges have complimented me on my manner of giving evidence. And now to business. I arrived at the railway station here" (touching the non-descript building), "and took a room in the Villa Nuova here" (he laid a finger on the mansion), "which, as you see, is quite close to the Hotel de Londres here" (a flourish over the hotel), "at which, as I expected, Mr. Capella took up his abode. According to your instructions I obtained a competent assistant, a native of Naples, and we both awaited Mr. Capella's arrival. He reached Naples at 10.30 a.m. the day following my advent at night, and after breakfast drove straight to the Reclusorio, or Asylum for the Poor, situated here" (he indicated the institution), "close to the Botanical Gardens. Mr. Capella arranged with the authorities to withdraw from the poorhouse an elderly woman named Maria Bresciano. It subsequently transpired that she was a nurse employed by a certain English gentleman named Fraser Beechcroft, who became entangled with a beautiful Italian girl named Margarita di Orvieto some twenty-eight years ago."

Mr. Holden paid not the remotest attention to the looks of amazement exchanged between Brett and Winter. He merely paused to take breath and peer benignantly at the map, following lines thereon with the index finger of his right hand.

"It appears further," he resumed, "that the Englishman and the Signorina di Orvieto could not marry, on account of some foolish religious scruples held by the young lady, but they entertained a very violent passion for each other, met clandestinely, and a female child was born, whose baptism is registered, under the name of Margarita di Orvieto, in the church of the village of La Scutillo here." (He tapped a tiny spired edifice on the edge of the map.)

"The two were living there in great secrecy, as they were in fear of their lives, not alone from the young lady's relatives, but from her discarded lover, the Marchese di Capella, father of the present Mr. Giovanni Capella, who has dropped his title in England. The old woman, Maria Bresciano, attended the signorina and her child, but unfortunately the mother died, and her death is registered both by the civil authorities in the Minadoi section here" (lifting a small house bodily off the map), "and by the ecclesiastical here" (he touched another spire).

"The affair created some stir in the Naples of that day, but Beechcroft's suffering, the calm daring with which, after the girl's death, he defied those who had vowed vengeance on him, and the generally passionate nature of the attachment between the two, created much public sympathy for him. Among others who were attracted to him were a Mr. and Mrs. Somers, and their daughter, then resident in Naples. Oddly enough,

Beechcroft did not content himself with securing efficient care for his child, but brought the infant to the Hotel de Londres—you note the coincidence—where it was nurtured under his personal supervision."

Brett drew a long breath. So this was Margaret's secret and Capella's vengeance! He was aroused, as from a dream, by Mr. Holden's steady voice.

"Mr. Beechcroft always held that the Signorina di Orvieto was his true wife in the eyes of Heaven, for their marriage was only prevented by a most uncalled-for and unnatural threat of incurring her father's dying curse it she dared to wed a Protestant. Eighteen months after her death he married Miss Somers at the British Consulate, and revealed his real name and rank—Sir Alan Hume-Frazer, baronet, of Beechcroft, near Stowmarket, England. His lady adopted the infant girl as her own, and local gossip had it that this was a part of the marriage contract, whilst the ceremony took place at an early date to give colour to the kindly pretence. The pair lived in a distant suburb, at Donzelle here" (another church fixed the spot), "and in twelve months a boy was born, birth registered locally and in the British Consulate. After four more years' residence in Naples, Sir Alan and Lady Hume-Frazer left Italy with their two children. Mr. Capella found two of their old servants, Giuseppe Conti and Lola Rintesano, living in these small houses here and here" (the remaining houses were lifted into prominence).

"Mr. Capella married Miss Margaret Hume-Frazer in Naples last January, the marriage being properly registered. His estates are situated in the South of Italy, and his father retired thither permanently during the scandal that took place twenty-eight years ago. Mr. Capella has brought with him the persons named as the nurse and servants, together with certified copies of all the documents cited. I also have certified copies of those documents, I now produce them, together with a detailed statement of my expenses. Mr. Capella is residing in a neighbouring hotel."

The methodical police-sergeant laid some neatly docketed folios on the table near the map, and sat down for the first time since entering the room.

As a matter of fact, he had not uttered an unnecessary word. Other men, describing similar complexities, would have given particulars of their adventures, how this thing had been done, and that person wheedled into confidences.

Mr. Holden rose superior to these considerations. His mission was all-important, and he had certainly fulfilled it to the letter.

"If ever a grateful country makes me a judge, Mr. Holden," said Brett, "I will add another to the encomiums you have received from the Bench. Indeed, before this affair ends, that pleasant task may be performed by an existing judge, for I do not see now how we are going to keep out of the law-courts. Do you, Winter?"

"Looks like a murder case plus a divorce," commented the detective.

"You are leaving out of count the biggest sensation, namely, the title to the Beechcroft estates. Under her father's will, if it is very cleverly drawn, Mrs. Capella may receive £1,000 per annum. She has not the remotest claim to Beechcroft and its revenues or to her brother's intestate estate."

Winter whistled.

"My eye!" he exclaimed. "What is Capella going to get out of it?"

"Revenge! His is a legacy of hate, like most other benefactions in the Hume-Frazer family. The next move rests with him. I wonder what it will be!"

28
MR. AND MRS. JIRO

Chance, at times, tangles the threads on which human lives depend, and creates such a net of knots and meshes that intelligent foresight is rendered powerless, and plans that ought to succeed are doomed to utter failure.

It was so during the three days succeeding Capella's return from Italy. Reviewing events in the lights of accomplished facts, Brett subsequently saw many opportunities where his intervention would have altered the fortunes of the men and women in whom he had become so interested.

Although he endeavoured to keep control of circumstances, it was impossible to predict with certainty the manner in which the fifth act of this tragedy in real life would unfold itself.

Would he have ordered things differently had he possessed the power? He never knew. It was a question he refused to discuss with Winter long after everybody was comfortably married or buried, as the case might be.

To divide labour and responsibility, he apportioned Ooma and his surroundings to Winter, Capella to Holden. The strict supervision maintained over the Jiro family was relaxed. Brett proposed dealing with them summarily and in person.

Holden had barely concluded his remarkable narrative when Hume's reply came from Whitby, giving the address of the hotel where Fergusson resided.

Brett went there at once, and found the old butler on the point of retiring for the night.

Fergusson was at first disinclined to commit himself to definite statements. With characteristic Scottish caution, he would neither say "yes" nor "no" until the barrister reminded him that he was not acting in his young master's interests by being so reticent.

"Weel, sir, I'm an auld man, and mebbe a bit haverin' in my judgment. Just ask me what ye wull, an' I'll dae my best to answer ye," was the butler's ultimate concession.

"You remember the day of the murder?"

"Shall I ever forget it?"

"Before Mr. David Hume-Fraser arrived at Beechcroft from London, had any other visitors seen Sir Alan?"

This was a poser. No form of ambiguity known to Fergusson would serve to extricate him from a direct reply.

"Ay, Mr. Brett," came his reply at last. "One I can swear to."

"That was Mr. Robert Hume-Fraser, who met him in the park, and walked with him there about three to four o'clock in the afternoon. Were there others whom you cannot swear to?"

The butler darted a quick glance at the other.

"Ye ken, sir," he said, "that the Hume-Frazers are mixed up wi' an auld Scoatch hoose?"

"Yes."

"Weel, sir, there's things that happen in this world which no man can explain. Five are dead, and five had to die by violent means. Who arranged that?"

"Neither you nor I can tell."

"That's right, sir. I know that Mr. David or Mr. Robert never lifted a hand against their cousin, yet, unless the Lord blinded my auld een, I saw ane or ither in the avenue when I tried to lift Sir Alan frae the groond."

"You said nothing of this at the time?"

"Would ye hae me speak o' wraiths to a Suffolk jury, Mr. Brett? I saw no mortal man. 'Twas a ghaist for sure, an' if I had gone into the box to talk of such things they

wad hae discredited my evidence about Mr. David. I
might hae hanged him instead o' savin' him."

"Suppose I tell you that the man you saw was no
ghost, but real flesh and blood, a Japanese descendant of
the David Hume who fought and killed the first Sir Alan
in 1763, what would you say?"

"I would say, sir, that it had to be, were it ever so
strange."

"Have you ever, in gossip about family records, heard
anything of the fate of the David Hume I have just
mentioned."

"Only this, sir. My people have lived on the Highland
estate longer than any Hume-Frazer of them a'. My
father remembered his grandfather sayin' that a man
who was in India wi' Clive met Mr. Hume in Calcutta.
There was fightin' agin' the French, an' Mr. Hume would
neither strike a blow for King George nor draw a sword
for the French, so he sailed away to the East in a Dutch
ship, and he was never heard of afterwards."

This was a most important confirmation of the theory
evolved by the barrister. For the rest, Fergusson's
reminiscences were useless.

Next morning Brett went to Somerset House to
consult the will in which Margaret's father left her £1,000
a year. Her brother died intestate.

As he expected, the document was phrased adroitly. It
read: "I give and bequeath to Margaret Hume-Frazer,
who has elected to desert the home provided for her, the
sum of" etc., etc.

The fact that she was, in the eyes of the law, an
illegitimate child could not invalidate this bequest. For
the rest, he imagined that when her brother died so
unexpectedly, no one ever dreamed of inquiring into the
well-intentioned fraud perpetrated by Lady Hume-Frazer
and her husband. Margaret was unquestionably accepted
as the heiress to her brother's property, the estate being
unentailed.

Then he drove to 17 St. John's Mansions, Kensington, where Mr. and Mrs. Jiro were "at home." They received him in the tiny drawing-room, and the lady's manner betokened some degree of nervousness, which she vainly endeavoured to conceal by a pretence of bland curiosity as to the object of the barrister's visit.

Not so Numagawa, whose sharp ferret eyes snapped with anxiety.

Brett left them under no doubt from the commencement. He addressed his remarks wholly to the Japanese.

"You have an acquaintance—perhaps I should say a confederateresiding at No. 37 Middle Street, Kennington" he began.

"I do not understand," broke in Jiro, whose sallow face crinkled like a withered apple in the effort to display non-comprehension.

"Oh yes, you do. The man's name is Ooma. He is a tall, strongly-built native of Japan. He sent you to Ipswich to watch the trial of Mr. David Hume-Frazer for the murder of his cousin. He got you to write the post-card to Scotland Yard on the type-writer which you disposed of the day after my visit here. You recognised the motto of his house in the design which I showed you, and which was borne on the blade of the Ko-Katana. For some reason which I cannot fathom, unless you are his accomplice, you made your wife dress in male attire and go to warn him that some person was on his track. You see I know everything."

As each sentence of this indictment proceeded it was pitiable to watch the faces of the couple. Jiro became a grotesque, fit to adorn the ugliest of Satsuma plaques. Mrs. Jiro visibly swelled with agitation. Brett felt that she was too full, and would overflow with tears in an instant.

"This is vely bad!" gasped Jiro.

"Oh, Nummie dear, have we been doing wrong?" moaned his spouse.

The barrister determined to frighten them thoroughly.

"It is a grave question with the authorities whether they should not arrest you instantly," he said.

"On what charge?" cried Jiro.

"On a charge of complicity after the act in relation to the murder of Sir Alan Hume-Frazer. Your accomplice, Ooma, is the murderer."

"What!" shrieked Mrs. Jiro, flouncing on to her knees and breaking forth into piteous sobs. "Oh, my precious infant! Oh, my darling Nummie! Will they part us from our babe?"

The door opened, and a frowsy head appeared.

"Did you call, mum?" inquired the small maid-servant.

"Get out!" shouted Brett; and the door slammed.

"Mr. Blett," whimpered the Japanese, "I did not do this thing. I am innocent. I knew nothing about it until—until–"

"You verified the motto on the blade by consulting the 'Nihon Suai Shi' in the British Museum."

This shot floored Jiro metaphorically, and his wife literally, for she sank into a heap.

"He knows everything, Nummie," she cried.

"Evelything!" repeated her husband.

"Then tell him the rest!". (Yet she was born in Suffolk.)

Brett scowled terribly as a subterfuge for laughter.

"Tell me," he said, "why you helped this amazing scoundrel?"

"I did not help," squeaked Jiro, his voice becoming shrill with excitement and fear. "He was my fliend. He is a Samurai of Japan. We met in Okasaki, and again in London. I came to England long after the clime you talk of. He told me these Flazel people were bad people, who had lobbed his father in the old days. He wanted them to be all hanged, then he would get money. He said they might watch him and get him sent back to Japan, where he belongs to a political palty who are always beheaded when they are caught. So when you come, I think, 'Hello, he wants to find Ooma!' I lite Ooma a letter, and he lite me to send Mrs. Jilo, dlessed in man's clothes, to tell him evelything. I did that to save my fliend."

"Have you Ooma's letter?"

"Yes; hele it is."

He took a document from a drawer, and Brett saw at a glance that Jiro's statement was correct.

"You appear to have acted as his tool throughout," was his scornful comment.

"But, Mr. Brett," sobbed the stout lady, "I ought to say that when I–when I–put on those things–and met Mr. Ooma, I disobeyed my husband in one matter. I–liked you–and was afraid of Mr. Ooma, so instead of describing you to him I described Mr. Hume-Frazer from what my husband told me of his appearance in the dock. He was the first man I could think of, and it seemed to be best, as the quarrel was between them. Only–I gave him–a beard and moustache, so as to puzzle him more. Didn't I, Nummie? I told you when I came home."

So Mrs. Jiro's unconscious device had undoubtedly saved Brett from a murderous attack, and Ooma had probably seen him leave the Northumberland Avenue Hotel more than once whilst waiting to waylay David Hume. Hence, too, the partial recognition by Ooma when they met by night in Middle Street.

The barrister could not help being milder in tone as he said:

"I believe you are both telling the truth. But this is a very serious matter. You must never again communicate with Ooma in any way. Avoid him as you would shun the plague, for within three or four days he will be in gaol, and you will be called upon to give evidence against him."

29
MARGARET'S SECRET

At his chambers Brett found Holden awaiting him, with the tidings that Capella had gone to Whitby. The Italian's agents, Messrs. Matchem & Smith, had evidently ferreted out Margaret's whereabouts. Her husband, full of vengeful thoughts and base schemings, hastened after her, rejoicing in the knowledge that her cousins and Miss Layton would also be present.

"As I knew exactly where he was going, and assumed his object to be a domestic quarrel, I did not think it necessary to accompany him until I had first consulted you, sir," said the imperturbable Holden.

"You acted quite rightly. Wait until the little beast returns to London!" exclaimed the barrister, with some degree of warmth.

Capella's conduct reminded him of a spiteful child which deserved a sound spanking. He telegraphed to Hume to inform him of the fiery visitor who might be expected at the hotel that evening.

Oddly enough, Helen, David, and the Rev. Mr. Layton, tempted by a marine excursion to Scarborough and back, left Whitby Harbour on a local steamer at 11 a.m., and were timed to return about 9 p.m. Margaret was not a good sailor, so Robert Hume-Frazer remained with her, the two going for a protracted stroll along the cliffs.

During their walk, the golden influences of the hour unlocked Margaret's heart. She was overwhelmed with the consciousness of the wretched mistakes of her life. She could not help contrasting the manly, gallant, out-spoken sailor by her side with the miserable foreigner whom she had espoused under the influence of a genuine but too violent passion. The knowledge that Robert might, under happier conditions, have been her husband was crushing and terrible.

There came to her some half-defined resolve to show her cousin how unworthy she was of his affections. Stopping defiantly at a moment when he casually called her attention to a lovely glimpse of rock-bound sea framed in a deep gorge, she said to him:

"Robert, I have something to tell you. I was on the point of telling Mr. Brett the last time I saw him in London, but he would not permit it. You are my cousin, and ought to know."

"My dear girl," he cried, "why this solemnity? You give me shivers when you speak in that way!"

"Pray listen to me, Robert. This is no matter for jesting. I am your cousin, but only in a sense. In the eyes of the law I am a nameless outcast. My mother was not Alan's mother. I was born before my father married the lady who treated me as her daughter until her death. My mother was an Italian, who died at my birth, and whom my father never married."

Frazer looked at the beautiful woman who addressed these astonishing words to him, and amazement, incredulity, a spasm almost of fear, held him dumb.

"It is too true, Robert. I did not know these things until a few short months ago. Some one, I believe, told my husband the truth soon after our marriage, and it was this discovery that so changed his feelings towards me. At first I was utterly unable to explain the awful alteration in his attitude. Not until I returned to England and settled down at Beechcroft did I become aware of the facts."

"Surely, Rita, you are romancing?"

"No, there can be no doubt about it. I have seen the proofs."

"Proofs! How can you be certain? Who made these statements to you?"

"I have been blackmailed, bled systematically for large sums of money. At first I was beguiled into a correspondence. My curiosity was aroused by references to my husband and to my father's will. Finally, I received copies of documents which made matters clear even to my bewildered brain. More than that, I was sent a memorandum, written by my father, in which he gave Alan all the particulars, corroborated by extracts from registers, and explaining the reasons which actuated him in framing his will so curiously. We were never closely knit together, as you know. I think now that he regarded me as the living evidence of the folly of his earlier years, and perhaps my sensitive nature was quick to detect this hidden feeling."

"May I ask who blackmailed you?"

Robert's face grew hard and stern. The woman experienced a tumultuous joy as she saw it. She had at least one defender.

"That is the hard part of my story," she murmured, in a voice broken with emotion. "The correspondence took place with a man named Ooma, a person I never even met at that time, and—can you believe it, Robert—within the past few days I have good reason to know that he is the murderer of my brother, the man who endeavoured to kill both you and David."

Frazer caught her by the shoulder.

"Rita," he said, "what has come to you? Are you hysterical, or dreaming?"

"Oh, for pity's sake, believe me!" she moaned. "Mr. Brett knows it is true. What is worse, he knows that I know it. I cannot bear this terrible secret any longer. I went to this man's house in London the other night, and boldly charged him with the crime. He denied it, but I could see the lie and the fear in his eyes. To avoid a terrible family scandal I came here with you all. But I can bear it no longer. God help me and pity me!"

"He will, Margaret. You have done no wrong that deserves so much suffering."

For a little while there was silence. Frazer was only able to whisper gentle and kindly words of consolation. He would have given ten years of his life to have the right to take her in his arms and tell her that, let the world view her conduct as it would, in his eyes she was blameless and lovable.

But this was denied him. She was the wife of another, of one who, instead of shielding and supporting her, was even then engaged in plotting her ruin.

"I nearly went mad," she continued at last, "when I first became acquainted with the truth concerning my parentage. With calmer moments came the reflection that, after all, I was my father's child, the sister of Alan, and entitled morally, if not legally, to succeed to the property. My wealth has not benefited me, Robert, but at least I have tried to do good to others."

"You have, indeed," he said tenderly. "But tell me about this fiend, Ooma. You say you saw him. Then you were in possession of his address?"

"Yes, during the past five months. When Mr. Brett first appeared on the scene, I feared lest he should discover my secret. How could I connect it with the death of my brother? The explanation given to me was that the documents were purloined by a servant years ago. It was not until the attacks on you and Davie, and the chance mention he made of some curious marks in a type-written communication received by Mr. Winter, that a horrible suspicion awoke in my mind. I had received several type-written letters" (Mr. Jiro, it would appear, had not told "evelything" to Brett), "and I compared some of those in London with the description given by Davie. They corresponded exactly! Then I resolved to make sure, no matter what the risk to myself, so I went to a place in Kennington the last night we were in town, and there I saw Ooma. Oh, Robert, he is so like you and Davie that at first it seems to be a romance! Only you two look honest and brave, whereas he has the appearance of a demon."

Frazer looked at his watch.

"Brett ought to know all these things at once," he said. "Let us walk back to the hotel and wire him. Perhaps it will be necessary for David and me to return to London immediately."

"Why? You are safe here? Why should you incur further risk?"

He could not help looking at her. A slight colour suffused her face. Then he laughed savagely.

"There will be no risk, Rita. Once let me meet Mr. Ooma as man to man and I will teach him a trick or two, if only for your sake. The law will deal with him for Alan's affair. He has an odd name! It has a Japanese ring, yet you say he resembles our family?"

Margaret, of course, could only describe him in general terms. As they returned to the hotel she explained her strange story in greater detail, largely on the lines already known to Brett.

In the office they found a telegram addressed to David, but his cousin opened it, believing it might be from Brett. It was, and read as follows:

"Capella arrives Whitby five o'clock. I know everything he has to tell you. If he becomes offensive, boot him."

Robert did not show the message to his cousin. He gave her its general purport, and added:

"Prepare yourself for an ordeal, but be brave. Perhaps your husband is in the hotel now, as he must have reached here half an hour ago."

He had barely uttered the words when Mrs. Capella's maid approached.

"Mr. Capella is here, madam," she said "and awaits you in your sitting-room."

Margaret became, if possible, a shade whiter.

"What about you, Robert?" she whispered.

"Me! I am going with you. Brett's telegram is my authority."

30
Husband And Wife

The Italian was glaring out of a window when they entered the room.

He turned instantly, with a waspish ferocity.

"So, madam." he cried, "not content with deceiving me from the first moment we met, you have left your home in company with your lover!"

Margaret looked at Robert beseechingly. The sailor's face was like granite. Only his eyes flashed a warning that Capella might have noted were he less blinded by passion.

"Do not attempt to shield yourself by the presence of others!" screamed Capella. "I know that Miss Layton and her father are here. That is part of the game you play. As for you, Mr. David Hume, or whatever you call yourself, your own record is not so clean that you should endeavour to cloak the misdeeds of others."

The Italian had never before seen Robert to his knowledge. He only met David for a few moments during an angry scene at Beechcroft, when Brett did most of the talking. The mistake he now made was a natural one.

"It does not occur to you," said Robert, in a voice remarkable for its calmness, "that not content with grossly insulting your wife, you are attacking the reputation of a man whom you do not know."

"Pooh!" Capella, in his excitement, snapped his fingers. "You Hume-Frazers are very fond of defending your reputations. A fig for them! You are not worthy to consort with honourable people. I feel assured that when Mr. Layton and his daughter know the truth about you they will decline to associate with you."

Whatever else might be urged against the Italian, he was no coward. Such language might well have led to a fierce attack on him by a man so greatly his superior in physical strength. But Robert sat down, near the door.

"You have some object in coming here to-day," he said. "What is it?"

Margaret remained standing near the fire-place. Capella produced a bundle of papers.

"I am here," he said, "to unmask the woman who unfortunately bears my name, and at the same time to prevent you from getting Miss Layton to marry you under false pretences."

"A worthy programme!" observed Frazer suavely. "You may attain the second part of your scheme, I admit, but the first seems to be difficult."

"Is it? We shall see!"

Capella flourished his papers and began a passionate avowal of the "treachery" practised on him in the matter of Margaret's parentage, ending by saying:

"That woman's mother was the affianced bride of my father. She deceived him basely. On his death-bed he made me vow my lifelong hatred of her betrayer and all his descendants. To you, a cold-blooded Englishman, that perhaps means nothing. To me it is sacred, imperishable, dearer than life. And to think that I have been tricked into a marriage with the daughter of the man who was my father's enemy. How mad I was not to make inquiries! What a poor, short-sighted fool! But I will have my revenge! I will expose your accursed race in the courts! I will not rest content until I am free from this snare!"

Margaret would have spoken, but her cousin quickly forestalled her.

"You bring two charges against your wife," Robert said. "The first is that she deceived you before marriage; the second that she is deceiving you now. You contemplate taking divorce proceedings against her?"

"I do."

"But you are lying on both counts. There is no purer or more honourable woman alive to-day than she who stands here at this moment. You are a mean and despicable hound to endeavour to take advantage of circumstances attending her birth of which she was in profound ignorance."

"She can tell that to a judge," sneered the Italian. "I know better."

Robert rose, his face white with anger.

"Margaret," he said, "you have heard your precious husband's views with regard to you. What do you say?"

She looked from one to the other—no one knows what tumultuous thoughts coursed through her brain in that trying moment—and she answered:

"I am his true and faithful wife, Robert. I have never been otherwise in word or deed."

Capella started, as well he might, when he heard the Christian name of the man who was treating him with such quiet scorn.

"So," he laughed maliciously, "I have again been fooled. You are not David, but"

Frazer strode towards him, and the words died away on his lips.

"Listen, you blackguard!" he hissed. "Were it not for the presence of your wife I would choke the miserable life out of you. Go! We have done with you! You have unmasked your real character, and I cannot believe that a spark of affection can remain in your wife's heart for you after your ignoble conduct. Go, I tell you! Do your worst. Spit your venom elsewhere than in this hotel. But first let me warn you. If you dare to approach Miss Layton, I cannot promise that my cousin David will treat you as tenderly as I propose to do. He will probably thrash you until you are unconscious. I simply place you outside this room."

He grabbed the Italian by the breast with his right hand, lifted him high in the air, gathered the papers from the table in his left hand, and carried his kicking, cursing, but helpless adversary to the door.

Then he set him down again, opened the door, and remembering Brett's advice, assisted him outside, flinging the documents after him and closing the door.

With impotent rage in his heart, Capella rushed from the hotel and caught the last train to the south. He had not been in Whitby two hours, but he was now embarked upon his vengeful mission, and bitterly resolved to push it to the uttermost extremity.

Margaret had not uttered a sound during the final scene. She stood as one turned to stone. Robert did not dare to speak to her. How could he offer consolation to a woman whose tenderest feelings had been so wantonly outraged?

"Robert," she said at last, "he spoke of getting a divorce. I believe he can do this by Italian law. Here it should be impossible."

"In that case," he said calmly, "you and I will go and live in Italy."

She placed her hands before her face, and burst into a tempest of tears.

"Now, my dear girl," he murmured, "try and forget that pitiful rascal and his threats. You are well rid of him. I will leave you now for a little while. In half an hour we will go and listen to the band until dinner. Really, we have had a most enjoyable afternoon."

He went out, placid and smiling, and Margaret sobbed plentifully—until it became necessary to go to her room and remove the traces of her grief. So it may be assumed that her tears were not all occasioned by grief for the contemplated loss of her ill-chosen mate.

When the others returned from their excursion, Frazer explained to them all that was needful with reference to Capella's visit. Helen was very outspoken in her indignation, and even the rector condemned the Italian's conduct in plain terms.

He warmly approved of the resolution arrived at by Robert and David to return to London next day, and not leave Brett until a definite stage had been reached in the strangely intricate inquiry they were embarked on.

They sat late into the night, discussing the pros and cons of the situation; yet among these five people, fully cognisant as they were of nearly every fact known to the able barrister who had taken charge of their affairs, not one even remotely guessed the pending sequel.

Whilst they were talking and hoping for some favourable outcome, the night express from York was hurrying Capella to a weird conclusion of his efforts to discredit his wife. Had he but known what lay before him he would have left the train at the first station and hastened to Margaret, to grovel at her feet and beg her forgiveness for the foul aspersions cast upon her.

It was too late.

31
To Beechcroft

Thenceforth, as the French say, events marched. Robert Frazer faithfully recounted Margaret's statement to the barrister and the detective. The "documents," copies of which Ooma sent to the ill-fated woman whose sudden accession to wealth had proved so unlucky for her, were evidently those stolen from the drawer in the writing-desk at Beechcroft.

Here, at last, was the motive of the murder laid bare.

The Japanese, by some inscrutable means, became aware that the young baronet possessed these papers, and held them *in terrorem* over his reputed sister. In the hands of a third person, an outsider, they were endowed with double powers for mischief. He could threaten the woman with exposure, the man with the revelation of a discreditable family secret.

He visited the library in order to commit the theft, probably acting with greater daring because he mistook the sleeping David for his cousin. Having successfully wrenched open the drawer and secured the papers, still holding in his hand the instrument used for slipping back the tiny lock, he turned to leave the room by the open window, and was suddenly confronted by the real Sir Alan, who recognised him and guessed his object in being present at that hour.

Brett had gone thus far in his spoken commentary on the affair as it now presented itself to his mind when Winter asked:

"Why do you say 'recognised' him, Mr. Brett? We have no evidence that Sir Alan had ever seen Ooma?"

"What, none? Search through your memory. Did not the stationmaster see a third David Hume leave the station that day when the movements of only two are known to us. What became of this third personage during the afternoon? Where did he change into evening dress? Why did Sir Alan leave documents of such grave importance in so insecure a hiding-place?"

"There is no use in asking me questions I can't answer," snapped the detective.

"Perhaps not. I think you said that you amused yourself in your Middle Street lodgings by taking to pieces a small electrical machine fitted together by your companion?"

"Yes, sir; but what of that?"

"Let us suppose that, instead of a complex machine he built a small arch of toy bricks, and you were well acquainted with the model whilst each brick was numbered in rotation, don't you think you could manage to reconstruct the arch after repeated efforts?"

"I expect so."

"Well, my dear Winter, we have now got together every material stone in our edifice. Mrs. Capella's yielding to blackmail is the keystone of the arch. Every loose block fits at once into its proper place. The Japanese, Ooma, must have met Sir Alan and discussed this very question with him. The baronet must have unwittingly revealed the family secret, and the Jap was clever enough to perceive its value. Further, the murder was unpremeditated, the inspiration of a desperate moment, and the weapon selected shows a sort of fiendish mandate suggested by family feud. Ooma is undoubtedly"

But Smith entered, apologetic, doubtful.

"Mr. Holden is here, sir, and says he wishes to see you immediately."

Holden's news was important. Capella had left Liverpool Street half an hour ago for Beechcroft, and in the same train travelled Ooma.

"Are you sure of this?" demanded Brett, excitedly springing from his chair.

"Quite certain, sir. Mr. Winter's mate followed him to the station, and told me who the Japanese was. Besides, no one could mistake him who had ever seen either of these two gentlemen."

He indicated Robert and David.

"Quick," shouted the barrister. "We must all catch the next train to Stowmarket. Winter, have you your handcuffs? This time they may be needed. Smith, run and call two hansoms."

He rushed to a bureau and produced a couple of revolvers. He handed one to Holden.

"I can trust you," he said, "not to fire without reason. Do not shoot to kill. If this man threatens the life of any person, maim him if possible, but try to avoid hitting him in the head or body."

To the Frazers he handed the heaviest sticks he possessed. He himself pocketed the second revolver, and picked up the peculiar walking-stick which Ooma dropped in Northumberland Avenue.

"Now," he said, "let us be off. We have no time to lose, and we must get to Beechcroft with the utmost speed."

Winter and he entered the same hansom.

"Why are you so anxious to prevent Capella and Ooma meeting, sir?" asked the detective, as their vehicle sped along Victoria Street.

"I do not care whether they meet or not," was the emphatic reply. "It is now imperatively necessary that the Japanese should be placed where he can do no further harm. The man is a human tiger. He must be caged. If all goes well, Winter, this case will pass out of my hands into yours within the next three hours."

The detective smiled broadly. At last he saw his way clearly, or thought he saw it, which is often not quite the same thing. In the present instance he little dreamed the nature of the path he would follow. But he was so gratified that he could not long maintain silence, though Brett was obviously disinclined to talk.

"By Jove," he gurgled, "this will be the case of the year."

The barrister replied not.

"I suppose, Mr. Brett," continued Winter, with well-affected concern, "you will follow your usual policy, and decide to keep your connection with the affair hidden?"

"Exactly, and you will follow your usual policy of claiming all the credit under the magic of the words 'from information received.'"

Winter could afford to be generous.

"Mr. Brett," he cried, "there is no man would be so pleased as I to see you come out of your shell, and tell the Court all you have done. You deserve it. It would be the proudest moment of your life."

Then the barrister laughed.

"You have known me for years, Winter," he said, "yet you believe that. Go to! You are incorrigible!"

The detective did not trouble to extract the exact meaning from this remark. He understood that Brett would never think of entering the witness-box. That was all he wanted to know.

"Are you quite certain," he asked, with a last tinge of anxiety in his voice, "that Ooma will be arrested to-day?"

"Quite certain, if we can accomplish that highly desirable task."

Winter pounded the door of the hansom with his clenched fist

"Then it is done!" he cried. "I'll truss him up like a fowl. If he tries any tricks I'll borrow the leg-chains from Stowmarket police station."

At Liverpool Street they all made a hasty meal. They caught the last train from London and passed two weary hours until Stowmarket was reached.

There on the platform stood the station-master. He approached Brett and whispered:

"A man who came here by the preceding train told me that you and some other gentlemen might possibly follow on. He intended to telegraph to you, but he asked me, in case you turned up, to tell you that the Japanese has gone on foot to Beechcroft, and that Mr. Capella has not arrived."

"Not arrived!" cried Brett. He turned to Holden. "Can you have been mistaken?"

Holden shook his head. "I saw him with my own eyes," he asseverated, "and to make sure of his destination I asked the ticket examiner where the gentleman in the first smoker was going to. It was Stowmarket, right enough."

"There can be no error, sir," put in the stationmaster. "Mr. Capella's valet came by the train, and assured me that he left London with his master. Besides, the carriage is here from the Hall. It was ordered by telegraph. There is the valet himself. He imagines that Mr. Capella quitted the train on the way, and will arrive by this one. But there is no sign of him."

The mention of the carriage brought a look of decision into the barrister's face.

"One more question," he said to the official. "Did you see the person described as the Japanese?"

"Yes, sir, I did. As a matter of fact, I thought it was somebody else. It was not until the stranger who arrived by the train used that name to distinguish him that I understood I was mistaken."

The stationmaster looked into Brett's eyes that which he did not like to say in the presence of the Frazers. Of course, he had fallen into the same error as most people who only obtained a casual glimpse of Ooma.

Brett hurried his companions outside the station. There they found the Beechcroft carriage, and a puzzled valet holding parley with the coachman and footman. David Hume's authority was sufficient to secure the use of the vehicle, and Brett made the position easier for the men by saying that, in all probability, they would find fresh instructions awaiting them at the Hall.

Before the party drove off Winter noticed a local sergeant of police standing near.

"Shall I ask him to come with us, sir?" he said to Brett.

The barrister considered the point for an instant before replying:

"Perhaps it would be better, as we have not got a warrant."

Winter grinned broadly again.

"Oh yes, we have," he cried. "Mr. Ooma's warrant has been in my breast-pocket for three days."

"What a thoughtful fellow you are," murmured Brett. "In that case we can dispense with local assistance. We five can surely tackle any man living."

"What can have become of Capella?" said David Hume, when they were all seated and bowling along the road to Beechcroft.

"It is impossible to say what such a mad ass would be up to," commented his cousin. "He has probably gone back to London from some wayside station, and failed to find his servant to tell him before the train moved on."

"What do you think, Mr. Brett?" inquired Winter.

"I can form no opinion. I only wish Ooma was in gaol. For once, Winter, I appreciate the strength of your handcuffing policy."

32

THE FIGHT

It was almost dark by the time they reached the lodge gates. Brett, moved by impulse, stopped the carriage in the main road. The others alighted after him. Mrs. Crowe, the lodge-keeper's wife, opened the gates, and evidently wondered why the carriage did not enter.

"Good evening, Mrs. Crowe," said Brett, advancing. "Have you seen a telegraph messenger recently?"

"Lawk, sir," she cried, "I didn't recognise you in the gloom! No, sir, there's been no messenger, only"

Then she uttered a startled exclamation.

"Why, there's Mr. David an' Mr. Robert! I could ha' sworn one of you gentlemen walked up to the house five minutes ago, an' I wunnered you never took no notice of me. Well, of all the strange things!"

"It was a natural mistake," said the barrister quietly.

Then he told the coachman to wait where he was until a message reached him from the house.

He did not want to disturb the visitor who had caused Mrs. Crowe to "wunner," nor was there any use in sending the carriage back to Stowmarket. Somehow, he felt that Capella would not come to Beechcroft that night.

The five men went rapidly and silently up the avenue. As they approached the lighted library, they could see a servant parleying with the Japanese.

A motion of Brett's hand brought the party into the shade of the sombre yews.

"You and Holden," he said to Hume, "go round to the main entrance, proceed at once to the library door, enter the room, and lock the door behind you. Be ready with your stick, and do not hesitate to lunge hard if Ooma attacks you. You, Holden, keep the revolver handy. It must only be used to save life. The moment you appear at the door we will rush to the window, which is open. Ooma must have entered that way. You both understand?"

They nodded and walked off, clinging to the line of the trees. The others closed up. Timing their approach with perfect judgment, they crept over the gravelled road at the bend, and gained the turf in front of the window.

Ooma's back was towards them. They could hear his voice—a queer, high-pitched, yet strident voice—whilst he questioned a somewhat scared footman as to the whereabouts of his mistress.

The man had evidently perceived the remarkable resemblance borne by this uncanny stranger to the Frazer family. His replies were respectful, but stuttering. He was alarmed by those fierce eyes, more especially because his inability to give satisfactory information seemed to anger the new-comer.

"You are not a child," they heard Ooma say, with menace in his tone. "You must have heard, from her maid or some other source, where Mrs. Capella has gone to?"

"Nno, sir," stammered the man. "I really 'aven't I ttthought Mrs. CCapella was in London. The bbutler says we are all to 'ave a 'oliday next week."

"Is there no way in which I can find out where your mistress is at this moment? I must see her. My business is important. It cannot wait. It is of the utmost importance to her."

Brett, straining without like a hound in the leash, could note a slight accentuation in the perfect English spoken by Ooma. There was just a suspicion of the liquid "r" so strongly marked in Jiro's utterance. What an uncanny thing is heredity! It even alters the shape of the roof of the mouth. The Japanese of English descent could necessarily pronounce English better than the pure-born native.

The servant within seemed to rack his brains for a favourable reply.

"You might ask Mr. Capella, sir," he said at length, with some degree of returning confidence. "He was expected here by the last train, but missed it in London, I expect. He is sure to come to-night, and he will tell you, if you care to wait."

"Mr. Capella! Coming by the last train! What is he like?"

"Do you mean in appearance, sir? He is a small, dark-complexioned gentleman, with wavy black hair and a very pale face. He"

But Ooma turned away from the man, and looked through the window, with the lambent glare of a wild animal in his eyes. He instantly saw the three motionless figures, Brett, Winter, and Robert Hume-Frazer.

They sprang forward. Robert was quickest, and reached the open window first. The Japanese jumped back and made for the door, but it opened in his face, and David entered the room. Behind him was Holden, who made no secret of the fact that he carried a revolver.

Ooma caught the astounded man-servant by the waist, lifted him as though he were a truss of straw, and threw him bodily at Robert Frazer and Winter, bringing both to the ground by this singular weapon.

It was a fatal mistake to attack the readiest means of exit. Had he used his human battering ram against Holden and David he might have escaped. But now he looked into the muzzle of another revolver, and heard Brett's stern demand:

"Hands up, Ooma! If you move you are a dead man?"

Nevertheless, he did move. He seemed to have the agility as well as the semblance of a carnivorous animal. He bounded sideways towards the wall of the library, picked up the writing-desk, and barricaded himself behind it. In the same second he produced a small, shining article from his waistcoat pocket, and shouted, in a voice now cracked with rage:

"Stand back, all of you. You may shoot me! I will not be arrested!"

Winter, swearing, scrambled from the floor. Robert, too, threw off the yelling servant, and rose to his feet. Alarmed not only by the curious entry made by David Hume and Holden, but also by the racket in the library, other servants were now clamouring at the locked door, for Holden had slipped his left hand behind him and turned the key. Brett similarly closed the window. They were five to one, but the one seemed to defy them.

"That be blowed for a tale!" roared the infuriated detective, whose blood was fired by the manner in which he had been floored. "I arrest you in the King's name for the murder of Sir Alan Hume-Frazer, and I warn you"

Robert Hume-Frazer waited for no preliminary explanation of an official character. He wanted to feel that man's bones crack under his grasp. He had the strong man's ambition to close with an opponent worthy of his thews and sinews. Without any warning, he made for the Japanese, who seemed to await his oncoming with singular equanimity, though otherwise quivering with baulked hate.

But Brett had seen something that aroused a lightning-like suspicion. Twice had the Japanese looked at a small, shining thing in his hand, as though to make sure it was there. So the barrister was just in time to grasp Robert's shoulder and hold him back.

"No," he cried, "you must not touch him. I command it. He cannot escape."

"Then let me have a go at him first," growled Frazer, whose face was pale with passion.

"No, no. Leave him to me. Winter, do you hear me? Stand back, I say."

Brett's imperative tone brooked no disobedience. Thus, in a segment of a circle, the five enclosed the one against the wall–Ooma barricaded by the table, the others ready to defeat any stratagem he might endeavour to put in force.

"Now listen to me, Ooma," said the barrister sternly. "You must drop that thing you have in your right hand. You must hold both your hands high above your head. If you move either of them again I will shoot you. If you do not obey me before I count five I will shoot you. One! Two! Three!"

The Japanese, gasping a horrible sort of sob, three times plunged the instrument he held into his left arm. Then he flung it straight at Robert. One would have thought his vengeance would be directed against Brett, whom he must have credited by this time with his capture.

No; he singled out a Hume-Frazer for his last attack. The instrument struck a button on Robert's coat and fell to the floor, where it lay twisted out of shape by the force of the impact.

It was a hypodermic syringe.

Again Ooma uttered that weird cry.

"This is the end," he said. "You have not beaten me. It is Fate."

He folded his arms and looked at them. A change came over his face. He was no longer a tiger at bay, but a human being, calm, dignified, almost impressive.

"I arrest you" began Winter.

"You fool!" laughed the Japanese, with a quiet contempt in his tone; "I shall be dead in twenty minutes. That syringe contained snake poison, the undiluted venom of the karait. Put away your pistols. They are not wanted."

Quite nonchalantly he leaned back against the bookcase that lined the wall. He turned his eyes to Robert.

"You have the luck of your race," he said "If that point had reached your skin no human skill could have saved you. As it is, you are spared, and I must go. The same blood flows in our veins, yet you are my enemy. I wish I could once get my fingers round your throat before my strength fails."

"Come from behind that table and try," was the quick rejoinder.

Ooma made to accept the challenge, but Brett intervened.

"If you are telling the truth," he said, "you can spend your brief remaining span of life to better purpose than in a mad combat with one who has done you no harm. Where is Capella?"

"I killed him," was the cool reply.

The footman, who had slowly regained his senses, uttered a groan of horror. By this time several men, not alone house servants, but gardeners, grooms, and others, had gathered on the lawn.

"Send away that slave," cried Ooma impatiently, "and tell those others to go to their kennels. This is no place for such."

Brett knew that the Japanese was in truth about to die. Afterwards Winter and Holden confessed that they thought the pretence of injecting snake poison was a mere ruse to gain time. Robert and David intuitively agreed with the barrister. It was in their breed to know when eternity yawned for one of them. The very calmness of the criminal, his magnificent apathy, his dislike of vulgar witnesses, foreboded a tragedy.

Brett motioned to Holden to open the door, and the footman gladly made his escape. In response to a wave of the barrister's arm the other servants disappeared from view, though they probably only retreated to a greater distance, and could see well enough all that happened.

"Yes," continued Ooma, "I killed Capella. It was a mistake. Everything is a mistake. It was foolish on my part to kill Alan Hume-Frazer, even though he was my enemy. I should have let him live, and tortured him by fear. You English dread these scandals worse than death. We Japanese fear neither. For I am a Japanese, and I am proud of it, although my ancestor was David Hume of

Glen Tochan, who fought and killed the man who robbed his father."

"But how and why did you kill Capella?" asked Brett.

"I saw him in the station at London. He followed me. I puzzled him, I suppose. He perceived the likeness between me and my dear cousins. We are like one another, are we not, we Hume-Frazers?"

He laughed mirthlessly, and stared at David and Robert alternately. Winter broke in with a hasty question:

"If he is speaking the truth about the snake poison, shouldn't we send for a doctor?"

No one had thought of this previously. Brett reproached himself for his forgetfulness. So strange are our civilised notions that we strive to save a man's life in order to hang him by due process at law.

It was Ooma who answered.

"Doctor!" he cried. "Bring him! Bring the whole College of Surgeons. They can watch me die, and tell you learnedly why the blood curdles and the heart refuses to act, but not all their science can beat the venom of the little karait. It is an Indian snake, more deadly than the cobra, with mightier tooth than the tiger. I meant to use that syringe on the whole cursed brood of Frazers in this country. No one would have known what happened to them. But look you, Fate is too powerful. The karait stored his poison for me only. I killed only one of the race, and him I stabbed with a Ko-Katana of my own house."

Holden left the room to send a messenger post-haste for the village doctor.

"About Capella?" persisted Brett.

"Ah, Capella. He sought his own death. He looked at me so oddly that I thought him a spy. I was alone in a carriage when, half-way here, he ran along the platform at a small station and joined me. He began to question me. I looked out of the window and saw that we were coming to a viaduct over a stream between deep cliffs, so I took the little man and cracked his neck. Then I flung him over the bridge. It was a mistake. He should have left me alone."

He described this cold-blooded murder of the unfortunate Italian with the weary air of one who recites a tedious episode. The lids drooped heavily over his eyes.

"I am tired," he said. "That was a good little snake. He knew his business. He could make the best of poison."

"Surely," said the barrister solemnly, "you are not so utterly inhuman that at the very point of death you still maintain the attitude of a disappointed avenger. What wrong had all these people done you to demand your murderous hate?"

Ooma seemed for a moment to rouse himself from lethargy. Once again the black eyes sparkled with their menacing gleam.

"It is you," he cried, "you, the thinker, who question me. I never gave a thought to you, or I would not now be slowly sinking into death. I might have guessed that a higher intelligence was at work than that which saw the Ko-Katana with its motto, and yet failed to read its story. You ask my motives. Can a man explain heredity? Here"— and he threw a packet of papers on the writing-desk—"are the proofs of my identity. It is not long ago, only one hundred and fifty years, since David Hume was robbed of his birthright, and what is such a period to the old families of England and Japan? There are men living in Japan to-day who saw his son in the flesh. I am his lawful descendant. I came to England and resolved to be an Englishman. But I needed money. Do you remember our motto, 'A new field gives a small crop'? The first Japanese Hume did not prosper. He was a good fighter, but he saved no yen. So I applied to my family. I came here on the New Year's Eve, and Sir Alan Hume-Frazer saw me walking up the avenue. He stepped out through that window to meet me. He was surprised at my appearance, and thought I was his cousin Robert, whom he had not seen for years."

At this remarkable statement the four listeners chiefly concerned looked wonderingly at each other. The main incidents of the family feud were repeating themselves in a ghostly manner.

Ooma paid no heed to their amazement. He staggered unsteadily to a chair and sank into it limply. It was the chair which David Hume occupied when he slept, and dreamed. Not even Winter saw cause for suspicion in the act. Ooma was dying. His yellow skin was now green. His lips were white. His whole frame was sinking. At this phase he became a Japanese, and lost all likeness to the Frazers.

He continued, with an odd cackle:

"I kept up the error. I demanded money as my right, and from his words I gathered that the Frazers had been at their old tricks and defrauded another relative."

Robert started.

"Do you hear?" he murmured to Brett. "That accounts for Alan's strange reception of me the same day."

Brett held up a warning hand. Ooma was still talking.

"I taunted him with thriving on the plunder of his own people. That made him furious. He raved about the world being in league against him. The only relative he loved, one who was more than brother, had stolen the woman he wished to marry; his sister was a living lie; his cousin a blackmailer. I laughed. 'Do you disown your sister, then?' I asked. He took from his breast-pocket some papers—you will find them there, on the table—and told me, in great anger, that he possessed proof that she was not his sister. I was cooler than he, and saw the value of this admission I pretended to go away, but hid among the trees and saw him walk about the library for nearly an hour. I meant to enter the house if an opportunity presented itself, and, trusting to my appearance, go to his bedroom, if he changed his clothes and went out. But he helped me by placing the papers in the drawer which I afterwards broke open. I saw him

meet you"–he feebly pointed to Robert. "I saw you arrive
in the carriage," and he indicated David. "Then I
determined to wait until the night I went back to
Stowmarket, where I left a portmanteau at a small
hotel"–Brett knew that Winter stole a look at him, but he
ignored the fact"–and changed my clothes. In England, at
night, a man in evening dress can enter almost any
house. When I returned I carried my bag with me, as I
did not know how I might wish to get away subsequently.
I saw the preparations for the ball. They helped me.
David Hume's unexpected appearance at midnight upset
my plans. Waiting near the gate, I witnessed Alan's
meeting with a girl in a white dress. Whilst they were
talking, I ran up to the house and found David asleep in
the library. I resolved to act boldly. Even he would not
know what to do if he suddenly discovered another Frazer
in the room. To force open the drawer I picked up the
Japanese sword, and knew it as belonging to my house by
the device on the handle of the Ko-Katana. The thing
inspired me. I obtained the papers, and was going out
when I met Alan. He had seen what I was doing. He
called me a cur, and the memory of my ancestor's
vengeance rushed on me, so I struck him with the knife,
and left it resting in his heart as he fell. Afterwards it
was easy. No one knew me. Those who had seen me
thought that I was either David or Robert Hume-Frazer. I
depended on the police and the servants to complete the
mystery. They did. I saw David meet the same girl in a
white dress near the lodge, so I sent the post-card which I
made Jiro write for me. He wrote it badly, which was all
the better for my purpose. I meant David to be hanged by
the law; then I would marry Margaret. That is all. Give
me some brandy. I am dreaming now. I can see curling
shapes. Ah!"

He gulped down half a tumblerful of raw spirits
hastily procured by Brett. Again he attempted to shake
off the torpid state that was slowly mastering him. He

lifted his eyes feebly to Brett's face, and his face contorted in a ghastly smile.

"You!" he croaked. "I should have killed you! You carried my stick that night in Middle Street. Why was I not warned? Did you follow the girl from the hotel? I was a fool. I tried to stop the inquiry by getting rid of David Hume-Frazer. As if he had brains enough to get on my track! About that girl! She believes in me. She does not know anything of my past. Do not tell her. Try to help her. She is coarse, one of the people, as you say here, but she has courage and is faithful. Help her!"

His head drooped. The action of the brandy, whilst momentarily stimulating the heart, helped the stupefaction of the brain. It was a question of a minute, perhaps two.

"Why did you come here to-day?" asked Brett quickly.

"To see Margaret She would give me money. I was going away. That man—I threw from the train—was her husband? He was not—a proper mate—for a Frazer—or a Hume. We are—an old race—of soldiers. We know—how to die. Four of us—fell fighting—in Japan. I am dying! What a pity!"

His head sank lower. His breath grew faint His voice died away in unintelligible words. After a brief silence he spoke again.

The words he used were Japanese. In his weakened consciousness all he could recollect was the language he learnt from his Japanese mother—the mother he despised when he became a man and knew his history.

Winter and Brett were now holding him. The others drew apart. They afterwards confessed that the death of this murderer, this tiger-cub of their race, affected them greatly. He was fearless to the end. The way in which he quitted life became him more than the manner in which he lived.

There was a bustle without, and the local doctor entered. He looked wise, profound, even ventured on a sceptical remark when the barrister explained that Ooma had injected snake-poison into his arm. But he lifted the eyelids of the figure in the chair and glanced at the pupils.

"Whatever the cause of death may be, he is undoubtedly dead!" was his verdict.

33
THE LAST NOTE IN BRETT'S DIARY

Winter and Holden were invaluable during the trying hours that followed. Acting in conjunction with the local police, they caused a search to be made for Capella's body. It was found easily enough. Only once did the line cross such a place as that described by Ooma, and a bruised and battered corpse was taken out of the boulder-strewn stream beneath the viaduct.

Meanwhile Winter, writing from Brett's dictation, drew up a complete statement of all the facts retailed by the Japanese in relation to the murders of Sir Alan Hume-Frazer and the unfortunate Italian.

This they signed, and went to obtain the signatures of the two cousins, Holden, and the man-servant, for whom a special short statement had been prepared.

"This is for use at the coroner's inquest, I suppose?" inquired David.

"Yes," said Brett. "We must seize that opportunity to publish all the evidence needed to thoroughly acquit you of suspicion in relation to your cousin's death. By prior consultation with the coroner we can, if you think fit, keep out of the inquiry all allusions to Mrs. Capella."

"It would certainly be the best thing to do," agreed David, "especially in view of the fact that Robert and I have burnt those beastly papers."

He pointed to some shivering ashes in the grate of the drawing-room, for Ooma occupied the library in the last solemn stateliness of his final appearance on earth.

"What!" cried Brett. "Do you mean to say that you have destroyed the documents deposited by the Japanese on the writing-desk?"

"Not exactly all," was the cool reply. "We picked out those referring to Margaret, and made an end of them. We hope to be able to do the same with regard to papers discovered on Capella's body or among his belongings. Those bearing on Ooma himself are here"–and he pointed to a small packet, neatly tied up, reposing on the mantelpiece.

"You have done a somewhat serious thing."

"We don't care a cent about that. Robert and I have both agreed that what Margaret has she keeps. There may, in course of time, be very good reason for this action. Anyhow, I have acted to please myself, and my father will, I am sure, approve of what I have done."

Brett shook his head. No lawyer could approve of these rough-and-ready settlements of important family affairs.

"Has anyone telegraphed to Mrs. Capella?" he inquired.

"Yes," said Robert, "I did. I just said 'Ooma dead; Capella reported seriously ill. Remain in Whitby. I will join you to-morrow evening.' That, I thought, was enough for a start."

It certainly was.

Soon there came excited messages from both Margaret and Helen demanding more details, whereupon Brett, who knew that suspense was more unbearable than full knowledge, sent a fairly complete account of occurrences.

During the next few days there was the usual commotion in the Press that follows the opening up of the secret records of a great and mysterious crime.

It came as a tremendous surprise to David Hume-Frazer to learn how many people were convinced of his innocence "all the time." Being the central figure in the affair, he was compelled to remain at Beechcroft until Capella and Ooma were interred, and the coroner's jury, at a deferred inquest, had recorded their verdict that the wretched Japanese descendant of the Scottish Jacobite was not only doubly a murderer, but guilty of the heinous crime of *felo de se.*

Brett, in the interim, saw to the despatch of the Italian witnesses back to Naples. These good people did not know why they had been brought to England, but they returned to their sunny land fully persuaded that the English were both very rich and very foolish.

Winter, in accordance with Brett's promise, secured a fresh holiday towards the close of August, and had the supreme joy of shooting over a well-stocked Scotch moor.

At last, one day in September, Brett was summoned to Whitby to assist at a family conclave.

He found that Margaret was firm in her resolve never again to live at Beechcroft. She and Robert intended to get married early in the New Year and sail forthwith for the Argentine, where, with the help of his wife's money, Robert Hume-Frazer could develop his magnificent estate.

Beechroft would pass into the possession of David, and Helen and he, who were to be married in October, would settle down in the house after their honeymoon.

But on one point they were all very emphatic. That ill-fated library window should pass into the limbo of things that have been. Already builders were converting the library into an entrance hall, and the main door would occupy its natural place in the front of the house.

Let us hope that the return of the young couple after their marriage marked a new era for an abode hitherto singled out for tragedy. Their start was auspicious enough, for true love, in their case, neither ran smoothly nor yielded to the pressure of terrible events.

Mr. and Mrs. Jiro went to Japan. With them they took the girl, Rose Dew, and the last heard of them was that the trio were running a boarding-house in Yeddo, where Mrs. Jiro advertised the excellence of the food she supplied, and Miss Dew sternly repressed any attempt on the part of the lodgers to obtain credit.

The last entry in Brett's note-book, under the heading of the "Stowmarket Mystery," is dated six months after the departure of Mr. and Mrs. Robert Hume-Frazer for the Argentine. It reads:

> *"To-day is the anniversary of David Hume's first visit to my chambers. This morning I discovered in a corner, dusty and forlorn, Ooma's walking-stick. It reminded me of a snake that was hibernating, so I gave it to Smith, and told him to light the kitchen fire with it. Then I telegraphed to old Sir David Hume-Frazer, saying that I gladly accepted his invitation for the 12th. His son, it seems, cannot go North, as he does not wish to leave his wife during the next couple of months. I suppose I shall be a godfather at an early date."*

THE END

Resurrected Press Mysteries From Louis Tracy

The Albert Gate Mystery
Four men murdered and a fortune in diamonds belonging to the Turkish Sultan stolen, while the Foreign Office official in charge has gone missing. Was it a common jewelry theft or was it a case of international intrigue? This is the question that barrister detective Reginald Brett must solve.

The Bartlett Mystery
When Ronald Tower is murdered on his way to a bridge game on the yacht Sans Souci it at first appears a common crime. But as Rex Carshaw finds, a tragic case of mistaken identity leads to political scandal among the rich and powerful of New York.

The Strange Case of Mortimer Fenley
When the wealthy Mortimer Fenley is struck down by a shot from an express rifle on the steps of his mansion, detectives Winter and Furneaux of Scotland Yard must find the culprit. Was it the artist who claimed he was painting a picture at the time of the shot? The disaffected younger son? Or is there another suspect?

The Stowmarket Mystery
For five generations the Fergus-Hume family has been cursed. Each of the baronets has met a violent end. When the fifth baronet is found slain by a ceremonial Japanese dagger, suspicion falls on his cousin David. It falls to barrister detective Reginald Brett to prove his innocence and find the real murder in a case that spans two continents and as many centuries.

Resurrected Press Mysteries by J. S. Fletcher

The Orange-Yellow Diamond
When an elderly pawnbroker is murdered in the London parish of Paddington, a young, down on his luck writer is accused of the crime. But then it's found the pawnbroker had had in his possession an extraordinary South African diamond worth over eighty-thousand pounds — a diamond that's now missing. It falls to Melky Rubenstein to unravel the mystery and prove the young man's innocence.

The Middle Temple Murder
When an elderly man's body is found on the steps of chambers in the Midde Temple, one of the Inns of Court, it falls to newspaperman Frank Spargo and Detective-Sergeant Rathbury to solve the crime. The murdered man, for indeed it was murder, was found with no money or identification on his person except for a piece of paper with the name and address of a young barrister. Who is the victim? Why was he killed? Who is the murderer?

Scarhaven Keep
Bassett Oliver, the famed actor, has gone missing. When Oliver fails to show for a rehearsal, aspiring playwright Richard Copplestone finds himself sent to the small village of Scarhaven on the northern coast of England to track down the actors movements. What he finds is mystery. Find the answers as Copplestone unravels the mystery of Scarhaven Keep.

Visit www.resurrectedpress.com

Resurrected Press Mysteries by Fergus Hume

The Green Mummy

Professor Braddock hoped to compare the burial practices of the Egyptians with those of the ancient Peruvians with his latest acquisition, the mummy of the last Inca, Caxas. But on arrival, the packing case proved to hold not the mummy, but the body of his assistant Sidney Bolton. It falls to Archie Hope to discover the murderer if he is to marry the professors step-daughter, Lucy Kendal. Who killed Bolton and where is the mummy? Was it the sea captain Hervey? The mysterious Don Pedro? Cockatoo the Polynesian servant? The professor, himself? And what has become of the emeralds? These are the questions that Hope must answer amongst the secrets of the past in The Green Mummy.

The Mystery of a Hansom Cab

"Truth is said to be stranger than fiction, and certainly the extraordinary murder which took place in Melbourne Friday morning goes a long way towards verifying that saying." Thus opens The Mystery of a Hansom Cab, the best selling mystery of the nineteenth century. When a man is found dead in a hansom cab one of Melbourne's leading citizens is accused of the murder. He pleads his innocence, yet refuses to give an alibi. It falls to a determined lawyer and an intrepid detective to find the truth, revealing long kept secrets along the way. Fergus Hume's first and perhaps most famous mystery... The Mystery Of A Hansom Cab.

Visit www.resurrectedpress.com

Resurrected Press Mysteries from the Dr. John Thorndyke Series

Dr. John Thorndyke - Lecturer on Medical Jurisprudence and Forensic Medicine. Before Bones, before CSI, before Quincy, M.E – there was Dr. John Thorndyke solving the most baffling cases of Edwardian London using the latest tools of medical science. Read about his cases in:

The Eye of Osiris
John Bellingham, noted Egyptologist has vanished not once but twice in the same day. Now Dr, Thorndyke must unravel the tangled claims on his estate, solve the riddle of the missing man and find the "Eye of Osiris".

The Mystery of 31 New Inn
When Dr. Jervis is whisked away in a coach with no windows to an unknown location to treat a man in a coma from undivulged causes it is Dr. Thorndyke who must come up with the solution.

The Red Thumb Mark
The first of Dr. Thorndyke's cases finds him trying to prove the innocence of a young man accused of being a diamond thief despite the fact that his finger print was found at the scene of the crime.

John Thorndyke's Cases
More cases of medical mysteries as told by his trusted assistant Jervis, M.D. Eight stories of crime and deduction in Edwardian London.

Visit www.resurrectedpress.com

Resurrected Press Mysteries by John R. Watson & Arthur J. Rees

The Hampstead Mystery

High Court Justice Sir Horace Fewbanks found shot dead in his Hampstead home, a butler with a criminal past, a scorned lover and a hint of scandal. These are the elements of the Hampstead Mystery that Detective Inspector Chippenfield of Scotland Yard must unravel with the assistance of the ambitious Detective Rolfe. But will he be able to sort out the tangled threads of this case and arrest the culprit before he is upstaged by the celebrated gentleman detective Crewe. Follow the details of this amazing case at it plays out across Hampstead, London and Scotland until it reaches a stunning conclusion in the courts of the Old Bailey.

The Mystery of the Downs

When Harry Marsland was caught in a sudden down pour he sought shelter at Cliff Farm. Met at the door by a young woman clearly expecting someone else he is only too glad to get inside to wait out the storm. When they hear a noise upstairs in the deserted house they investigate only to discover the body of the farm's owner, Frank Lumsden, dead of a gunshot wound. Who then, killed Lumsden, and why? Who was the woman expecting and did she have any roll in the murder? These are the questions that private detective Crewe must answer in The Mystery of the Downs.

Visit www.resurrectedpress.com

Other Resurrected Press Mysteries

Mysteries on a Train

Before the Orient Express there was:

The Rome Express by Arthur Griffiths
A man is found dead in his first class sleeping compartment on the express from Rome to Paris. Who was his murderer? The Countess? The English General? His brother the clergy man? The maid who has disappeared? Is the French justice system up to solving the crime? Read about it in The Rome Express.

The Passenger from Calais by Arthur Griffiths
Colonel Basil Annesley finds he is the only passenger on the train from Calais to Lucerne. That is until a mysterious woman shows up at the last minute to book a compartment. Who is after her? What is her secret? Is she a criminal or a victim? Read about it in The Passenger from Calais

Visit us at www.resurrectedpress.com

About Resurrected Press

A division of Intrepid Ink, LLC, Resurrected Press is dedicated to bringing high quality, vintage books back into publication. See our entire catalogue and find out more at www.ResurrectedPress.com.

About Intrepid Ink, LLC

Intrepid Ink, LLC provides full publishing services to authors of fiction and non-fiction books, eBooks and websites. From editing to formatting, from publishing to marketing, Intrepid Ink gets your creative works into the hands of the people who want to read them. Find out more at www.IntrepidInk.com.